Cake & Cocktails

The Men of Haven Grove

A.D. ELLIS

Cover Photo of Michael H. by
Eric McKinney- 6:12 Photography

Quotes of Inspiration

"The moment our paths crossed, everything felt inevitable."

~*A.A. Milne*

"The best love story is when you fall in love with most unexpected person at the most unexpected time."

~*Alfiya Shaliheen*

"Sometimes, someone comes into your life, so unexpectedly, takes your heart by surprise and changes your life forever."

~*Unknown*

"I never knew what love was until you came into my life without any hint, so unexpected."

~*Maria Bastida*

Chapter 1
Henry Riggs

AN UNKNOWN LIQUID DRIPPED FROM MY HANDS as I thought about the mess out back in the trash area. The stench of hot, wet garbage clung to my nose as I scraped what appeared to be a soggy pretzel from my boot before walking back into the Roadhouse.

"You still good with me stealing Hudson away a little early tonight?" Lance asked from his perch on the bar stool, my eyes adjusting to the dim light inside the bar.

"What?" I glanced at my hands and curled my lip. "Oh, yeah, sorry."

"What's that?" Lance asked. The man had known me since I was born, and he knew my big, gruff-ish exterior was just a façade. I didn't get close to people easily, but in all actuality, I was a big softie.

"Someone or something has been going through the trash. Made a huge mess and I've got garbage juice all over me."

Lance wrinkled his nose. "Gross. Animal?"

"That's what I thought at first, but animals usually eat pretty much anything they find. This seemed to be picked through." I washed my hands, the heavy-duty hand soap slicking away the putrid liquid. Not sure the smell would ever be washed from my nose. "Never mind, sorry, what were you saying?"

"Still willing to help me get Hudson away early today?"

Lance was my dad's lifelong best friend, but ever since he'd returned to Haven Grove a while back there'd been something simmering between Lance and my younger brother, Hudson.

I wasn't sure it was a great idea, but I also wasn't convinced it was a bad idea.

I wasn't a fan of my brother's "hookup and never develop feelings" approach to dating—especially because it stemmed from our traumatic past, domestically speaking—but the thought of Hudson and Lance together when there was *a lot* of history there had me waffling. On one hand, I knew no one would treat Hudson better than Lance. On the other hand, I wasn't sure anyone could be ready for the blow up when my dad found out his best friend was fucking his son.

But in all honesty, Hudson's dating life wasn't really my business. I trusted Lance. Hudson was a big ol' golden retriever even if he insisted on never letting his heart get involved in things. The two of them could figure out their own shit.

As long as my brother was safe and taken care of, I wasn't going to get too much involved.

"You remember he doesn't date, right? I don't know how you think you're going to get him to agree to a date."

I also didn't really date—as in a little when I was younger, and not at all these days—but I opted to keep myself pretty much closed off from anyone other than family, while Hudson slept around. Bisexuality in a small town didn't really afford a person a lot of dating options, even if Haven Grove was a pretty accepting place *if* I'd wanted to date. Yeah, I could find someone on one of the apps—*not* ClickC*ck, which is what Hudson used for hookups, but maybe one of the other ones known more for finding relationships—but the thought of meeting strangers and doing the whole get to know you thing just sent shivers down my spine. If I was ever going to find someone, I wanted it to happen naturally. Just two people drawn together and learning about each other.

Not that I expected that to happen in our little town, but that's the way I'd like it to play out if it ever did.

"He's not going to know it's a date," Lance said with a shrug. "It's an undercover date."

"You're going to *trick* him into a date?"

"That's the plan."

I eyed Lance with a smirk. "I don't see how it's going to work, but yeah, I'll tell him to head out early and you can do what you need to do."

Hudson walked into the main bar from the back a couple minutes later. "What's up with the trash?" he asked. "Looks like some panicked kid went through each bag searching for a retainer or something."

Nostalgia washed over me, and I remembered Hudson at about thirteen frantically searching for his retainer with Lance. Luckily, they'd uncovered the missing mouthpiece before Dad found out. Honestly, Lance had been our savior as kids more than once. Dad may have been physically present, but he was often absent emotionally back then, and having Lance around had been exactly what Hudson and I needed. He took Dad's place sometimes, acted as a buffer other times; he kept our little family together, and I knew the Riggs family was better off because of him.

Just wasn't sure how everything was going to play out now that Lance was back in town and had plans to trick Hudson into a date.

Again, though, not my business.

"Yeah," I huffed. "I don't know. Kinda worried we've got a hungry person dumpster diving, but they've been getting in the bags by the door before I even get them to the dumpster." I frowned, thinking about the situation. "Hate the idea someone is that hungry."

I had some picnic plates with domed screens. I could put some food out for the person. We always had extra from the bar's kitchen even after I saved some for leftovers. Something pulled in my heart at the thought of a person being desperate enough to dig through trash.

Hudson's eyes softened. My brother knew me too well. "Well, at least it's warm right now. Would hate for you to have to give them five blankets instead of the pillow and two blankets I can already see you planning on."

Clearing my throat, I set to work wiping down the bar. There was no reason to argue my brother's comment. If it came down to it...if the mystery person didn't move on in a day or so...I'd leave a blanket and pillow for him. The old booth we'd moved outside a few years ago would serve as a decent little place to curl up and rest.

I'd wait to see how things played out.

Hudson, Lance, and I talked for a few more minutes before they headed out, and I got busy with the lunch rush.

As things died down, a flash of golden blond hair caught my attention at the end of the bar. I hadn't noticed the guy earlier, but he was finishing off a piece of chocolate cake and a large glass of milk.

Tossing the bar towel over my shoulder, I headed his way. "Sorry about that," I started, but stopped midsentence when he turned the most gorgeous blue eyes my way. Ten seconds earlier, I would have told you blue eyes were blue eyes. Maybe there was a difference between dark blue and light blue, but nothing more. Looking into this guy's eyes, I suddenly realized I'd missed out on all the ways to describe blue.

Icy aquamarine flecked with deep sapphire.

I nearly swallowed my tongue, but I cleared my throat and tried again. "Sorry about that, I didn't see you down here. Didn't mean to ignore you."

The man smiled.

Holy.

Shit.

If I thought I'd nearly choked on my own tongue over his eyes, the smile would be what knocked me on my ass.

"No worries." His smooth voice and casual words brought me back from the daydream I was having about his smile.

Those lips were probably illegal. At least in a couple states.

"I was at a booth, but a group came in. I moved to the

bar to finish my cake, so they didn't have to wait." He fidgeted with the collar of his t-shirt before brushing a hand down the open denim button-up he wore.

Gorgeous *and* kindhearted.

"Thanks for that. Can I get you anything else?" I asked.

"No, I'm good. Thank you."

My brain attempted to tell my feet to walk away, but my chest squeezed tight while my mouth tried its best to find something to say.

I was a bar owner. Of course, I enjoyed chatting with customers.

But this was different, and I didn't know why.

He glanced up at me with a question on those perfectly sculpted brows.

"Well, I'll let you eat your cake in peace," I mumbled before heading to the back hallway next to the kitchen. What the hell was going on? I didn't get all flustered over an attractive customer. He hadn't even been flirting.

Let the man eat his cake, Riggs, for fuck's sake.

I blew out a breath.

"You okay?" Kayla asked as she came around the corner. "Why are your cheeks all red?"

"The guy at the end of the bar." I tipped my head.

"Yeah?"

"What did he order?" Least I could do was comp his meal.

"Just the cake and milk."

"Tell me when he's ready to pay, I want to cover it since he moved for that group, and because I didn't realize he was at the bar."

"Can't. He asked if cash was okay when he ordered and

paid with a ten when I brought his cake and milk." Kayla shrugged.

"Damn. Okay, thanks." I glanced toward where the guy sat. I'd never seen him in town before. Would it be too forward to offer him a meal on the house next time he came in? Just to thank him for his kindness. Maybe he was just passing through, and wouldn't ever be back in. What about a free drink? The peach sours and lemon drop martinis were popular right now.

Yeah. A free drink. Keep him at the bar, get him talking.

I turned toward the bar, and my heart sank.

Cake crumbs and an empty glass.

The guy was gone.

A few days later, Hudson pored over some paperwork for our family's peach orchard and the family general store, the Juicy Peach, but he looked loopy and unfocused.

"Man, you don't look so hot," I said.

"Just a headache," Hudson muttered.

"Your cheeks look like you've got a fever," I said, reaching out a hand to touch my brother's forehead like I'd done a million times as he was growing up. "You're burning up. Go home and sleep."

"I'm fine."

"Damn it, Hudson, go home before you get me or my customers sick."

Hudson glanced up with a frown.

"Seriously, go home. I've got enough going on here with the trash bandit—"

"That's still a thing?" he asked.

"Yeah, but I'm just leaving food on plates now. Whoever it is has started using the blankets and pillow I left out. They're eating at the booth out back," I said, "and they must be curling up there to sleep. They keep everything neat and tidy."

"Just stay out there and catch them," Hudson muttered.

"I mean, I'm not trying to *catch* anyone. Not like they're in trouble. Wouldn't mind helping them, but I don't want to spook them and have them run away. If they're eating food and sleeping, I at least know they're somewhat safe. Haven Grove isn't dangerous. Maybe I'll meet them at some point."

A weird little *something* tugged in my gut whenever I thought of my mysterious stranger. I was a caregiver at heart, and protecting my brother had been something I took very seriously after our mom fucked off, so it wasn't surprising I already had a soft spot for this person. I found myself thinking about them, worrying, wanting to *happen* outside to see who was sleeping on the old booth out back in the wee hours of the morning.

But they seemed skittish, and I was a big guy who could come off as gruff if a person didn't know me, so I'd wait.

They weren't disrupting anything.

Hell, I'd had employees leave bigger messes out back than this guy did.

Guy? Gal? I guess I didn't know.

Either way, my helper's heart was happy as long as they were safe and somewhat comfortable for the time being. If the situation needed something else, the right direction would likely show itself.

"Could call the marshal," Hudson said, his teeth chattering.

"Why? I don't want them in trouble. As long as they aren't hurting anything or doing anything illegal, I don't mind it." I pointed a finger at my brother. "Get out of here. You're sick."

"S'posed to meet with Lance," Hudson slurred. "Gotta look at numbers."

"I'll tell him you're sick. Dad and I will take care of the orchard and the store for a few days. Go. Home. Don't come back here until the fever has broken. If it gets worse, get to the doctor."

My brother gathered his things, stumbled from his stool, and gave a halfhearted wave as he headed out the door.

The Riggs family was known for a few things.

The small-town drama my mom stirred up when she wrote a goodbye note and left my dad with two little boys thirty-plus years ago.

The scandal shortly after when Dad went to confide in his brother and found Mom in bed with Uncle Billy.

The feud that raged between Casey Joe and Billy Riggs for years until my uncle drank himself to death.

And peaches.

We owned the biggest, most successful peach orchard in the entire Midwest.

Uncle Billy almost ran it into the ground before he

died, but Hudson was working his ass off to save the orchard and the Juicy Peach general store.

Those peaches inspired many a drink at the Riggs Family Roadhouse where I manned the bar and ran the place. Dad used to be more involved, but he'd been going downhill lately. Not because he was *that* old—he and Mom got pregnant with me pretty young—but he'd never been the same since our mom left, and even more so since Billy died.

Casey Joe Riggs needed a change in his life.

I wasn't sure exactly what that was going to be, but he couldn't go on the way he was. Dad was a good guy who had been dealt a shit hand. He had a lot of love to give if the right person ever came along and convinced him to give it another chance.

Anyway, Dad and I could handle the orchard, the store, and the Roadhouse while Hudson slept away whatever illness had him down. My brother was a newer full-time addition to the business, taking over for Billy and trying to overcome our uncle's fuck ups, so it wasn't like Dad and I weren't used to doing a lot of it on our own anyway. Billy hadn't been a lot of help in the years before his death; too busy drowning in his drink and almost letting the orchard go to shit.

That night, as I packed up leftovers for myself and made a plate for my mystery person, I checked the radar. Storms were predicted over the next few days to weeks thanks to an unstable atmosphere, but the forecast for that night was just a gentle, soaking rain.

Good for the orchard.

Bad for a person roughing it.

Placing the plate under the little screened picnic dome, I glanced around the area outback. The booth was partially covered, but a pouring rain would soak anyone trying to curl up on the bench.

I yanked open the utility cabinet, the scent of citronella, polyethylene, old paint, and varnish assaulting my senses. I rummaged through for something I hoped was still there. Ah, yeah, there it was. The tarp. We'd used it a couple years ago when a limb fell and busted through the roof of the Roadhouse during a storm.

The tarp was folded neatly and wrapped up with four elastic cords complete with hooks. Surely a person as resourceful as my mystery man would be able to figure out a way to rig up a little shelter.

Just in case, I headed inside and grabbed a notebook from my office.

Supposed to rain tonight, thought you might want some protection from the weather. Use it however you want. Is the food okay?
Henry

It was already getting dark; I'd gotten myself lost in thought as I'd cleaned up the bar. If I didn't go upstairs soon, the stranger might just skip dinner and head on out of town.

And for reasons I couldn't quite explain, I didn't want that to happen.

Didn't want that to happen at all.

I put the notebook on the edge of the table where it would most likely stay dry, checked that the plate of food was covered and protected from bugs, and tossed the tarp onto the bench seat.

"Stay safe," I whispered into the midwestern summer night, my words barely audible over the intense buzz of cicadas as dusk fought to hold on for a few more moments.

I didn't understand the pull I had toward this mystery person, but my gut told me they needed protecting.

I didn't date. Didn't let myself get involved in relationships. Didn't have any desire to end up in a situation where someone leaving could rip my heart out again.

But protecting those I cared about was what I did. It was my thing, and I was good at it.

The only thing that kept me from checking on the stranger overnight was the fact my bedroom window in the apartment above the Roadhouse looked out over the front of the building, not the back.

But come morning, I found the tarp spread out and a note.

Thank you. The food is good. Letting the tarp dry.

. . .

The handwriting was closer to chicken scratches, and he hadn't left a name.

That was okay, he didn't owe me his name.

He knew mine, and maybe he'd start to trust me.

I kept an eye on the weather over the next week. The expected storms had fizzled out, but the forecast had another round predicted to pop up. The tarp wouldn't do anything in a storm.

My mystery guy and I wrote notes every day. Mostly just hello, thank you, superficial stuff. It was clear handwriting was a struggle for him, and he almost never wrote more than a few words. Finally, I gave him my number and suggested texting might be easier.

That night, I kicked myself.

You fool. This guy is sleeping on a bench, and you think he has a cell phone?

But my phone buzzed about an hour later.

> Unknown Number: Thanks. Texting is a lot easier.

After staring at my phone with my brow wrinkled for much too long, I finally realized who it was and saved his number to my phone.

> Me: There's supposed to be a storm tonight. Not telling you what to do, but that tarp isn't going to keep you dry when the wind starts up. You're welcome to come to my place. I can give you the couch.

The typing bubbles appeared.

Disappeared.

Appeared.

And then nothing.

Shit.

If he'd seen me around, he maybe thought I looked intimidating. Over six feet tall, broad shoulders, beard, and a heavy, sometimes scowly brow would do that sometimes.

Or maybe he just wasn't super trusting. Would I sleep on a stranger's couch in a town I didn't know? Probably not.

> Me: Or I can leave the backdoor to the bar open. You can stretch out in one of the booths inside. There's a shower in the back bathroom. Nothing fancy, but there's soap and a towel. And you'd be dry inside.

What the hell was I doing?

> Mystery Guy: Doesn't seem smart to let a stranger into your business.

> Me: You going to rob me?

> Mystery Guy: Not me. But others might.

> Me: I'm offering it to you, not others. Door will be unlocked.

> Mystery Guy: Beggars can't be choosers. Don't feel right about it but can't turn down a shower.

My heart tugged in my chest. Poor guy. How long had he been living out of a bag, sleeping outside, hiding out, and just needing a warm shower along with a comfortable place to sleep?

My mind was still on my mystery guy when the blond with a killer smile walked into the Roadhouse the next day. He looked a bit rumpled, but his hair shone in the bar lights, and he could have been a model in a toothpaste commercial.

"Welcome back," I greeted when he took a seat at the bar and pushed his backpack under the stool. "What can I get ya?"

"Water to start, please." He wore faded jeans, tennis shoes that definitely weren't new, another t-shirt, and the denim button-up left open again.

"You got it." As I filled a water glass, I noticed the kid thumbing through some bills in his wallet. When I placed his glass on the bar, I went with my usual instead of worrying about his finances. "Special today is the Roadhouse burger, onion rings, and peach cobbler for dessert."

He wrinkled his nose. "Don't really like peaches." He fiddled with the t-shirt collar again, pulling it up to rub it along his bottom lip.

I chuckled. "He says to part owner of the Riggs Family Orchard, one of the largest peach orchards in the area."

Blondie winced. "Sorry."

"How can you not like peaches?"

He shrugged. "Just never took a liking to them."

I crossed my arms. "You ever have fresh, ripe peaches?"

Another shrug. "Just whatever school had in the fruit cocktail."

I slapped my hand to my forehead, and the guy snorted.

"What?" he asked, grinning as he took a drink.

"Canned peaches? You've only ever had canned peaches, and you let that determine if you like them?"

He stared at me, big blue eyes blinking over his water glass.

"Okay, challenge accepted. I'm going to treat you to *fresh* peaches."

"Oh, um, I was just going to get something small," the guy started.

I waved him away. "The Great Peach Challenge is on the house, and so is your lunch."

He wrinkled his nose. "Is a free lunch supposed to sway me toward your peachy ways?"

"The free lunch is because you were helpful when we were packed the other day," I said, rubbing my hands together. "Okay, do you want to order your own lunch, and I'll provide the peach-themed desserts? Or do you entrust me with the entire meal?"

The guy narrowed his eyes, but the sapphire flecks sparkled with humor. "Well, if it's on the house, I guess beggars can't be choosers."

I slapped my hands on the bar. "That's the spirit." A tickle of something played at the back of my head, but I ignored it, too excited about the challenge ahead of me. "Now, are you allergic to anything?"

He shook his head.

"Do you drink alcohol?"

"Not daily, but on occasion."

"Perfect. I'm gonna set you up with an appetizer and drink first, then I've got the perfect idea for your main course, and dessert will be a sampler." My chest bubbled with excitement. I loved to cook, loved to see people truly enjoy a meal. Throughout the week, we served the usual bar fare. On the weekends, I upped my game with some higher-scale dinner options. And today, my skills were going to be put to the test.

I decided to make a little flight of drinks for him to try. "My name's Henry, by the way." Peach Sour, a peach cider, Sex on the Beach, Fuzzy Navel, and just for the fun of it since I'd been playing around with something citrusy, a Lemon Drop Martini. Just small samples of each, I didn't want the guy going on his way tipsy.

He hesitated, watching me create his drinks. "Um, I'm Jackson. Usually Jack. Never Jackie."

Hmmm, there was a story there.

Maybe I'd hear it someday.

I refilled his water and placed the drink sampler in front of him. "Good to meet ya, Jack. All the peach drinks are made with our very own peach simple syrup—no fake peach flavor here. You've got a Peach Sour, peach cider, Sex on the Beach, and a Fuzzy Navel." I pointed to each drink as I named them, loving the way he cocked a brow at Sex on the Beach. "This one is a Lemon Drop Martini I've been playing around with. Keep drinking your water, and I'll be back with an appetizer."

Jack gave a little shake of his head and a smile before picking up the cider.

I rushed through the swinging doors to the back, the

warm, fragrant air blasting me in the face. Hot oil, fresh onions, searing meat mixed with the scents of heavy-duty dish soap and bleach water.

Fueled by the gleam in Jack's eyes over whatever game this was we were playing, I quickly plated up four boneless wings with a side of our sweet and spicy peach barbeque sauce. I wanted to toss the wings in the sauce, but in case he wasn't a fan, I opted to let him dip.

Ignoring my cook's confused look, I headed back toward the bar.

"If you don't care for them, I don't expect you to eat them," I said as I placed the plate in front of him. "You like any of those drinks?"

"The lemon drop thing was awesome. The rest were good."

I smirked. "Just determined not to like peach, huh?"

Jack grinned. "I just really liked the lemon."

"Okay, you enjoy the wings. I'm going to work on your meal. You okay with a flaky white fish? I can do chicken too, but I thought you might want something different after the wings."

"I like fish," he said with a shrug before dipping a wing in the sauce.

Trying to hide my smile at the way his eyes lit up with his first bite, I glanced around to make sure my servers had all the tables covered and headed back to the kitchen.

"Any reason you're back here messing up my kitchen when you're supposed to be manning the bar?" Sam asked, his beefy arms crossed over his chest, two different smears of today's lunch on his crisp white apron.

"You know I like to cook just as much as I like to mix

drinks and chat with customers." I grabbed two filets of the white fish, sprinkled them with a fragrant seasoning, and tossed them on the grill. "Just wanted to try out this fish taco recipe before we put it on the menu." Sam and I were beyond competent at the grill, and we took turns as needed, but it was usually me coming up with the ideas, and Sam executing the cooking.

"Got anything to do with the cute guy you've been drooling over at the end of the bar?" Sam's eyes twinkled before he returned to his work.

"What? No." Hoping my face was as neutral as I meant for it to be, I mixed up a peach and mango salsa.

"Kayla said you were bummed when he left before you got to comp his meal the other day," Sam continued.

"My employees need to mind their own damn business," I grumbled, adding cilantro, onion, and lime to the peach salsa while the fish sizzled on the grill. The mix of scents wafted on the steamy air and added just the right punchy zest to the meal.

Sam chuckled. "I had an order for steamed veggies earlier, you want some of those?"

I glanced at the colorful mix of red peppers, carrots, zucchini, yellow squash, and cauliflower. "Yeah, that looks amazing." I chunked the fish, loaded three tortillas with thinly shredded cabbage and the flaky pieces of grilled fish, and spooned the peach and mango salsa into a ramekin. With a large scoop of the steamed and seasoned veggies finishing the picture-perfect plate, I tossed a couple limes atop the fish tacos.

"Looks good," Sam said.

"Jack says he doesn't like peaches." I wiped the edge of the plate.

"Jack, huh?" Sam winked.

I huffed. "Everyone has a name."

"And this person with a name doesn't like peaches?"

"Correct."

"And he's in Haven Grove?" Sam asked with a smirk.

"He's only ever had canned peaches."

Sam winced.

"Right?"

"So, you're going to prove him wrong?"

I smiled. "The Great Peach Challenge. Peach drinks, peach BBQ wings, peach salsa, and the most important part, peach desserts."

"You gonna ask him out?" Sam elbowed me.

Snorting, I picked up the plate. "I don't even know the guy. And I don't do the whole dating thing."

Sam shrugged. "If he keeps coming in, you'll know him before long."

"Even if I was interested, he's at least ten years younger than me."

Sam eyed me like he knew something I didn't. "Hudson and Lance don't seem to mind the gap." He waggled his brow at the mention of one of the worst kept secrets in Haven Grove. "And age is just a number."

I rolled my eyes and flipped him off.

When I reached the bar, Jack's appetizer plate was empty, the flight of drinks drained, and he slurped the last of his water before wiping a napkin over his mouth.

"Lunch is served." I placed the tacos in front of him. "Let me get you more water. You want another drink?"

"Water is good," Jack said, his eyes greedily taking in the tacos. "These look amazing."

"Grilled fish tacos with peach and mango salsa, fresh steamed veggies. You don't *have* to use the salsa, but it's the perfect addition to the fish." I grabbed his water glass and refilled it. "Enjoy. I'll let you be while you eat. Don't fill up too much, you've still got dessert."

I made a round through the Roadhouse, chatting with locals, clearing a couple tables, and taking a few drink orders. Keeping an eye on Jack without hovering, I waited until he looked to be nearing the end of his meal and headed to the kitchen to start his desserts.

Citrus grilled peaches, peach pound cake, and peach crisp with ice cream from The Sweet & Creamy Dairy Palace in town. Just a tiny bit of each, but hopefully enough to give him a better impression of peaches.

"Dude, there's no way I can finish all of this." Jack had two tacos left on his plate when I emerged from the kitchen with dessert. "Do you do doggie bags?"

"Sure thing. I'll pack you up good." I placed the tiny bowls of dessert in front of him. "Citrus grilled peaches, peach pound cake, and peach crisp with ice cream from right here in town."

Jack dug right in starting with the citrus grilled peaches. He chewed, swallowed, and took another bite.

I waited while the din of voices and silverware rang in my ears and sweet peachy goodness teased my nose.

And waited.

Finally, he grinned. "Fine, these are fucking delicious."

Letting out a whoosh of air, I sagged. "Hell, yeah they

are." I gestured toward the tiny bowls. "Try the rest. I'll get a box for your tacos."

When I returned with a to-go box, Jack had eaten most of the grilled peaches, half the pound cake, and was scooping up the last bit of peach crisp and ice cream.

"Oh my god," Jack said. "I never knew."

I cocked a brow.

"Never knew how good real peaches were. All this time, I swore I didn't like them. And this ice cream is fuckin' amazing."

"I'll be sure to let Lance know. His family owns The Sweet & Creamy Dairy Palace. They've been making ice cream longer than I've been alive."

"I probably can't pay for everything, but at least let me pay something." Jack reached for his wallet.

"Nope. I said it was on the house. Plus, converting you to the peachy side is payment enough."

Jack grinned. "The peachy side, huh?"

"Yep. You can't live in Haven Grove and not love peaches." I wanted to ask what brought him to town. Wanted to know where he was staying.

"Well, I guess it's a good thing you converted me."

So, he lived here? The Haven Grove rumor mill would work its magic and provide information about Jack soon enough. But I didn't want gossip and rumors. I wanted to learn about Jack from Jack.

And what was that about? Since when did I want to learn more about a person? I had my brother, my dad, and Lance in my life. Beyond that, I'd never really felt the need for more people getting close to me. Arm's length was good enough for me.

Hudson was a pro at hooking up and sending people on their way.

Me? My heart got too involved too easily, so I just shut most people out.

But really, it was no big deal. I got to know bar patrons all the time. Maybe not on a deep level, but I was friendly enough with most people in town.

Getting to know Jack was no different.

And it wasn't like I had a *thing* for him. He was way too young for me even if I was looking for something romantic.

Which I wasn't.

I kept most people on the outside of my close circle.

And I planned to keep it that way.

There was just something about Jack that made me want to delve a bit deeper than the usual superficial bar chatter.

It didn't mean anything.

Chapter 2
Jackson Garner

TAKING A DEEP BREATH OF THE WARM, STICKY late summer air heavy with fresh-cut grass, honeysuckle, and the nearby sweet scent of peaches, I let the peacefulness of this place wash over me. The calmness in my soul was new. I hadn't yet gotten used to the fact no one was yelling at me, and my anxiety had dropped by several degrees.

I got a couple curious glances and a few friendly smiles as I stretched my legs in the parking lot outside the Roadhouse. I'd taken to getting up super early, filling my water bottle, washing up a bit, and then strolling around town. I'd been here long enough people recognized me, but it was clear they didn't know who I was. Some whispered, but most still offered me a friendly nod and wave. I'd always heard small towns were friendly, and Haven Grove was proving that adage true.

I glanced at the restaurant I'd come to consider my home base. The Roadhouse was a bi-level building. From the front, the single level stretched out to the right. That's where the bar, dining room, open area for pool and darts, kitchen, and restrooms for patrons were located. The far end of the single level looked to be an extra space of some sort, but it appeared to be empty.

The two-story part of the building came up off the back area. On the ground level, there was a workroom, storage room, office, and private restroom. The outside back area housed an old booth, a storage cabinet, and wooden stairs leading up to what I assumed was the owner's apartment. The apartment's shape was boxy from the outside, but it appeared large enough to provide a nice living area on the inside.

The Roadhouse was neat and clean, but it looked every single bit like what you'd expect a small-town bar and restaurant to look like. It wasn't a five-star eatery; there was absolutely nothing fancy about it. But the food was delicious, and the owner was one of the kindest people I'd ever met. Plus, he made an amazing Lemon Drop Martini, and his other cocktails were pretty good as well.

This town was nothing like the huge city I'd come from. Nothing about that place was friendly—namely the people I was forced to call my family. For years, I'd dreamed of leaving, striking out on my own, realizing my own dreams, but fear held me back.

No more, though.

It was close enough to lunch time I thought I could wander into the Roadhouse and kill some time—which seemed like all I'd been doing lately, but no one had scolded me for it. And I enjoyed the people watching and friendly atmosphere.

Being on my own, being allowed to make my own decisions, being treated as a trusted adult...all of that was going to take some getting used to. But I already knew I liked it. The giddy butterflies flitting around my gut told me leaving had been the right decision, and I was on the right track. It was just going to take some time to overcome two decades of conditioning that had my head and heart doubting nearly everything.

I placed my backpack under the bar stool. I'd reached a point where I *had* to make a decision one way or another. Haven Grove was a place I wanted to stay, but I had no idea how to go about making that a reality.

When I'd arrived in the little town, I'd opted to hang out for a bit to get my bearings. I liked the name of the town. I liked the idea of a haven, a place to rest and reset. Thought I'd maybe chill for a while before moving on if the initial good vibes wore off.

But then I met Henry Riggs.

Henry offered me kindness and generosity—a complete stranger, yet he took care of me better and more genuinely than anyone in nearly twenty years. Henry kept me safe and protected—although, he didn't know that part yet. And he helped me realize I actually liked peaches—the real kind, not the canned ones we got at school.

Not to mention he was drop-dead gorgeous.

But I obviously wasn't thinking about staying in Haven Grove because of a handsome bartender. I'd spent too many years just going through the motions of life based on what others wanted instead of living for me.

No. If I stayed, it would be because of more than just Henry.

But that didn't stop me from thinking about making this little town my home.

At twenty-five, I hadn't felt *at home* anywhere since I was six. And even those memories had faded to the point I barely trusted them anymore. From time to time, I'd catch a whiff of perfume—something like roses—and it would wake something inside me trying to recall if that was what she smelled like. Or I'd hear a woman's laughter, and I'd wonder if that was how she sounded.

Each passing year chipped away more and more of my tiny treasure trove of memories. Even the two photographs I carried in my wallet, corners ragged and colors fading, were only artifacts—proof of a good life I once lived, but so far removed from who I was now it was hard to imagine I was ever that small. Or that we were ever that happy.

She would have wanted me to be happy. I didn't need vivid memories to confirm the one thing my heart knew deep down. My mother didn't want to leave me. She fought tooth and nail to stay with me, and she wouldn't have ever wished for me to go to the home I ended up in. But even with the fading scent of her perfume, longing to hear her laughter one more time, and the disconnect when I gazed at those long-ago photos, I knew without a doubt that she would have been supportive. My biggest fan.

Like a poem on a loop, I heard her tired, weak, fading voice every single day.

Be safe. Be healthy. Be happy, sweet boy. Never let anyone dull your zest for life. Live life to the fullest, and love until your heart is bursting.

Despite the smeared ink on her last words to me, the

paper worn thin by my fingers and tucked tightly behind my two most treasured pictures, I'd lost her words over the years. No, *lost* wasn't the right word. Her words had been drowned out in a toxic environment. In the quiet moments, few and far between, heavy-laden with anxiety, worry, and fear, I'd pick up her refrain. I'd hold on tight. I'd promise myself *one day*.

And *one day* finally happened.

So, there I was in a Podunk-but-welcoming town the size of a postage stamp.

Unsure of what the hell I was going to do.

Homeless and jobless.

But enjoying a sense of peace the likes of which I couldn't remember in…well, ever.

Haven Grove was picture-perfect, exactly what you'd think a small-town centering around a peach orchard would look like. Old farmhouses, clapboard buildings built long ago mixed with newer ones, vehicles meant more for work than flash and swagger, average people just living their best lives, rolling hills, a scenic orchard spread out over several acres, and even a couple actual dirt roads leading here and there.

So very different from what I was used to, but I loved how quiet it was. Not like the town wasn't full of life, but there weren't the usual big city noises overtaking the background. Birds, crickets, frogs, and cicadas sang their melodies with the same gusto as those auditioning for the next big stage production here in Haven Grove. After years of big city cacophony and domestic dissonance, I'd taken to the small town quiet like a duck to water.

More than anything, I loved how quiet my soul could

be here. Relaxed. At ease. Not on constant guard. From the moment I stepped off that bus it was like I could actually take a deep breath and know things were going to get better.

I needed to look around town and see if anyone was hiring. I'd seen the Juicy Peach orchard and general store, the Sweet & Creamy Dairy Palace, Glazed Buns, and the Riggs Family Roadhouse. There was also a rundown gym, a little gas station and auto repair shop, a tiny school, and a few other small businesses. Surely, one of them was in need of a new employee.

The Roadhouse or Glazed Buns would likely be my best bet if I ever wanted to get a foot in the door to making my dream come true. A dream I'd been forced to quell, shamed into hiding, and bullied into never mentioning it. But that hadn't stopped me from dreaming and honing my skills. I'd just had to get creative.

And now I was ready to put my talents into action with the perfect job.

But a job usually required proof of residence. And getting a place to stay usually required proof of income.

I had neither because I'd left home with no plan. Just grabbed a tiny suitcase, shoved whatever I could into it, and fled without looking back.

And I'd do it all over again.

But being stuck in an unfamiliar town with no job or place to live wasn't the best way to start out on my own.

I'd come to town with every single dollar I could pull from the ATM back home packed in a hidden pocket of my backpack. It wasn't a lot, but I'd been stretching it, and I could make it last a while longer.

The day I left, I'd vowed to never go back, but I couldn't just hang out in the Roadhouse every day. I needed to either make something happen in Haven Grove, or head out of town and look for something else.

A tiny twinge in the center of my chest had me thinking sure I could leave this pretty little town and start over somewhere else. But Haven Grove was beautiful; I couldn't even begin to imagine it in the autumn. Something about the place had me feeling more settled and at peace than I'd been in nearly two decades. And I'd seen a lot of people coming and going at the Roadhouse. Everyone seemed friendly enough.

Henry was the only person I'd say I actually knew, but I'd seen people I assumed were his family. I was pretty sure the guy with lighter hair than Henry's was his brother—I'd heard one of the servers call him Hudson. He was taller, slightly less broad in the chest, and kinda reminded me of a golden retriever puppy who hadn't grown into his feet yet. The brothers laughed and talked whenever Hudson came into the bar. They seemed close.

An older guy was often with Hudson. If I'd overheard correctly, his name was Lance, which made him the guy who owned the Sweet & Creamy Dairy Palace. Lance and Hudson looked a bit more like father and son based on their ages, but the way they touched and smiled had me thinking they definitely weren't related.

Then there was a guy who looked to be about Lance's age. He had to be Henry's father. I'd heard a couple of the townsfolk call him Casey Joe or Casey, and one guy called him CJ. Lance called him Case a couple times. Casey Joe looked like the perfect mix of Henry and Hudson. He was built broader like Henry, but his features matched more with Hudson.

One thing I noticed sitting at the bar and moving about town was that Lance and Hudson were flirty—there was definitely something between them—but they never touched or flirted when Casey Joe was around. Interesting.

I'd always been good at watching people. In school, I struggled *terribly* with reading and writing. My uncle wouldn't allow the school to test me for anything that maybe would have gotten me some extra support. *"The Hills don't do charity. This family doesn't need any extra help in school or life. We take care of ourselves."*

He threw in some other words that weren't worth repeating.

In one of my earliest life lessons, I learned that *we take care of ourselves* didn't mean they took care of *me*. Just that they refused to get me any help.

But I watched in school and figured out quickly which kids were getting extra support. I made sure to sit near them—I'd pull my chair next to their small group. Soon enough, the teachers who came in to help included me in their groups. I got the extra support I needed with my uncle being none the wiser.

Thankfully, my struggles with reading and writing eased a bit as I got that help, and high school wasn't *as* terrible. But I took advantage of every single offer of tutoring and extra help available.

Same with college. While I didn't get to go to the school I really wanted to attend, I recognized that the business degree my uncle required me to get would come in handy in my future endeavors. The tutors and study tables at college were where I spent almost every moment of my free time.

Now that I was on my own, I had every intention of turning my hobby into a career. I just had to find the right place to put down roots and get my start.

I knew Haven Grove felt right. There was a draw to this place, a pull toward these people. I'd never been taken care of, and maybe this was the place I could find that. But more than anything, this tiny town and the people in it, felt like the perfect place for me to spread my wings. After so many shitty years, maybe I could finally learn to be true to myself rather than barely living life.

Chapter 3
Henry

My eyes landed on Jack coming in the front door just as my brother and Lance headed out the side door.

So far, I'd been spared from Hudson's questions regarding Jack since they hadn't run into each other in the lengthening time the new guy had been in town.

On one hand, I honestly didn't have much to say.

On the other hand, I wasn't ready for Hudson to meet Jack.

Which was ridiculous.

We weren't dating. We barely knew each other. He was just a customer.

But Hudson would make it a thing.

And I just wasn't ready for that.

For all I knew, Jack would leave Haven Grove before Hudson finally pulled his head from Lance's ass and realized the sunny blond was in town.

And frequenting the Roadhouse daily.

While looking like a damn sunshine grenade blew up on him.

Those fucking aquamarine eyes and gleaming smile were an absolutely lethal combination.

I gave a quick wave toward Jack as I took orders for a couple guys at the other end of the bar. I already knew Jack would order water and a sandwich. I got the feeling he was eating on a very thin budget.

Glancing toward a few patrons and noticing their whispers and narrowed eyes, I couldn't help but chuckle. Haven Grove was a friendly, welcoming place, but that didn't mean the good townsfolk weren't in a tizzy trying to figure out who the sunshiney man was and what he was doing in our little town.

I entered the order I'd just taken and made my way toward Jack. "You know, you've got the whole town abuzz with questions."

He cocked a brow. "Why's that?"

"So far, I've heard you're an exotic dancer. Not sure where they think you're going to dance, maybe in the orchard." I pretended to consider it. "I bet I could get Hudson to install a pole..."

The flush of pink on Jack's face stirred something in my gut. "No dancing here. Exotic or otherwise."

"Well then, how about an undercover agent?" I slid a glass of ice water in front of him. "Heard someone say you'd come to town to solve a murder. Maybe our very own Jack Reacher in the form of Jack Garner."

"Not even close." His eyes flashed with humor. "I don't even like the unsolved mystery type shows on TV."

I slapped a menu in front of him. "Big rig driver whose truck broke down and you're just waiting for repairs?"

"Been here an awful long time waiting for the repair guy." Jack huffed out a chuckle. "They're going to be disappointed to find out I'm just a regular guy looking for a new place to live." He cleared his throat. "And a job," he muttered.

It was my turn to cock a brow.

He shook his head. "Never mind. Can I get the BLT, please?"

I let him change the subject.

For now.

"You want fries or onion rings?" I offered, knowing he'd say no. He always turned down a side.

"No, just the sandwich, thanks." He handed me the menu.

I couldn't *accidentally* bring him fries every time he ordered something.

And I could only knock so much off his bill without him knowing something was up.

But I couldn't help wanting to feed him.

And now I knew he needed a job and a place to stay.

Did that mean he planned on staying in Haven Grove?

Shit.

I needed to play it cool. If I started asking a bunch of questions, I might spook him.

Slow and steady.

I tapped my pen on the little notebook. "Let me get this put in. I'll be back with some more water."

Jack was looking at his phone when I returned with a pitcher of water and two small bowls. I got the feeling he came to the Roadhouse so often because he could hang out for hours, fill up on water and peanuts aside from his tiny meal, charge his phone in the outlet near his stool, and use the Wi-Fi.

Not that I minded him sitting at my bar looking like sunshine personified every day. I'd gotten kinda used to it. Seeing him walk through the door brought a smile to my face and a zing of *something* to my heart. Jack had inexplicably become the highlight of my days.

"Sam and Kayla both fixed sides for an order, so these are extras. You want them?" I wasn't sure my intended nonchalance hit its mark based on the way Jack studied me, but he eventually shrugged and let me place two bowls of cottage cheese and applesauce in front of him.

I took care of drying some glasses, filling the ice, and clearing a few plates at the other end of the bar while Jack polished off the cottage cheese and started in on the applesauce.

"Order up," Sam called, framed by the kitchen window, billowing steam, grill smoke, and the sizzle of burgers providing the perfect backdrop.

When I grabbed the plate and noticed chips nestled around the BLT, my eyes flew to Sam's.

He shrugged. "My bad. I was plating another order and got carried away."

"Gotcha. Thanks."

Sam was good people. Most of Haven Grove was the same.

If Jack was going to stay, he'd be hard pressed to find a better place.

If he was going to stay.

Placing the plate in front of Jack, I caught his furrowed brow. "Sorry about the chips. Sam had a bunch of orders and threw chips on yours too."

Jack looked like he wanted to argue. What was he going to do? Ask me to remove the chips from his plate?

Jack picked up a chip and popped it in his mouth. "Thanks."

I gave a little nod. "Enjoy your lunch." Forcing myself to leave him to eat in peace, I rang up a couple bills, made my rounds through the dining room, chatted a bit with some guys playing pool, and gathered up some dishes.

As much as I would have liked to comp Jack's meal, I'd run out of viable excuses to give him free food. So, I printed his ticket and placed it on the bar as he finished the last of his chips and water.

"Hey, listen," I started.

Jack glanced at me, a hint of wariness in his pretty blue eyes.

"I'm not sure where you came from or what the rent situation was like there. Small town living is a lot cheaper than elsewhere, but that doesn't mean it's not gonna cost ya. There might be a few places available around here, but most of them aren't going to be affordable without at least a few months' worth of paychecks under your belt. I've got a pretty comfortable couch I'm willing to let you borrow if you plan on sticking around town."

He cocked his head. "You offer your couch to a lot of strangers?"

When I hesitated, he raised a brow.

"Not often." It wasn't a lie, but it *was* ironic I'd offered my couch to two strangers in such a short time.

"You barely know me."

"I've got good instincts." I knocked my knuckles on the bar. "Think about it. It's yours for however long you need if you want it."

He chewed on his lower lip, pulling the collar of his shirt up and rubbing it over his chin—something I'd noticed seemed to be a nervous or anxious response. "Yeah, okay. I'll let you know."

The kid stayed mum on the subject for several days. He came in to eat a midday meal, hung out for a few hours, and left without so much as a word about the offer to stay on my couch.

Just as I was about to bring it up again—where the hell was he staying?—Jack cleared his throat one day as he paid his bill.

"You still got that couch?" he asked, his cheeks a pretty pink as he chewed his bottom lip.

Remembering how Hudson would shut down if he thought I was excited about something back when he was younger, I schooled my features. "Yep. Couch, pillow, and I can even throw in a blanket."

"Once I get a job, I'll pay you back—"

I held up a hand. "That's not part of this deal."

"But—"

"No, I'm offering the couch with no strings attached. You get a job and want to move on to something bigger and better? That's your choice. But the couch is yours, no payment." I handed him his change. "Now, if you want to wash any dishes you make and maybe gather up the trash from time to time, I'm not gonna complain about that."

Jack studied me with those big blue eyes for several heartbeats before he bit his bottom lip and smiled. "Yeah, I can do that."

Chapter 4
Jack

THE OLD BOOTH OUT BACK HAD A LOOSE BENCH seat that lifted, the shriek of the cicadas *almost* drowning out the squeak of the hinges. I'd stowed my suitcase there the first night I curled up outside the Roadhouse—living mostly from my backpack—but, for the occasion of moving to the apartment upstairs, I hefted the tiny case out as twilight fell on Haven Grove. Once I had the dust and cobwebs brushed off, I gripped the handle of my suitcase and adjusted my backpack.

The flutters in my belly were nothing new, but I took a moment to really feel them. This wasn't nerves and fear rumbling through me like it had for so many years at home. This was excited anticipation.

I was actually doing this. Staying in Haven Grove. Taking my shot. Making a go of it.

But, if I was being honest, the excitement in my gut shared space with worry, both emotions roiling into a frenzy.

Henry had unknowingly offered me his couch not once, but twice. I had no plans to sleep in the man's apartment without letting him know I was the person who'd been sleeping on the old booth out back and eating the food he'd been leaving.

How to bring it up was something I still needed to figure out.

But I had to tell him and soon. It wasn't so much shame, although that feeling tinged the very edges of my being. It was more just that I knew I had to come clean.

I'd been raised for six years to know right from wrong. Then I'd spent the next nineteen being on the bad side of people who didn't know—or care—about the difference between right and wrong.

Guilt wracked me because I was essentially lying to the man who had done nothing but help me. It would have been one thing if I was leaving town. But I was staying, at least for now, and I didn't want to start anything with Henry with a lie of omission hanging between us.

Not that I thought anything was starting between us. Not like romantically.

Yeah, he was gorgeous in a big, kinda growly, protective way, but the point of hanging out in his restaurant and sleeping on his couch wasn't to get in his pants.

I mean, I wasn't against it, just wasn't the reason I accepted the offer of his couch.

My brain buzzed with way too many thoughts, a ton of hopeful excitement, and a mess of emotions as I rounded the building and headed toward the entrance.

Walking into the Roadhouse at closing time was a

stark contrast to the hustle and bustle of the place at lunchtime. The air hung heavy with fryer oil that needed to be changed after a long day, the yeasty smell of beer— probably what was making the floor sticky under my feet —and the garlicky breadsticks left over on a table waiting to be cleared.

The clack of pool balls signaled the end of a rousing game followed by laughter and hands slapping friends on shoulders as the little group cleaned up the game area. A couple walked out the door calling their friendly goodbyes to the staff. A teen bussed dirty dishes, stacking them in a tub carried tightly against a hip. Kayla wiped down tables, while Sam could be seen cleaning up the kitchen.

And then there was Henry.

He stood at the register, a scowl of concentration on his bearded face.

But he smiled when he glanced up and met my gaze.

Damn.

That smile did things to me.

From an early age, I'd known I was different, but then I lost my mom, and my whole world turned upside down. Being an orphan, living with toxic people, and struggling through grief and learning difficulties didn't leave a lot of time for exploring my sexuality.

I'd kissed a boy behind the bleachers in middle school. It had been quick and awkward, but it had cemented the fact I wanted to kiss boys in a way I definitely didn't feel about kissing girls.

My cousin Douglas somehow found out about the kiss and bullied me relentlessly about it. Degrading words, physical acts, and all-around threatening vibes were

Douglas's M.O. He was a few years older than me, and he had lackeys all around the school who were more than willing to spy on his little cousin and report back, probably to keep his wrath away from them.

Douglas had never been kind to me, but when he found out about that kiss, his mean streak shifted into high gear. Of course, my uncle Joseph egged it on, and then laughed it off with the tired old mantra of *boys will be boys*.

My aunt Chrissy, Mom's sister, wasn't a bad person. She'd just been caught up in her own personal demons and stuck with an asshole and his son—Mom hadn't really known Joseph as she was too sick by the time Chrissy married him. I'd like to think Mom wouldn't have let me go to Chrissy if she'd known, but I wasn't sure what other options she really had.

Chrissy was usually so high on whatever prescription medication she could get her hands on that she didn't stand a chance of cooking dinner let alone standing up to Joseph and Douglas for me. I didn't really blame her for my situation. She had a lot of mental health struggles, and losing her sister made things worse. Joseph was willing to keep her in money and didn't question the medication as long as his wife performed her duties as he saw fit.

So, knowing I was gay and living with homophobic assholes meant I had very little opportunity to spend time with other guys. I branched out a bit in college, but by that point, I was so stunted in my personal journey, I found myself keeping my distance from the dating scene after quickly finding out that a large majority of the guys on apps, and even around campus, were pretty much jerks.

I wanted to kiss, hold hands, go watch a show and grab dinner. Most guys I met wanted to fuck me into a mattress and walk away before morning. At nineteen and twenty, on my own for the first time and learning who I was and what I liked, casual sex wasn't where it was at for me.

At twenty-five, I'd had a bit more time to discover myself, and I wasn't completely against being fucked into a mattress. But I'd also figured out I'd always be the type of guy who wanted to know someone first. I wanted those flirty smiles and glances, those soft first touches and kisses, holding hands, going to dinner, watching a show. If sex developed from that, I was all for it—and if it didn't, that was fine by me—but I knew myself enough now to know I *needed* the rest of it before sex was on the table.

Lost in the thoughts brought on by Henry's killer smile, it took me a moment to realize he'd said something and was waiting on me to reply. I flinched internally as I recalled how Douglas would punch me right in the chest or slap the back of my head when I got lost in thought.

But Henry just grinned, his care and patience a warm blanket wrapping around me. He quirked a brow, cocked his head, and just waited.

"Sorry, what?" I asked, hearing Douglas's harsh words in my head as I pulled the collar of my shirt up to hold it tightly between my lips while I collected myself.

Henry had no hateful words, no violent hands, just a sweet chuff of laughter. "I asked if you wanted to eat dinner down here or with me upstairs. I usually take leftovers home and eat while I watch the late news."

After nineteen years of never feeling like anyone gave two shits about me—nineteen years of being surrounded by *family,* but feeling so damn lost and alone—the thought of heading upstairs with this gentle giant sent an ooey-gooey warmth to my belly.

I dropped my shirt collar and cleared my throat, hating that my painful past was a constant drum beat in my head. "I can eat upstairs."

Henry gave a wink and a nod. "Sounds good. I'll gather us up some to-go boxes here in a minute."

I sat on my usual stool and watched as the crew worked together to close down the place. With several lights off, all the patrons headed home, and the music turned off, the atmosphere morphed from busy and fun to cozy and calm. I lost myself in watching Henry count the cash drawer, pull receipts, and scratch notes while the scent of dish soap and bleach danced on the air.

"Come on, you can help me pick out dinner." Henry gestured for me to follow him.

As I fell in step beside him, a thought zinged through me. *I'd follow this man anywhere.* I didn't hate the idea, but it was something new to ponder. Aside from my mom, I'd never had anyone in my life I trusted and would *truly* follow anywhere.

And then I'd found myself in Haven Grove and met Henry.

I'd been here a while, but these swirly feelings in my gut were way too much and way too soon.

Right?

Of course they were. Henry hadn't indicated an interest in me. Whatever I was feeling needed to stay tamped down lest I ruin my chances at making a life in Haven Grove.

I took a deep breath to settle my nerves.

He led me to the back area where I'd taken advantage of the unlocked door to get a shower and slightly better sleep for so many nights.

"So, this area is just for employees mostly." His eyes caught on the booth—my bed—and he frowned. "The bathroom back here has a shower." He pointed to the backdoor I'd slipped through so many times. "That leads to a little area out back. Trash, smoke breaks, stuff like that. Also, the way I go home." He nodded toward the door. "Go ahead and put your stuff there. We'll grab it on the way out."

Right then.

I should have told him right then. He clearly had no idea I was the person he'd been leaving the door open for. No clue I was the person he'd been giving leftovers to every night.

Something caught in my throat. I *had* to be honest with him. But what if I told him, and he changed his mind about me staying on his couch?

Instead, I cleared my throat and blurted, "You should do outdoor dining."

"Huh?"

I gestured toward the backdoor. "Set up some outdoor dining. On nice days, people would probably like to eat outside. Get some local live music. Even on cooler days, you could have some of those heaters set up."

Henry eyed me for a moment as he mulled over my words. "Thought about it before, just never took the time to make it happen."

"Well, you should."

Henry's eyes twinkled, making the scowl lines between his brows seem so much less grouchy. "Come on, we'll pack up some dinner."

Dinner first.

Then I'd tell him instead of tossing out business ideas.

Henry placed three carry-out boxes on the counter as Sam gave a wink and waved goodbye on his way out. I'd watched the comings and goings of the Roadhouse enough to know Sam would walk Kayla to her car before he climbed in his old truck and headed home.

"Burgers and lasagna sound okay?" Henry asked. When my eyes locked with his, he huffed out a laugh. "Weird combo, I know, but it's what's left."

I shrugged. "Beggars can't be choosers."

He fumbled a serving spoon, the utensil clattering on the metal countertop, but Henry recovered quickly and handed me a box. "Let's do this." He nodded toward the container. "Put the burgers in this one."

I loaded the box with two of the three leftover burgers. "Two or three?"

"Do three if they'll fit." He scooped two heaping helpings of lasagna into his box. "Put all the fixins' for the burgers in that other box." Henry grabbed a fourth box. "We can put green beans in this one. And the best way to pack up a couple pieces of cake is with those smaller containers."

"Do you always take this much food home?" I asked as I filled a container with lettuce, tomatoes, pickles, onions, and packets of mayo, mustard, and ketchup.

"Sure do, no reason to let food go to waste." He paused, his eyes traveling toward the backdoor. He scowled before shaking his head. "Look in the fridge. Should be cake in there."

By the time we had everything packed up, my stomach rumbled for dinner. "I'll come back down and get my bags," I said as we walked toward the backdoor with our arms laden with to-go boxes.

"No worries," Henry said. "I'll come back down here in a bit and grab them."

While you leave a plate of food and unlock the backdoor. I bit my lip. What would Henry do when the food he left on the picnic table wasn't eaten.

Tell him right now.

Instead, I swallowed a lump of guilt and followed Henry up the stairs to his place. The light, homey scent of cinnamon and cedar welcomed me like a warm hug into Henry's comfy little apartment.

"We'll eat first, and then I'll show you around," Henry said. He placed his boxes on the table. "Grab us some plates from that cabinet." He pointed toward a thin cabinet next to the sink.

I did as I was told, a strange ease and familiarity washing over me as we worked together seamlessly in his tiny kitchen.

"Want a drink?" Henry asked from his position peering into the fridge. "I've got peach cider, water, milk, juice, and some pop."

"Pop?"

He withdrew from the refrigerator with a playful grin. "Sorry, you're in the Midwest now, you better get used to it. Soda?"

"Ohhh," I drawled, and put on my absolute worst

southern accent. "I'd heard tell that folks in these parts called it *pop*, but never witnessed it myself until tonight."

Henry chuckled and elbowed me. "Smart ass. I grew up calling it pop but interchange it with soda just as often. I'll try to stick with pop to give you the true Midwestern experience."

"Peaches, pop…gee, what else in is store for me?" Back and forth with Henry was the easiest thing I'd ever done. A friendly, easy banter I'd never had with anyone else.

When our plates were full, Henry gestured toward the living room with his bottle of water. "I've got this little kitchen nook, but I find myself eating in front of the TV more often than not."

"I'm not picky." I followed him from the kitchen and sat down on the couch.

My bed?

The whole situation was surreal. I'd left home quickly and under somewhat strange circumstances—something I hadn't completely let myself relax enough to think about —but never once did I think I'd end up in a small town known for peaches and sleeping on the couch of the gruff-but-secretly-sweet bar owner.

Henry settled down in a recliner, and I fought the ridiculous urge to want to cuddle close to him.

"You okay with the news?" Henry asked as he pointed the remote toward the television.

"I'm good with anything."

He took a swig of water as the late-night news came on. "This is the most local channel we get. It's based about twenty miles up the road, but they'll cover Haven Grove happenings as needed." Henry scooped up a bite of lasagna. "What do you normally like to watch?" he asked before taking the bite and chewing.

I swallowed the sip of water I'd taken and shrugged. "Cooking shows, I guess. Mostly baking. Cakes and stuff."

"We'll get along just fine." Henry grinned. "I keep it on the news, the weather, or cooking shows ninety-nine percent of the time."

"Do you like to cook?" The soft couch—and Henry's presence—offered a level of comfort and protection I'd longed for since my mom died, and I savored a big bite of burger while I sank into the warm cushions.

"I do. Sam and I take turns sometimes. I like planning the meals the most. It's why Sam and I get along. He'd rather let me set the menu while he cooks it up."

"Good team."

"We are."

God, the way that little grin melted away the grumpy façade. Henry was such a study in contrasts. Big, burly, and scowly was what most people saw. But it was all just a front.

I didn't think he purposely tried to put up a false wall, it was just who he was, what his life had trained him to do. I could be way off base, but my vibes about people were usually right. Hope washed over me; maybe I'd get to know the man behind the scruff and scowl better.

Henry cleared his throat. "Do you cook?"

Biting my lip, I fought the engrained fear of admitting what I liked. But I took a deep breath and lifted my chin. "Bake."

"Hmm?"

"I like to bake."

"No shit?"

I shrugged. "Yeah."

"You any good?" He cocked his head, a playful smile teasing his lips.

"You know that cake we brought up here?"

"Yeah?"

"And the cake I had the first night I came in?"

Henry narrowed his eyes. "Yeah."

I pulled my collar up to brush it over my lips even though I wasn't the least bit anxious around Henry. "And the peach pound cake?"

He crossed his arms over his chest. Probably trying to look menacing, but the gesture just sent warm giddiness straight to my heart. *"Yeah?"*

"I could do better."

A flash of something crossed his face. Surprise, I think. Then he narrowed his eyes, and a bit of a grumble sounded.

A giggle bubbled up from deep within me and escaped before I had the chance to stop it. Nothing about this man scared me—except maybe the fact I knew nothing of his personal life, his sexuality, *anything* really—I was likely barking up the wrong tree and setting myself up for heartache...if I was interested in him like that, which I kept telling myself I wasn't.

But I knew I was safe with him. Knew it was okay to poke this particular bear a bit. He'd grumble, but he'd just as soon ruffle my hair or tickle me into submission than truly be mean. I didn't think there was a mean bone in Henry's body.

And some part deep within me wanted to see what

would happen. Wanted this man's protective, gentle reactions. His arms around me, his hands on me in any way he wanted to touch me.

"Is that a challenge?" Henry's words, rough and full of humor, pulled me from the beginnings of very inappropriate thoughts.

"You issued the Great Peach Challenge," I said. "It's my turn to lay out the Great Cake Challenge."

"It's a deal." Henry stood from his recliner and moved to stand in front of me. Allowing my gaze to travel up his tall body, I realized just how big and burly this man was. But for the first time in my life, I had no fear of a man standing before me. Henry wasn't Joseph. He wasn't Douglas.

I took his proffered hand and let him pull me to stand facing him. "What?" The word wasn't meant to be a breathless whisper, but that's the way it came out.

"Gotta shake on it."

Henry still held my hand. Warmth and awareness filled the space between us, a current of electricity humming through our skin. His large, rough hand engulfed my smaller and probably sweaty one based on my heart beating a million miles a minute.

"What's the prize? And how do we determine if my cake is better?"

A flash of humor twinkled in Henry's eyes like I'd missed out on a joke, but he just gave my hand a squeeze. "We'll figure it out. No need to rush anything."

My mind immediately started planning which cakes I would make. How could I best incorporate Henry's beloved peaches? Could I do a lemon cake like his Lemon

Drop Martini? Or a dark salted chocolate to complement the tartness of the lemon, or even to go perfectly with the Peach Sour he'd made.

When I finally realized Henry was talking again, we were still holding hands, still facing each other with very little room in our personal bubbles.

And I wanted to completely invade his space, wrap my arms around his broad body, snuggle into his rugged, protective warmth.

Instead, I blinked away the thoughts of cakes dancing in my head and pulled my collar up to my lips. "Sorry, what?"

Henry huffed a laugh. "One of these days, you can tell me where you go in there." He tapped a finger gently against my temple. "Help me gather up this trash. Then we'll get you settled for the night."

We set to work cleaning up from dinner, and Henry placed a bag of trash by the door.

"So, my bedroom is at the end of this hall. Bathroom is right here." He flipped on the light to show a tidy bathroom complete with a tub and shower combo, toilet, double sink, and mirror. The room was decorated sparsely, but the cocktail theme was cute. As if sensing my thoughts, Henry shrugged, a hint of blush brushing his cheek bones above his beard. "My brother likes to go antiquing from time to time. He found the cocktail stuff on sale in a bundle and decorated while I was working."

"It's cute, I like it."

Henry studied me a moment before giving his head a shake and turning off the light. The brush of his hand on my back as he directed me back into the hall did funny things to my knees and belly.

Shit.

Was I getting in way over my head here?

But the touch hadn't come across as romantic or sexual, just a soft push in the direction he wanted me to go. I needed to get my stagnant-until-the-most-inopportune-times libido under control and not ruin the situation with a guy who had shown me nothing but platonic kindness.

"This closet has soap, towels, shampoo." He opened the closet next to the bathroom. "Under the sink is toilet paper and cleaning supplies. I use bar soap, you're welcome to use it, open a new bar, or get yourself whatever kind you like. The shampoo isn't fancy, but it gets the job done, and you're welcome to it."

The thought of steamy water pouring down on me while surrounded by the warm, woodsy scent of Henry had me wanting to take a shower right then and there.

But I kept myself together and followed him back to the living room with its soft, cozy couch and worn but tidy light beige carpet. The couch was a dark plaid of black, gray with small bits of teal, red, and yellow. I liked the way the teal curtains picked up on the same color in the sofa cushions.

"This chest has blankets and pillows." Henry opened a chest as I moved to stand beside him. The clean scent of cedar wafted up, the scent reminding me of being wrapped in a warm blanket while an icy cold rain pelted the windows, and logs crackled in the fireplace.

Henry handed me a pillow and tossed two blankets on the couch.

"Thanks." The word caught in my throat. Vivid memories of the hospital social worker dropping me off at Chrissy's house played through my mind like a low-budget afterschool special. The social worker, Kim, had been thrilled to know I'd have my own room. In hindsight, it was one of the only things that kept me sane. My room was mostly safe, a respite from Douglas's mean streak and Joseph's disinterest and unpredictable anger.

Maybe it was a total inconvenience to have me move in and disrupt everything about their lives. A small part of my brain told me that was ridiculous. I was six years old, I didn't eat much, I barely took up any space in the McMansion Joseph bragged about to anyone who would listen.

But some days, when the nightmares of my past reared their ugly heads, it took a lot of distraction and logic to convince myself Joseph and Douglas had no real reason to despise me as much as they did.

As an adult, I could reason they were miserable people who had a lot of their own issues to work through. As a kid, it was hard not to think everything was somehow my fault.

I cleared the emotion from my throat and tried again.

"Thanks," I croaked. It was just a couple blankets and a pillow, but it was one of the kindest gestures anyone had ever offered me.

And Henry had done it twice now.

Just because he could.

No strings, no benefits for him.

He was just a good person.

Maybe down the road I'd realize I'd been duped, but my gut sang Henry's praises, and my heart led the charge for all things Henry.

"If that pillow is too soft, there's a firmer one—" Henry started.

"No," I blurted, "this one is great. Perfect for cuddling."

Something washed over Henry's face as I clutched the pillow to my chest and rubbed my chin against the soft material. He gave a quick nod and turned away, heading toward the kitchen.

I followed, still gripping the pillow firmly to my chest. The human brain and emotions were really weird. The onslaught of warm gooeyness Henry had set in motion had also stirred up a shit-ton of negative thoughts and heavy memories.

Breathing in deeply, I allowed the soft scent of cedar to calm me.

"You're welcome to anything in the place, don't ever ask. I usually get groceries on Sunday afternoons. If the Juicy Peach doesn't have what I need, I'll make a run up the road to the bigger grocery, but I like to keep things as local as possible." Henry opened the fridge, peered inside, and then let it swing closed as he wrote on a magnetic pad of paper on the side of the fridge. "If you need anything, you're welcome to put it on the list, or do your own shoppin' if you like that idea better."

"Think anyone would want to hire me?" I didn't like how unsure my voice sounded, but the only real job I'd ever had was one I was forced into by my uncle, and I hated it even though it made me decent money. "I have a degree and skills. I'm teachable."

Henry studied me for a moment, his fingers scratching over his beard—more than stubble, but not quite bushy. "What kind of job you think you'd want?"

"Honestly, at this point, anything. Beggars can't be choosers, ya know?"

He paused, something unreadable in his expression, but then he nodded. "We'll see what we can figure out."

Something in me deflated, and Henry must have noticed because he put a big hand on my shoulder and squeezed. "I don't mean you aren't employable. I just mean we need to make sure to get you a job worth your while; don't want to waste your talent and potential."

Something hot and sweet flamed to life in my belly. Whoa, what was that?

I'll take "Things Jack is learning about himself for one hundred, Alex."

The clue is compliments and praise.

What is "Things Henry does to make Jack weak in the knees?"

Ding-ding-ding.

Huh. Who knew?

Maybe *I* should have known. You know, the kid with no father in the picture, a deceased mother, and two men who spent the majority of their time mentally, emotionally, and verbally abusing him. Yeah, maybe that kid would grow up to be the type who really liked a gorgeous, gentle, caring man complimenting him.

I swear, I'm not a complete fool, just slow to catch on sometimes.

"Why don't you go ahead and shower. Get settled in

for the night. I'm gonna run down to the bar and finish up a couple things before bed. Sleep in as long as you want in the morning."

"I should start looking for a job..."

And a vehicle.

An apartment.

A fist gripped my heart. There was so much I needed to do.

"No need to rush things. You've got all the time in the world. You're welcome here as long as you need."

"Why?" I blurted.

Henry shrugged. "Why not? I've got the space. I'm used to helping people."

"You don't even know me."

A soft chuff of laughter escaped him. "I know you well enough to know you're a good person, and you need a moment to gather yourself. Nothin' wrong with that. I'm in a position to help, and it's what I do. It's what I *live* to do."

Something unsaid floated on his words. "Who takes care of you?" The words slipped out before I could think them through.

Henry gave me a wink. "That's not the way it works. Go ahead and get your shower. I'll be back up in a bit."

Once Henry was gone, I decided I'd shower, start some laundry, charge my phone, and wait for him to return.

It was time to tell him.

With a tsunami of emotions pummeling my heart, I pulled clean clothes from my suitcase and headed to the bathroom. The shower was nothing special, but using the woodsy soap and citrusy shampoo that smelled like Henry might have been the highlight of my day.

Once I'd dried off and pulled on a t-shirt and shorts—my long sleeve shirt and long lounge pants were in dire need of a washing—I pulled all the dirty clothes from my backpack and made a pile in the basket I found in a hall closet.

The first door I opened looking for the washer and dryer was the water heater. The second was a coat closet. But what I thought was a pantry turned out to house a stacked unit. Tossing everything in, I poured in a cap-full of the soap Henry kept stored on a little wire shelf and turned the knob to normal wash.

Glancing at the couch, I decided I'd make up my bed and chill out until Henry returned. I grabbed another blanket from the chest and spread it out over the cushions. Once I'd turned off the lamp, the TV cast just enough light in the room. After plugging in my dead battery and my phone, I settled onto the couch.

Five minutes later, I popped up and grabbed the firmer pillow from the chest.

Firm pillow for my head, squishy pillow to hug close, and two warm blankets tucked around me while the late-late news droned on was the perfect.

A perfect recipe for disaster.

I most definitely wasn't awake when Henry came back up.

Chapter 5
Henry

JACK WAS SOUND ASLEEP WHEN I GOT BACK upstairs that first night, and it was likely for the best. He was clearly exhausted from whatever had brought him to Haven Grove, and hanging out without a place to stay hadn't helped in any way.

Plus, I knew we needed to talk, but I wasn't sure how to bring it up.

Or maybe he'd bring it up.

Someone needed to bring it up.

The elephant in the room.

The big question.

But he'd been passed out when I snuck into the apartment, and I hadn't even thought about waking him.

I felt like the biggest fool in the world for taking so long to put two and two together. It wasn't until Jack was sleeping on my couch, and the food I put on the table outside the backdoor of the bar didn't get eaten, that the puzzle pieces finally clicked into place.

Jack was my mystery guy.

Insert facepalm here.

Sure, looking back, there'd been clues I shouldn't have missed. Maybe I didn't really miss them, I just wasn't in the right headspace to pick up on them.

But why hadn't he said anything? At first, I'd been irritated. Was he playing me for a fool? Trying to pull one over on me? What was in it for him? It wasn't like a crappy booth and leftover food was some big prize.

The realization came the morning after Jack moved in, but after a couple days of Jack sleeping on my couch, eating cereal as he watched baking shows, washing dishes, and gathering up the trash, I realized his reasons were all his own, and I couldn't push him to tell me.

Sure, I could ask, but it didn't feel right.

Jack needed to come to me on his own. It had to be in *his* timing and for *his* reasons. There were likely a hundred reasons Jack hadn't told me he was the guy sleeping out back.

Honestly, it was killing me to not know, but I stubbornly refused to push the subject until Jack was ready. Until then, he had a safe space, and I was left wondering just how long I'd be able to keep my secret boarder from Hudson.

As if my family had a sixth sense and knew I was thinking of them, my dad came rip roarin' into the bar before we opened, the backdoor slamming behind him. "Who the hell is sittin' out back? You hire someone new?"

Casey Joe Riggs was a good man at heart. Hudson and I resembled each other because we each got bits and pieces of our dad. The three of us were similar heights. I was broader than the two of them, but Dad wasn't far behind. Lance used to say if you merged Hudson and me together, we'd be the exact replica of Casey Joe.

But he wasn't known for being soft or quiet.

"Huh?" Dad's barreling in and launching questions startled me, I hadn't been expecting anyone but maybe Jack to come through the backdoor. Sam and Kayla weren't on the clock for another twenty minutes.

"Some damn kid out there, looking like a little lost lamb." Dad flung himself onto a barstool as he muttered something about *fleece of gold.*

"Did you say something to him?" I demanded. Not waiting for an answer from my clearly-in-a-very-foul-mood father, I marched out the backdoor.

Jack sat on the old booth bench, phone in hand, staring off into space.

"Hey, you okay?" I asked.

He flinched, and I immediately wanted to punch anyone in the face who had ever made him so jumpy. "Sorry, what?"

"No need to be sorry. Just checking on you. Looks like my dad is in a mood, and I wanted to be sure he wasn't an asshole."

Jack's eyes went wide as if he wasn't accustomed to anyone calling their father an asshole.

Standing next to him as the last of the morning breeze did its best to hold off the warm, muggy air, I rested my hip against the table. "You know how dads can be."

He shook his head. "Not really. Uncles maybe." He glanced toward the door. "Does he know you call him an asshole?"

I chuckled. "Sure, if he's being one. I'll leave you be. Come in when you feel like it. If not, I'll see you for dinner tonight?"

Jack nodded. "Yeah." Still lost in whatever thoughts had him tied up.

The bright morning sun blasted the stained-glass windows reflecting soft, colored light onto tables and the dining room carpet as my eyes adjusted to the dim interior of the bar. Dad had moved to the corner to launch darts at the bullseye. Either he sucked at darts, or his anger had him so pissed off his aim wasn't worth shit.

"What crawled up your ass?" I asked from behind the bar.

Dad jerked his attention to me, returned the darts to the board, and barreled his way back to his stool. "Fuckin' Lance. God damn traitor if you ask me."

Oh.

Shit.

Dad eyed me for a moment. "Fuckin' hell, you knew? Does the whole god damn town know? No one thought to let me know? Same ol' shit, different day."

I set to work putting away glasses, wiping down menus, and opening the register for the day. "They're adults, not really anyone's place to spread their business."

"My god damn best friend? With my fuckin' son?" He choked out a sarcastic grunt. "*Fuckin'* with my son more like it." Dad's arms flailed as he bellowed, his country boy twang all the heavier when he got pissed. "And no one thought I needed to know?" He rubbed a hand over red, swollen knuckles.

Glad there was a bit of time before we opened, I

figured I'd let him blow off some steam. "You want a drink?"

"Vodka."

I snorted. "Nah, it's too early."

"Beer."

He didn't need beer. He needed healthier food, regular exercise, a therapist, and the conviction to get his life back on the right track before he ceased to exist. But I wasn't gonna fight him. Not right then, and not on something as simple as a beer when he'd just found out what he'd found out.

Wincing inwardly at *how* he might have discovered Hudson and Lance were a thing, I grabbed an icy mug and filled it with Dad's favorite draft before sliding it in front of him. "If it helps, I'm pretty sure they were planning on telling you soon."

"Fuckin' hell," Dad grumbled before taking a long swallow of his beer. "God damn, fuckin' hell. No, it doesn't help. How long have you known?"

I shrugged, not wanting to get Hudson and Lance into deeper shit than they appeared to already be in. "Can't say I've known anything official for all that long."

"Official? What the fuck is that supposed to mean? They gettin' hitched or somethin'?" Dad took another swig of beer.

Putting away a couple glasses, I made a noncommittal noise.

"Fuckin' traitor, that's what he is. God damn fuckin' snake in the henhouse. Think I'd learn by now; everyone fucks ya over. Don't go thinkin' your god damn best friend won't because just when you least expect it, he'll go and weasel his way into your baby boy's bed. Fuckin' disgusting, that's what it is—"

"Whoa, hold up a damn minute." I cut off Dad's bitching. "First things first, Lance and Hudson are grown ass men who can make their own decisions about who they do or do not spend time with. Second, Lance has been your best friend since long before Hudson and me were around." I crossed my arms over my chest. "What the hell do you mean by *it's disgusting?*"

Dad opened his mouth like he was about to say something, caught my eye, and snapped his mouth closed. "I'm not talkin' about the gay thing," he started, "although, I gotta say seein' Lance in bed with *any* man would have thrown me for a loop."

I sighed. "I'm sure seeing him with your son was a shock."

"You boys both know I'm not against your sexualities. Straight, bi, gay, whatever, I don't care." Dad took another pull from his beer. "In the beginning, I can't say I understood it at all. Maybe still don't. But all I've ever wanted is for my boys to be happy. The rest of it doesn't matter. Hell, somedays I think I maybe even get it on some level—finding that person...no matter who they happen to be...gettin' that chance to live your true, authentic life with a person you love who loves you right back. Somedays, it makes sense." He ran a hand over his face.

For a moment, I thought maybe he was simmering down. It wasn't the time to ask, but I wanted to know more about his changing attitude—not so much about Hudson and me being queer; he'd always been decently okay with that—but about this new openness to loving a person and living an authentic life.

That would have to be a later conversation because Dad grunted angrily and slammed his mug down on the bar. "But fuckin' hell," he said, his voice already ramping up into a roar. "Of all the people my son and best friend could have found to fuck, they had to find each other?"

"It's kinda cool if you think about it," I said. "Of all the millions of people in the world, two people you love the most found their way to each other."

Dad rolled his eyes. "Fuckin' Judas. Came home like everything was the same, but he's a backstabbin' bastard. Sneakin' around, fuckin' with Hudson's life."

I took his empty glass. "If I had to guess, this thing isn't just some sort of casual fling."

Dad snorted. "Hudson doesn't do serious. Hell, both you boys are just as fucked up as me."

I held up my hand. "Look, we all know she did a number on all of us. Hudson has his way of dealing with it. I have my way." Scratching my fingers through my beard, I offered, "Not sure you've ever really dealt with it."

"What the fuck is that supposed to—"

I cut him off. "All I'm sayin' is I know finding out this way was a shock, and maybe it would have gone over better if they'd had a chance to sit you down and tell you, but it's water under the bridge now." Letting Dad sit in his anger and stew a bit over what I'd said, I walked to the back and turned on the ovens. When I returned, Dad's fists clenched—open, close, open, close—and his agitated state had clearly *not* decreased any. "Hudson doesn't do relationships. He barely does repeats. We all know this. Maybe that should be our clue this is something more."

"So, what, they gonna fuck up a friendship—fuck, he was *family*—just for some good dick?" Dad bitched.

"Are you more upset about Lance sleeping with a guy or the fact that guy was Hudson?"

"Both," Dad grumbled. "Fuck, I don't know. I didn't see it comin' with Lance. But he shoulda kept his dick in his pants around my kid."

Shaking my head, I wiped up the mug's lingering condensation on the bar. "Lance isn't a player. He's not the type to fuck around."

"What's your god damn point?" Dad demanded.

"My point is maybe you should go home, cool off, and think about that fact that Lance and Hudson are adults. They're good people. Smart. If Hudson has thrown out the *no relationship* rule, maybe what he and Lance found together is real."

Dad's eyes caught mine as my words hit home. "God damn fuckin' Judas. Backstabbin' bastard. Fuckin' liars— all y'all. Leavin' me in the dark like it's some big fuckin' joke."

Pinching the bridge of my nose, I muttered, "Gee, wonder why no one wanted to tell you..."

Dad stood and pushed away from the bar, the stool nearly toppling over. "Gonna kick his fuckin' ass, that's what I'm gonna do."

"You need to take your ass home and calm the fuck down. I'm sure they'll want to talk to you, and you need to be ready to have an *adult* conversation when they come over." I placed my palms on the bar and leaned into my words. "Go. Home."

Dad shoved the barstool in, unnecessarily slamming it against the underside of the bar. "Fuck all y'all. I'm goin' home because I can't trust a damn fuckin' person in this town. Not gonna calm down. Not gonna talk to the backstabbin' Judas. Punch him in his damn mouth is more like it."

"Dad—" I started, but he turned and stormed toward the backdoor, his middle finger raised in way of goodbye.

Only because I worried he'd snap at Jack, I followed him.

Jack wasn't out back anymore.

But the damn trash bandit had returned. Dad kicked at a wet piece of garbage warming in the sun. "Get this shit figured out," he bellowed. "Smells like shit out here."

Staring at the open bag with trash spilling from it, I ran a hand over my face. "Thought I *had* this shit figured out," I muttered.

My phone buzzed in my pocket at the height of the lunch rush. With sweat prickling my forehead, and a headache building between my eyes, I grabbed at the interruption, set on swiping away the offending message in favor of concentrating on serving food and keeping customers happy.

Instead, the words caught my attention, and a brick settled in my stomach.

Dad: What the fucks wrong with your beer?

Me: Wdym?

Dad: Been sick ever since I got home. Damn beer.

Me: What's wrong? Puking?

Dad: Need a nap. Stomach hurts, can't get a good breath. Dizzy.

Well, fuck.

I quickly delivered dinner to a table and made my way back to the kitchen.

"Can you two cover things?" I asked Sam as Kayla took a plate from the window.

"What's up?" Sam asked, glancing my way.

"Need to check on my dad. He's not feeling well." Dad wasn't in the best of shape, but he wasn't usually one to text about feeling bad unless he was down with something like killer pig flu—his words, not mine.

Sam must have seen worry around my edges because he gave a quick nod as he expertly plated a meal. "Sure, man. No problem. Let me know what's up."

"Thanks." Heading to the back, I tossed my towel next to the washer, grabbed my keys, and headed out the backdoor.

Pounding up the stairs, I rushed inside my apartment. Jack sat curled on the couch, wrapped in a blanket, eating cereal. His eyes went wide, and a little squeak escaped him.

"Sorry," I said.

"What's wrong?" He uncurled himself and put the mostly empty bowl of cereal on the coffee table

"Gotta go check on my dad."

"The asshole?" Jack asked.

Chuckling, I nodded as I grabbed my wallet. "The one and only. He's not feeling well. May end up taking him to the hospital."

"Can I help?"

I hesitated. It wasn't really Jack's place to help me out, but he'd been in the bar enough lately to know Sam, Kayla, and several of the regulars. "Maybe check in with Sam, see if he needs any help? I'll pay you for your time."

Jack stood and crossed his arms over his chest. "Nope, that's not a part of this deal. Go on, go check on your dad. I'll help Sam."

Gratitude washed over me, and I fought the urge to pull Jack into a hug. Instead, I gave his shoulder a squeeze and headed back down the stairs.

By the time I reached Dad's place, I was half convinced I'd find him on the floor, and half sure he'd tell me he burped and felt better.

Unfortunately, he wasn't feeling better.

"You look like shit."

"Feel like shit," Dad said, rubbing his chest. "Can't get a good breath. Like a fuckin' elephant sittin' on my chest." He wiped sweat from his forehead. "Fuck. Damn skunk-ass beer."

"This isn't the beer. Come on, we're gonna go." I grabbed the remote, turned off the TV, and searched the hall table for his wallet.

"Go where?" Some of his usual obstinance tried to break through his words, but it lacked conviction.

"Hospital."

"The fuck I am." He stood, rubbed his chest, and tried to speak around catching his breath. "What the fuck do I need a hospital for?"

"Well, you look like shit. You feel like shit. Your chest hurts, you can't breathe, and you're nauseous."

"Yeah, so?"

"Jesus fuckin' Christ, Dad. Get in the damn truck." I grabbed his elbow and marched him down the front steps. It spoke volumes that Dad's bitching and fighting didn't make it beyond a few halfhearted protests and complaints, barely heard above the dental drill shriek of the cicadas.

The hospital wasn't too far up the state highway that ran through our county, but the distance seemed like a day-long journey for my nerves as I drove well-over the speed limit while Dad hunched himself against the passenger door. A fist of fear gripped me, and worry coursed through my veins. Dad was quiet, but I could tell he was uncomfortable.

And scared.

Fuck.

Even as an adult, no kid wants to see their dad scared for his life.

I parked in a temporary spot outside the emergency room main entrance and helped Dad into the waiting room as quickly as his condition would allow. His feeble attempt to shake off my hand on his elbow was yet another sign he felt like shit. "I think he might be having a heart attack," I said to the guy at the check-in desk trying my best to sound calm, but the fear demanding attention.

To their credit, everyone acted quickly. Dad was settled into a wheelchair—his large frame suddenly small and frail as he sank into the seat. The young nurse, who looked as if she'd worked every single bit of her twelve-hour shift and then some, expertly maneuvered the chair and whisked Dad through a swinging door. My chest squeezed tightly as I watched, his tired, pained words reaching my ears as he disappeared down a long hall. "That's my son. I want my son with me. Henry..." And then he was gone, the doors swinging shut behind him.

The rest was a blur of fear and nerves.

Fear that the last I'd see of my dad was him being taken away in a wheelchair looking every bit as sick as I'd feared he was for the last several years. The last words I'd hear from him were *I want my son with me*. I needed to call Hudson. Needed to let Sam know I wouldn't be back.

Move my truck.

Jack.

Fuck.

Chapter 6
Jack

"DAMN MAN, THIS IS THE BEST CAKE I'VE EVER eaten." Sam forked another bite of the salted caramel dark chocolate cake into his mouth.

"Thought it would go well with the peach sours and the Lemon Drop Martini Henry makes." I'd been taught to doubt everything about myself most of my life, but confidence in my baking skills was the one thing they never took from me. Probably because I fell in love with cake baking and decorating at a time when I promised myself I'd get away from them one day. They knew about the baking, but I let them think it was just a silly little hobby. They laughed at me, called me names, and shamed me for such a *girly* pastime.

They had no clue I soaked up baking basics, recipes, and expert techniques like a damn sponge. Squirreling them all away, breaking them out to practice anytime the opportunity arose, honing my craft slowly but surely.

And it paid off because my cakes were the best.

Period.

When Henry raced off to help his dad, I found myself hanging out with Sam at the Roadhouse. He mentioned he wasn't sure what dessert Henry had planned for that evening, and I offered to make a cake.

Sam had been skeptical, but he'd cleared space for me to work.

Soon, I'd had two cakes. The one Sam was already gaga for and a peaches and cream concoction I had a feeling would be super popular with the Roadhouse crowd.

As the dinner crowd started to trickle in, Sam had checked his phone, shrugged, and tossed me an apron. I'd loved helping Sam in the kitchen while Kayla and a couple other employees had covered the bar and dining room.

More than anything though, I just wanted to see Henry.

But it wasn't like I could ask Sam a bunch of questions. Mainly because he'd straight up mentioned he hadn't heard from Henry while we were in the middle of prepping for the dinner rush. But also because too many questions would make it look like I had something for Henry aside from just being grateful for the use of his couch.

And I didn't.

Really.

The guy had been nice. He'd helped me out. I enjoyed spending time with him.

Sure, he was big, burly, and gorgeous. For real, look up the word *bear* in any slang dictionary, and you'd find a picture of Henry.

But I mostly just wanted to know Henry's dad was

okay. The older Riggs had nearly scared me out of my socks when he came barreling through the little back patio, but that didn't mean I wanted him to be sick.

Or worse.

Sam split his time between the bar and the kitchen during the dinner rush. He had Kayla serving and mixing drinks while he cooked, then Sam would leave me to plate up the food while he relieved Kayla so she could help the others deliver food to tables.

We didn't run like a well-oiled machine, but most of the customers knew Casey Joe had gone to the hospital, so they cut us some slack. At least staying busy meant I didn't have a lot of time to think about Henry and what he might have been going through.

I'd only baked and decorated the two cakes. We likely could have sold every slice of at least three times as many. Not everyone wanted to order dessert, and several went with items other than cake—the peach crisp was a popular one. But every single bite of both cakes was gone by the time the last table closed out their check.

"Damn, man." Sam slapped me on the back. "Next time, you better make more cake."

Next time.

My heart leaped at the thought of working with Henry, baking cakes customers raved over, and making my home in Haven Grove.

But I shrugged, pulling the collar of my shirt up to rub it over my bottom lip—Sam felt safe, and I liked him, but that didn't stop the past from stirring up my anxiety. "Just helping out. Not sure Henry wants me working here full time."

"Hell if he won't," Sam said. "We'll tell him about the cake and how much you helped tonight. He'll hire you on the spot."

I dipped my head to hide the fire in my cheeks. As much as I loved Sam's praise, and as much as I longed to think Henry might hire me, I didn't want to get my hopes up. It would hurt too much to let my dreams start taking root only to have Henry act like hiring me would be the most ridiculous thing he'd ever heard. "Maybe."

Sam just chucked me on the shoulder. "Head on home, I'll wrap things up here. If you don't have anything else going on, plan on being here tomorrow. Still haven't heard from Henry, but I can't see him being able to work a full shift no matter what's going on with Casey Joe."

My heart dropped. Was Casey Joe in bad shape? Would he get better? When would Henry be able to come home? Selfishly, I wanted to think Henry would be back home soon. I liked knowing he was just down the hall while I slept. Liked the fact I could pop into the Roadhouse and see him anytime I wanted. It was wild how quickly he'd become my favorite person, my safety net, and my happy place all rolled into one.

Not for the first time, I thought about texting him. I had his number. He had my number, even though he didn't know it was *me*. But that was a conversation we needed to have face-to-face, so I refused to entertain it as an option.

Later that evening, after a hot shower, I sat curled up on Henry's couch wearing one of his huge flannel shirts over a bright pink pair of trunk style underwear. The shirt engulfed me, and the black, blue, and gray of the flannel complemented the fun splash of color underneath. The woodsy, citrusy scent of Henry surrounded me, and I pulled the soft material tightly around my body.

The sound of the TV kept me company, the local news reporting the weather forecast for the next day, while I tapped furiously at my phone. Ideas for cakes flooded my mind, mixing with concern for Casey Joe and wishing Henry was home. I made lists of flavors of cakes, fillings, and frostings, being sure to note which of Henry's cocktails the different cakes would go well with.

Between the soft clicking of the ceiling fan, whatever game show came on after the news droning on, and the cozy warmth of Henry's shirt cocooned around me, I must have drifted off to sleep.

The rattle of keys in the lock registered in my sleepy brain just as the front door crept open a crack. Kicking the blanket from my feet, I sprang up from the couch.

The door opened wider, and Henry's broad frame appeared, looking deliciously wrecked in the worn jeans and flannel I'd seen him in when he rushed to his dad's— sleeves rolled up, untucked, and rumpled. "Sorry, didn't mean to wake you." His eyes traveled down my body, paused on my naked legs under his borrowed flannel shirt and bare feet with toes curled into his living room carpet, and shot back up to my face.

Without even thinking about the clothes I wore or the possible inappropriateness of it, I launched myself into him, wrapping my arms around his neck and burying my face in his chest with an unintended whimper.

Henry grunted, his arms instinctively snaking around

to keep me from falling. "Whoa, you okay? What's wrong?"

The hug was a mistake on my part.

For a lot of reasons.

Reasons that probably needed examined, but that was something for a different time and place.

On the other hand, the hug was perfection.

And when it should have ended, mere seconds after it started, I couldn't bring myself to pull away. I breathed Henry in deeply, catching the antiseptic scent of the hospital and hand sanitizer mixed with his fading woodsy citrus scent.

"Jack." Henry's words were soft near my ear. "Are you okay?"

I shook my head, into his chest. "I'm sorry. I was just worried. I missed having you here; worried what might have happened with your dad." Trying to reset the situation from hella awkward to as close to normal as possible, I took a deep, shuddery breath. "I'm sorry."

Moving to loosen the vice grip I had on Henry, I tried to pull away, but my body tingled with awareness when he held me tighter. One hand traveled up and down my back while the other cupped my neck. His warm breath fluttered over my ear and the side of my face, his thick beard tickling my skin. "Shhhh, you're okay. I've gotchu."

God, I wanted his big hands to make their way to the bare skin of my back. Wanted his mouth on the sensitive skin of my neck while his strong arms pulled my nearly naked body flush against his big frame.

But what I got was so much better. At least for the

time being. Proving that, for me, an attraction to someone wasn't only sexual desire.

Henry shouldered the door to swing back toward its frame and pressed his big boot against the lower corner to shut it all the way before maneuvering us to the couch. When I should have wriggled my way out of his embrace, Henry lowered himself to the couch and pulled me onto his lap.

"Tell me what's going on," Henry said, his words soft, and his hand still caressing my back.

By this time, my cheeks were on fire because of the way I'd reacted to Henry coming home. I wanted to crawl into the cedar chest and hide forever.

Instead, I found my chin in Henry's big hand as he guided my face up to look him in the eyes. "Jack, talk to me."

"I'm sorry, it's silly. I'd just been so worried, and I kept making up the worst-case scenarios in my head for what happened to your dad." I curled into Henry's big, warm body. "And it's not like I felt unsafe here, but it's better when you're home." Freezing when I realized what I'd said, I backtracked. "Not like *home* home. I don't think I'm here forever or anything, I just meant—"

"This is your home for as long as you want it to be, and I like having you here." Henry let go of my chin, his free hand coming to rest on my bare thigh while his other hand kept up its constant stroking of my back. "Dad is going to be okay. He had a heart attack."

"Oh my god," I whispered. "Was it bad?"

Henry shook his head. "Could have been a lot worse.

Hoping this is the wake up call he needs to get himself in a better place."

"What happened to him?" I brought the cuff of the extra-long sleeve to my lips and rubbed it softly against the sensitive skin. "I mean, if it's not too nosey for me to ask."

"It's not. I forget you're not from around here. Most everyone in town knows." Henry absently brushed a thumb over the bare skin of my leg, and I had no intention of drawing attention to it for fear he'd stop touching me. "Dad and Mom got pregnant with me young. Mom convinced Dad to get married. Two years later, Hudson came along. By the time she'd been a small-town mom of two boys for four years, Missy decided she'd had enough. She left Dad, left Hudson and me."

"Shit, Henry. That sucks. I'm sorry." My gut clenched. Was this connection because we'd both lost our moms at a young age? Or was my heart just making up stories and hoping for something that wasn't truly there?

"I think that would have been enough to keep Dad down for quite a while, but he headed over to talk to his brother— my Uncle Billy—and found a drunk-ass Billy sleeping it off while Missy got dressed. Pretty much nearly killed him."

"Oh my god," I whispered.

"So, the three of us have a lot of baggage from the past. Hudson sleeps around—or he used to—and just never got attached before Lance. I pretty much keep everyone at an arm's length."

A slight smirk teased Henry's lips, tiny lines crinkling the skin around his pretty eyes, and I wondered if he was aware of how *not* arm's length he was keeping me. But I let him go on.

"And Dad." He smoothed a hand over his beard. "Well, Dad let himself go for way too long." By this point my head rested on Henry's shoulder, his soft words nearly lulling me to sleep.

"I'm sorry your mom left. I know how much it sucks to lose a mom."

Henry's hand stilled for a split second, but he recovered quickly. "I'm here if you ever want to talk about it."

I nodded.

I hadn't really talked to anyone about losing my mom. Hadn't had anyone care enough to listen. I recalled talking to a few counselors and social workers in elementary school, but Uncle Joseph had nipped that in the bud every time the consent papers came home.

Now wasn't the time to unload my past hurts, but my heart did a happy dance at the thought of having someone to talk to. The fact it was Henry made it one hundred times better.

The silence lasted just a smidge too long, but I worried once I started talking, I'd never stop.

"Talked to Sam on the way home," Henry said, and I was glad for the change in subject. "He said you were a huge help."

Hot emotion gathered in my chest at his words.

"And he said your cakes were to die for." Henry gave my leg a squeeze. "Sold out and left the customers wanting more."

I shrugged. "I just wanted to help. And staying busy kept my mind off things."

"Would you consider working for me?" Henry asked. "I'm not asking for a commitment. I know you'll probably want something better than what I can offer—"

"Yes," I blurted, cutting him off. "Yes, I want to work for you."

"And you'll make cakes? That's something you want to do?"

I nodded. "It's all I've ever wanted to do."

"Then it's settled."

"No."

Henry scowled. "What? Why?"

"I want to make cakes for you first. Before you hire me."

"The Great Cake Challenge?" Henry asked with a grin.

"The Great Cake Challenge."

"Sounds good. And maybe you can help me figure out who's going through the trash. It's not like it's a huge mess, but it's getting really annoying." Henry paused, his eyes catching mine as if he'd said too much.

"Wait." I shifted on his lap. It was actually ridiculous how much I liked being this close to him. "Are they still doing that?"

Henry cocked a brow, and I ducked my head.

"Explain," he demanded, tilting my chin up.

I bit my lip. "I'm sorry. I should have told you sooner."

Henry waited patiently. No anger, no threat, no disgust.

Just Henry being the caring, gentle man I'd grown to trust to the depths of my soul.

Swallowing down my guilt, I launched into my story. "I left home in a hurry. When I got off the bus outside of town, Haven Grove was the closest place to me based on signs. I liked the idea of a haven, so I walked this way. I had some money, but it wasn't enough to get a place to stay for more than a night or two, so I wandered around until I found the bench out back." I buried my face again. "Oh god, I'm so sorry. I've meant to tell you for so long, I just never could find the right time after I let it go on forever."

Henry smirked and brushed a hand over my hair. "It's okay. I should have figured it out a lot sooner. I feel ridiculous for how long it took me to put two and two together."

"You knew?" I asked.

He lifted one shoulder. "Not for long. Just since you moved in and the food I left wasn't eaten. But then the trash kept getting messed up, so I wasn't sure what to make of that."

"What? Oh god, no. I didn't do the trash." I chewed on the flannel cuff. "That first night, I saw them tearing into the trash. I should have run them off, but I saw you left a blanket and pillow, and I thought it was my lucky day. When you left out food, I nearly cried with relief. My money lasted so much longer because of those leftovers, thank you."

Henry's hand on my back detoured to give my hip a squeeze. "Glad I could help."

"I should have told you. Should have told them to knock that shit off." I squeezed my eyes shut. "But I didn't want to call attention to myself, and as long as you thought someone was digging through the trash for food, you kept the leftovers coming. You were my guardian angel."

Chapter 7
Henry

"Thank you for telling me," I said, loving the soft caress of his hair against my lips. "I'm glad the food helped."

"I thought it was outrageous when you offered me the booth inside the bar," Jack said, his words slightly muffled against my chest.

"Beggars can't be choosers, huh?"

He chuckled. "I don't think the trash bandits were trying to cause trouble. They were teens from what I saw. I never let them know I was around, but they looked like they were just fucking around."

"Well, I'm not gonna cause a big stink, but I would like to figure out who they are so I can tell them to stay out of my garbage. They're making a mess, and it's really not sanitary to be digging through trash."

We sat in silence for a while, Jack breathing so softly I wondered if he'd fallen asleep, as I did my best to ignore how good he looked in my shirt.

The pink underwear was really doing it for me too.

Which was a weird situation to find myself in. I'd experienced sexual attraction to a few people before, I'd even enjoyed sex with some of them. But none of that happened until we'd developed a close relationship. I wasn't against sex, it just wasn't something I *needed* or sought out.

But there I was, holding Jack on my lap with him in nothing but my shirt and tight pink underwear, and my body was torn between wanting to cuddle him all night long and wanting to make out with him until we couldn't catch our breaths. The idea of him making a mess of those pink trunks had my mind going wild.

Jack had quickly become one of my favorite people in the world, as evidenced by the easy way we sat together on the couch. Which was saying a lot, because I didn't really have favorite people outside of my dad, Hudson, and Lance. And even those three could work my nerves on the best days.

Sam and Kayla were good people, but we weren't close beyond a working relationship. My other employees came to work, did their jobs, and I treated them with respect, but we weren't ever gonna hang out.

I was courteous with people in town—it was good for business—and the Riggs family found ourselves invited to most of the events in Haven Grove because of our peaches and our family name. But I wasn't meeting townsfolk for coffee and chit-chat. I just didn't do that. It wasn't so much that I didn't *like* people. In fact, I enjoyed talking to folks just fine in the Roadhouse and around town. I just wasn't gonna risk getting too close to someone and then having to experience them walking away.

Until Jack.

Somehow, he'd appeared out of nowhere and turned my damn life upside down with his bright smile, sunshine gold hair, and aquamarine eyes.

And I wasn't even mad about it.

It wasn't just how gorgeous he was. I saw attractive people all day long. Haven Grove was a small town, so the numbers of good-looking people weren't breaking any records, but percentage-wise, I'd say we had our fair share of lookers.

Didn't mean I wanted to hold any of them on my lap while they wore tight pink undies and swam in my flannel shirt.

But sitting on my couch with Jack was absolutely perfect, and I was already thinking ahead to when I could make it happen again.

"So, when is this Great Cake Challenge going to take place?" I asked, hoping to keep my mind on less dick-hardening topics.

Jack shrugged. "Let's get your dad home and back on his feet first."

That sobering reminder sent guilt straight to my core.

"Shit." I knuckled my eye. "Yeah. Hoping he'll be back home soon."

"Then I'll wow you with my cakes when the dust settles."

The next couple days passed in an absolute blur. Trips to and from the hospital melded into short shifts at the Roadhouse. Listening to Dad grumble and taking turns with Hudson blended with submitting payroll and balancing the books.

Through it all, Jack kept me going.

Coffee waiting for me when I woke in the morning to head to the hospital.

A smile for me when I walked into the Roadhouse. No matter the time or what he was busy with.

An offer to clean up so I could finish paperwork at the end of a shift instead of staying late to get it all wrapped up.

Jack single-handedly got me through those days, and guilt coursed through me because no one in my family even knew about him yet. Well, Dad had seen him, but that didn't really count.

If Jack was going to be working for me, it was high time he met the rest of the Riggs family.

Once Dad was home from the hospital, I took a day off. The apartment needed a good cleaning, I needed to get groceries, and my brain needed a break from life for a moment.

"You wanna go with me to get groceries?" I asked Jack.

"I can stay and help Sam," he hedged. He was dressed in his usual faded blue jeans, a white t-shirt, and a denim shirt left open with the sleeves rolled up. His clothes—and the ratty tennis shoes he wore—had seen better days.

"Nah, he's got it covered. Come with me. We'll grab what we need, eat lunch, maybe get you some clothes for work."

Jack winced. "I probably need to wait until I get a few paychecks to buy new clothes."

"Let me get you a few things just so you don't have to do laundry so much. You're going to be bringing in business with your cakes, it's an investment on my part."

Those aquamarine eyes narrowed, the sapphire flecks almost glowing, but he finally relented. "Beggars can't be choosers," he said with a shrug.

Jack had two travel mugs of coffee ready by the time I emerged from the shower, and I fought the urge to hug him close and tuck him under my chin. The difference between recognizing some random person was physically attractive versus the warm, gooey ball of emotion oozing around in my chest for Jack was mind blowing. My past experiences with attraction, relationships, and sex hadn't even come close to preparing me for what I felt for Jack.

But I wasn't Hudson. I didn't just fall into bed to scratch some itch and then move on like nothing had happened. Until Jack, I assumed I'd continue on with life the way I had for thirty-five years. Sex was nice, but it wasn't something I needed. Falling in love wasn't part of my plan.

Whoa, whoa, whoa there, Riggs. Slow the fuck down. No one said anything about falling in love.

My head and heart were definitely on different pages when it came to my feelings for Jack. It was likely best to listen to my head. My heart had been trampled on. Could it really be trusted? It wasn't like that part of me had been involved in any real relationships before.

So, yeah. I needed to put the brakes on. There was no way I could truly be falling in love with Jack. Even if the age thing wasn't an issue—which it was. Right?—he was going to be working for me. He lived with me. And in reality, I barely knew him.

You know he's the person you look forward to spending time with every day. And you know him better than anyone in your life except your dad and brother. Pretty sure you know Jack just fine. Plus, you know he makes you feel alive for the first time in forever.

My heart wasn't going to be pushed aside so easily.

Okay, maybe it was for the best to just take things slow and see where we ended up. After all, it wasn't like Jack had made any declarations of love for me.

In fact, I was likely saving us both from me making a fool of myself. There was no way Jack felt anything for me. He probably looked to me as a father figure or something equally unsexy.

We headed down the stairs and climbed into my old truck. The 1987 black and grey Chevy Silverado had been my baby since I bought her to fix up several years earlier. She was a good girl, and I'd spent a lot of time getting her running and keeping her spruced up.

"I like your truck," Jack said, a blush spreading across his cheeks as he climbed in.

"Thanks." I patted the dash. "She's old, but she's got personality. I keep her happy, and she serves me well."

"She, huh?" Jack asked, his eyes boring into mine.

I shrugged. "I'm equal opportunity, I don't discriminate."

Jack bit his lip and brought the collar of his shirt up to rub it against his chin. "How do you keep her happy?" he asked as I pointed the truck up the road toward the big discount store.

"Oil changes mostly. Change her tires if they need it."

"I never learned how to do any of that." A soft frown formed between Jack's pretty brows. "Not that my uncle or cousin would have known how even if they'd been willing to teach me."

"I'll teach you," I said. "It's a good skill to have."

Jack didn't say anything, but he nodded, and a grin teased his lips from under the shirt collar as he rubbed it back and forth.

"So, you lived with your uncle and cousin?" The truck rumbled along; she was in great shape, but she wasn't a luxury ride. I didn't want to push Jack into talking, but he needed to know I was interested and willing to listen.

Jack's lips formed a thin line, the shirt collar pressed between them—I didn't think he realized how much he gave away with this quirky habit—before he nodded. "Yeah. And my aunt."

"Since you left, I'm guessing it wasn't a good set up?"

The snort was full of dark humor and pain. "You could definitely say that."

Withholding the questions I wanted to ask, I focused on the road for a few moments.

Finally, Jack said, "My mom died when I was six. I was sent to live with her sister, Chrissy." His words were barely audible over the truck's engine. "Mom never met Chrissy's new husband, Joseph; she was too sick by the time he came into the picture—at least, that's what I could figure out later. No way my mom would have been okay with her sister marrying him or me living with him. Joseph and his son, Douglas, were absolute pieces of shit. Chrissy was high as a kite on prescription medication most of the time. She wasn't a bad person, just caught up in her own personal demons, and married to a total jerk."

The urge to put my arm around Jack's shoulders and pull him close was strong, but I pushed it away. He was opening up, and I didn't want to risk something that might make him clam up. Although, based on the way he'd reacted when I got home from the hospital that first night, I wondered if he was starved for caring, protective, intimate touch.

"Joseph wasn't a car guy?"

Jack didn't reply for a moment, his gaze trained out the window, lost in thought. But then he blinked those pretty blue eyes and scoffed. "Not hardly. I mean, he was a car guy, but he didn't have the slightest clue how to change oil or take care of a car. He was a car salesman—owned Hill's Autos—and Douglas worked for him, but he would have died before he got his hands dirty in a car. He took his personal cars to the flashiest most overpriced service centers so he could brag about how much he paid. The cars he sold got serviced on-site before the sale was completed. But I doubt he ever got so much as a smear of oil on his bougie suits."

"So, they were both dipshits and wouldn't know a dipstick if it slapped them in the face?" My attempt at oil changing humor fell a little flat, but Jack smiled.

"Dipshits for sure."

"Are they still around?" We'd been talking about them in the past tense, but I didn't know if that meant they were out of the picture permanently or just because Jack had left home.

He nodded, looking miserable. "Unfortunately."

"I'm glad you got away from them." Unable to help myself, I reached out and squeezed his shoulder. Jack's warm smile went straight to my core.

We drove in silence for a bit longer. Just when I thought Jack was done with his trip down shitty-memory-lane, he huffed out a sardonic laugh. "They're the reasons I don't like *Jackie*."

I shot a glance his way but waited.

"My mom used to call me Jackie when I was little. When I had to go live with them, my aunt would call me Jackie when she cried about her dead sister." He rolled his eyes. "Don't get me wrong, I know she missed her sister, but I missed my mom too, and having her go on and on about 'My precious Jackie. My sister is dead, and she trusted me with her Jackie,' got really old. Like I couldn't even mourn my own mom because Chrissy so was so damn dramatic about all of it. Then Joseph and Douglas picked up on the name and used it to make fun of me." He shrugged. "They ruined the name for me. Can't even really remember my mom using it, just them degrading me. So, I never go by Jackie. Ever."

I gave a nod. "Understandable." Pulling into a parking spot at the discount store, I killed the engine. "You let me know if you ever want to talk. My mom didn't pass away, but I know what it's like to grow up without one." Giving his shoulder another squeeze, I went on, "I'm sorry you had to deal with those pieces of shit growing up."

Jack smiled. "Thanks. And I'm sorry about your mom too." He scowled, rubbing his shirt collar over his chin. "I know she didn't die, but..." His words trailed off as he caught my eye.

"It sucks for both of us, no matter how it happened."

He nodded. "Yeah. It does."

We spent the next forty-five minutes stocking up on groceries. I always tried to shop at the Juicy Peach when possible, but buying in bulk and getting big discounts made the trip up the highway worthwhile.

"Where you wanna eat?" I asked as we loaded our reusable grocery bags into the back of the truck, and I played Tetris filling up the cooler with ice and frozen goods.

Jack bit his lip. "Oh, it doesn't matter to me. I can wait until we get home."

"Fuck that." I slapped my hand against the side of the truck. "I can't wait that long. What do you feel like? Burgers? Pizza? Chinese? Subs?"

"Chinese? Oh my god, I haven't had good lo mein and crab Rangoon since college." Jack huffed and rolled his eyes. "Uncle Joseph was always going on about how 'The Hills are an American family, we eat good ol' fashioned American food.'"

"Damn, he sounds like an absolute ass."

"You have no idea," Jack agreed with a smile. "Makes your dad look like a saint, I swear."

I laughed, thinking back to the day I told Jack my dad was an asshole. "Chinese sounds great." I backed out of the parking spot and headed toward one of two Chinese restaurants in town. Both were good, but I knew one had the best crab Rangoon for a hundred miles. "What did you go to college for?"

"Business degree," Jack said.

I couldn't help the surprise on my face, and he chuckled.

"Yeah, I know, not what you expected, huh?"

Shrugging, I navigated the crowded parking lot in the strip mall. "Just figured it would have been something to do with baking."

"I wanted to go to culinary school for Baking and Pastry Arts."

"Let me guess, Uncle Douchebag wouldn't allow it."

Jack beamed. "Ding, ding, ding. He wanted me to take over Hill's Autos with Douglas, so he made me get a business degree."

"Did you have any interest in taking over the car lot?" The look Jack gave me made me laugh. "Well, then. I guess that answers that."

He smiled. "I had no desire to work with them, be around them, or even have my name associated with them." He sighed. "Probably sounds ridiculous since I stayed for so long."

I thought about that for a moment. "I think you probably had your reasons."

We climbed out of the truck and met by the tailgate.

"For the longest time, I was just too young. And Joseph did a great job scaring me into thinking I didn't have any options."

"People like him get off on taking away control and making you think there's no way out." We neared the door to Lucky Egg Roll #13. I wanted to stop right there in the parking lot and keep the conversation going.

"In high school, I started planning to leave, but Chrissy demanded Joseph pay for my college. He agreed as long as

I got a degree in business so I could work in the family business." Jack snorted. "Figured I'd let him pay for my degree first, then I'd make a plan to leave."

"Guess it worked out."

Jack pursed his lips. "Not exactly. I left before I meant to."

I cocked a brow.

"Don't get me wrong, I'm glad I left, I just wasn't prepared to leave when I did."

"Why?" I opened the door, a blast of cool, savory air washing over us.

Jack bit his lip. "I'll tell you sometime."

Chapter 8
Jack

Lunch was absolutely amazing.

Partly because of the best crab Rangoon I'd ever eaten, and partly because I wasn't sure there'd been a single moment since I met Henry that I didn't enjoy every single second I got to spend with him.

Was there very likely some Daddy complex shit going on there? Yeah, probably.

Did I plan on examining that too deeply? Nope.

Sure, Henry was going to teach me to change the oil in a car and change a tire, but that wasn't a strict dad skill. A brother or a friend could teach me how to do those things just as well. It just so happened that I'd had zero luck when it came to anyone filling the roles of dad or brother. I'd had a couple people in college I would have called friends, but none of them were into cars or anything like that.

I'd gone my entire life without a true father figure in my life. I wasn't looking to fill that spot with Henry. I had every belief that the universe had forced me to run that night, and fate had brought me to Haven Grove to meet Henry. Whether he was in my life for a short time as a comfort, a protector, and a friend, or it turned into something more, I wasn't going to question the solid connection we had just because of a difference in our ages. We had way too much in common to let whatever might be building between us slip away.

With our bellies stuffed with a delicious Chinese lunch, we headed out the door.

"You wanna drive over to the mall or walk?" Henry asked, pointing toward the smallest mall I'd ever seen across the parking lot.

"I need to walk if you're okay with it."

We browsed some of the little stores along the way. I got caught up in one, staring at the stand mixer and cake pans.

"These are good ones, huh?" Henry asked as he took in the baking display.

"Yeah, really good. When I have a place of my own, I'll have one of these mixers. And there are a lot of types of cake pans, but these are top of the line. Aside from having a great oven, a good mixer and cake pans are a must."

Henry rubbed a hand over his beard. "You'll get there. Pretty soon, you'll have all my customers just coming in for your cake."

As much fun as it was to daydream in the kitchen store, there was no reason to get my hopes up. Plus, I knew Henry wanted to get our shopping done and head back home.

We arrived at the main entrance of the mall, a cool

blast of air laced with the scent of new clothes, leather, and perfume smacking us in the face when the automatic doors slid open.

"Where do you usually shop?" Henry asked.

I glanced around the stores surrounding the area we'd walked into. "Um..."

Henry chuckled. "I'm guessing this is the least fancy mall you've ever been to, huh?"

My cheeks caught fire, and I brought the collar of my shirt up to rub against my chin. "I'm sure it's really nice," I started.

Henry ruffled my hair. "It's a tiny mall, but it's all we've got around here."

"No, it's fine. I just don't recognize any of the stores. It's not like I had designer clothes. I mostly had to wear Douglas's hand-me-downs until college. Then I just grabbed whatever I could find at the discount store when I got groceries." I gestured up and down my worn clothes. "Obviously, I'm not super picky."

"I think we'll get you some jeans, shirts, tennis shoes, and boots," Henry muttered as he started toward one of the stores.

"That's way too much," I protested. Even though I liked the clothes in the store window, I didn't like the idea of Henry buying me a bunch of stuff. I already felt like I owed him for the food and place to stay, I didn't want to add clothes to the debt.

"Stop," Henry grumbled.

"What?"

"I can hear you over thinking things. You don't owe me anything. A few pairs of jeans aren't going to break me, and you need to have clothes to wear without doing laundry every other day." Henry waved off the store employee offering to help. "We're good for now, thanks." He picked up a pair of dark wash jeans. "What size do you wear?"

"Did you buy your other employees clothes when they started working for you?" I bit my lip and crossed my arms.

Henry scowled. "Listen here, you little shit." Laughter glowed in his eyes, and I couldn't help the giggle that burst from me. He slapped a pair of jeans against my chest. "I didn't buy them clothes, but I provided uniforms back when we were doing the uniform thing. Moved away from that, but I still provide Roadhouse t-shirts. I'll give you a couple too. But you'll be doing something different than the rest of us, so you can opt to wear whatever you want. Stop arguing with me before I just buy five outfits I think you'd look good in and call it a day."

A protest was on my lips, but the set of Henry's brows told me he'd totally do it, so I tossed the jeans back at him. "At least get me the right size you big oaf."

Henry caught me in a headlock and gave me a noogie, but before I knew what was happening, he had his hands on my hips. Big, warm, strong hands gripped my hips, slid up to my waist, and back down. "I know what size I wear, and I know what size Hudson wears, so I'm going to guess you're about one size below him." He let go of me as quickly as he'd taken hold and rummaged through the jeans. "Here." He handed me three pairs in various shade of blue. "Try these." Henry messed with his beard before he turned his back on me to look at a rack of flannels.

After a couple moments of awkward silence, he cleared his throat. "Pick up a couple of those t-shirts and three of these flannels."

"What if I like your flannels better than these?"

Henry chuckled. "You can wear my flannels at home, but you'd be a safety concern in a jumbo shirt at work. Might get caught in the mixer or something."

I grinned. "True."

Home. Did Henry realize just how much his words affected me?

My heart did a little pitter-patter happy dance as I took the clothes to the changing room to make sure everything fit.

Henry paid for the jeans, t-shirts, and flannels, and we headed to a shoe store.

"You're gonna need a big coat come wintertime, but we've got some time for that. The boots we'll get today should be pretty good for any kind of weather; we might need to get you some warm coveralls. But those can wait."

"I usually just wear tennis shoes," I said, glancing down at my ratty shoes. They'd definitely seen better days. Damn, when had I bought them? Junior year of college?

"You'll need boots for outdoor stuff. If you're going to stay in Haven Grove and live with a Riggs, you'll end up spending time in the orchard. I don't make the rules, it's just the way it is." Henry's beard mostly hid the tiny smirk teasing his lips.

I rolled my eyes. "Fine. Let's get some boots."

"Atta boy." Henry cuffed me on the shoulder, his words sending warmth oozing through my veins.

By the time we reached the truck with a ridiculous amount of clothes and shoes, my feet hurt, and I wanted a nap.

"Climb in," Henry said from behind me on the passenger side. "These can't go in the back. Too light. Don't want them flying around."

I hauled myself up into his truck.

"Scoot over." Henry put two big bags on the passenger seat and two more on the floorboard before slamming the door.

When he hefted himself into the driver-side seat, I immediately realized just how close we were. Not that I was complaining, but had it been an accident or had Henry purposely pushed me toward the middle of the seat?

For about thirty seconds after Henry put the truck in gear and headed back toward Haven Grove, I kept my body tense so as not to lean into him. But the rumble of the engine and the passing scenery lulled me to sleep.

When I woke, the truck had stopped, and the sun was easing toward the horizon.

"If you're going to be a Riggs employee and boarder, you're going to need to meet the rest of my family," Henry said when we'd gathered the bags and headed up the stairs to the apartment.

"Would you rather I not?" I asked, stretching to work out the stiffness in my neck from my unexpected nap.

"What? No." Henry placed the bags in his big recliner.

"You just kinda sound like you're dreading it."

Henry huffed. "Hudson will give me shit."

"About me? Why?"

Henry opened his mouth like he wanted to say something, but then he snapped it closed and ran a hand over his beard. "He just likes to give people shit, and he'll want to know why I haven't introduced you already."

I shrugged. "I mean, I've been around. Maybe he just hasn't been paying attention."

"Exactly." Henry pointed a finger in my direction, the edges of his eyes crinkling with a smile. "He's been too far up Lance's ass to notice much of anything."

I followed Henry out the door and down the stairs. "So, they *are* dating?"

Henry chuckled. "They are. They have a lot of history, and I'm not completely sure how it all happened, but they're together. Dad's pissed, but I've honestly never seen my brother so happy."

"Guess they're proof that age is just a number, and some things are meant to be."

Henry caught me in a headlock and ruffled my hair. "Guess so."

Chapter 9
Henry

SOME THINGS ARE MEANT TO BE.

I tried to get Jack's sweet words out of my head, but they ran through on a loop, making it really hard to tell my heart to settle its ass down.

"You want a drink?" I asked as we headed into the Roadhouse. I wanted to check on a few things even though it was technically my day off.

"Are we staying here or going somewhere else?" Jack asked.

"'Bout twenty minutes here, then we can go walk the property. You can meet Hudson and Dad. Lance is probably around too."

"Can I have one of those lemon drop thingies?"

I frowned and gave Jack an elbow. "As long as you take a peach cider to go."

"Fine." He pretended to pout. "You and your peaches."

After making his lemon drop, I checked the register, did a quick inventory, and chatted with Sam for a bit. By the time I finished, Jack had polished off his drink and was talking to Kayla.

I poured us both peach ciders in frosty mason jar glasses and handed one to Jack. We said quick goodbyes to Sam and Kayla, I waved at a few of the regulars, and we headed out the door. I knew eyes were on us as we left, but Jack needed to meet my family before the townsfolk got their questions answered. And even then, it would be up to Jack if he wanted to answer any questions. Although, if he was going to be baking cakes at the Roadhouse, it would be best if he was friendly with the folks in town.

As we walked, I pointed out different businesses, where certain people lived, and points of interest in our small town. Jack asked questions, mentioned things he'd noticed about the people and places in town, and sipped his cider.

It made me sad to think about how lonely he'd been in the time he'd been sleeping out back and roaming Haven Grove when he first got to town. No wonder he spent so much time at the bar back then.

Jack lifted his chin toward a group of kids near the gas station. "That kid with the floppy red curls and the one with the frizzy black hair."

"Yeah?"

"They're the ones who were making a mess of your trash."

Shit.

"Of course, they are," I grumbled.

"Who are they?" Jack's wide eyes glowed with curiosity.

"Preacher's grandkid is the red head. The other one is the son of one of the guys on the town council who should have stepped down a long time ago." I sighed. "They aren't bad kids, and their fathers aren't terrible in general, I guess."

"But?" Jack pushed.

I shrugged. "Preacher isn't someone I talk to a lot. He tends to steer every conversation toward just how sinful the Riggs family is. But I think that's his usual pattern with most people."

"What? That's a load of shit. How is your family any of his business?" Jack took a long swig of his peach cider, kicked at a rock on the dusty ground, and swayed just a bit into my path. "No family is really his business unless he's helping to provide care for them."

"Yeah, he's not. He's more in the business of judging others, collecting money, and skewing the words of his favorite book to condemn folks around town." My words reminded me just how much I despised talking to Pastor Larry, and now I'd have to have a chat with him about his grandson, Randy. The pastor wasn't the worst of the worst, but I could think of at least fifty people in town I'd rather talk to before I talked to him.

Jack huffed. "Sorry, I'm not really religious. I guess I'm more spiritual than anything. Like, I believe someone, or something created all of this." He gestured broadly with a wild arc. "How could you not? But the churches I've had any contact with didn't give me good vibes. They were definitely more on the cultish side of things if I'm being honest. And not at all open and welcoming. Most of the people gave me the creeps. Joseph and Douglas were some of the worst people in the world, but they judged others up one side and down the other and thought they themselves could do no wrong—and the church seemed to back them up."

"I get that. Dad and Lance grew up with pretty religious parents, going to church, all that. But when Dad and Mom got pregnant with me, both sets of grandparents disowned them. Too worried about what the church might think. So, Hudson and I didn't really do the whole church thing when we were younger because Dad was done with it. I'm more like you though. I'm fairly spiritual in that I believe there's a higher power, but I have no interest in being involved with people who wear a smile while they exclude and shun whole groups in the name of God."

"Looking back on my time with Joseph and Chrissy, it pisses me off that not a single person at the church we went to ever stepped in to help me. Joseph kept most of his shit out of the public eye—like no one would have seen bruises on me at school—but he was terrible at church. And everyone there was so busy trying to make the right connections, raise the most money, and pop out the most kids, no one paid a lick of attention to me." Jack pulled his collar up to press it between his lips, and I wanted to pummel the people who made his life so traumatic that he'd picked up the anxious habit. "If just one person had really *seen* me and tried to help..." He chewed the collar for a second—never leaving it wet or wrinkled, just a movement that seemed to calm his anxiety. "But Joseph would have gone after them—he used to laugh about the people who tried to go up against him and how he'd ruin them."

"I'm sorry no one helped you," I said. "You didn't deserve that."

We were quiet for a bit before Jack spoke again. "Sorry, I just get worked up about church stuff. I'm sure there are a lot of people who go to church who are amazing. But people passing judgement when they have absolutely no right just goes straight to my gut." He sighed. "Tell me about your family."

I took the change in subject. "So, Hudson lives in the farmhouse closest to the Juicy Peach, and Dad lives in the one on the far end of the orchard," I explained from our stopping point between the two old farmhouses. "Hudson offered to let me have the house, but it makes more sense for me to live above the bar."

We climbed the steps to Hudson's door and knocked.

No answer.

"He's probably at the shop or in the orchard. The peaches are his babies. Which is kinda funny because he was never super attached to the orchard when we were growing up, but it got thrust on him when our uncle died, and we both knew our dad wasn't in the right frame of mind to take it over. So, it landed on Hudson, and he's really taken to it. Our uncle almost let the orchard go belly-up, but Hudson's been working his ass off to save this season's crop and the trees as a whole."

As we headed toward the back of Hudson's place and made our way to the orchard, Jack stopped.

"Wow," he whispered. "This is gorgeous. I've seen the edges of the tree rows, but I hadn't seen it from this view."

Standing next to him as we both finished our ciders, I

bumped my shoulder into his. "Yeah, it's pretty amazing." The sinking sun painted a mix of oranges and pinks, and thin clouds spread across the pale blue sky like wisps of cotton.

"Looks like it goes on forever, like an ocean of trees." Jack breathed in deeply of the earthy scents of green grass, leaves, and ripening fruit. "And it smells so good."

"I'm gonna make a peach lover out of you yet." I took the empty mason jar from Jack's hand and placed both our glasses on a tree stump. "Come on, let's find my brother."

"You guys are close?" Jack asked, weaving a tiny bit as we made our way down the sloping hill.

"We are. Kinda had to be after Mom left. It wasn't like Dad expected me to take care of Hudson—not like it was totally my responsibility—but it's just what I do. Making sure he was safe and taken care of was the most important thing to me, even as a kid."

Jack stumbled over a clump of grass and nearly went down, but I caught his elbow. "You okay?"

He giggled. "Yeah. I think I might be slightly buzzed."

Shit.

"Do you want to sit down?" Hell, I hadn't thought about him having two drinks. Neither was super strong, but two together was probably enough to have someone Jack's size feeling it.

"No, I'm good. I'm not drunk, just kinda tipsy. If I sit down, I'll probably want to sleep."

"We'll get you some water. Hudson probably has some." We continued down the gentle decline.

"Hudson's lucky to have you taking care of him," Jack said. "But I still wanna know who takes care of you."

I ignored his words, and I could tell Jack knew I was brushing him off, but he let it go. "You've seen Hudson and Lance in the Roadhouse, right?"

Jack nodded. "I've seen your dad and them a few times. You and Hudson are definitely brothers in that related but not identical way."

I chuckled. "He's the Travis to my Jason."

Jack's brows drew together. "Huh?"

"The famous football player brothers? The younger brother is the one everyone thinks is hot, and the older one is just the nice guy?"

Jack shook his head.

"The Clint to his Ron?" I tried again, although it was an even more obscure reference, but maybe he was a movie buff.

Jack's face was blank.

"Come on, the Howard brothers?"

Again, nothing.

"I'm the William to his Harry?"

Recognition lit Jack's face. "So, you were the attractive one when you were younger, and then he went and got hot as you both got older?"

I ran a hand over my beard to hide my smile. "Something like that, I guess."

Jack cocked his head. "But not really because you're still really handsome. Hudson is hot, but he's no better looking than you."

Luckily, we reached the trees because I wasn't sure how to answer that. No one in their right mind would ever think Hudson was no better looking than me. I had no issues with how I looked, but I knew my brother was considered more attractive by most. We were both broad, but he had more of a jockish otter vibe while I was definitely more on the bear side. Hudson wasn't super hairy, and his hair was lighter, but I had a full beard along with a hairier dad bod.

Hudson was more likely to catch second glances long before me.

But my gut flip-flopped at Jack's words.

With row upon row of peach trees stretching out for as far as we could see, Jack took a deep breath. "Everything smells so earthy and sweet down here." He stepped closer to a tree. "Is it okay to touch them?" he asked, his eyes lighting up when I nodded. Reaching out, he ran a finger over a peach and gasped. "Oh my god."

"What?"

"It's so furry. Like it's wearing a little fur coat."

I couldn't help the surprised laugh that escaped. "Yeah, I guess they are."

"So that's why you can't eat the skin?"

I shook my head. "You *can* eat the skin. Many people just don't care for it."

Jack grimaced. "I don't think I could eat their furry little coats."

All I could do was laugh and put an arm around him. "No one will ask you to eat the skins."

I savored the way he leaned into me and remembered how he'd cuddled against me on the couch. I'd never been one for a lot of physical affection outside of hugging my family or a good ol' slap on the back, but for Jack, I'd dole out the touches like candy on Halloween if it was something he needed.

After a quiet moment, a loud buzzing sound filled the air. Jack and I watched as a large bee, seemingly drunk on nectar, bobbed from one tree to the next.

Jack gasped again. "I didn't know they were real," he whispered.

"What?"

"Bubble bees." He pointed toward the insect.

"Say what?" I cocked my head, schooling my features.

"I didn't know bubble bees were real, I thought they were just in movies and stuff."

Bubble bees.

Oh.

My.

God.

This man was so damn adorable.

But also, how had he gotten to twenty-five not knowing very real insects existed outside of movies and television? My heart ached for the younger version of Jack and all the hurt he lived through.

"Yeah, bumble bees are an important part of what keeps the orchard going."

Jack's brow furrowed, and he wrinkled his nose. "*Bubble* bees?"

I cleared my throat. "They're actually called bumble bees."

He scowled. "But why?"

"I don't really know. I guess because they kinda bumble from flower to flower." Honestly, I had no idea where the insect's name had come from.

Jack shook his head. "No, they're bubble bees. Look at their little butts, they look like bubbles."

I couldn't even argue with him. The insect's round little butt was shaped just like a bubble. "I mean, you're not wrong."

Jack shrugged. "I like bubble bees better."

"Then bubble bees they are."

Peaches wearing tiny fur coats and bubble-butt bubble bees.

Fuck.

What this man was doing to my damn heart had to be illegal.

We walked further into the orchard until we reached the back corner where a creek crossed the land.

"Oh my god," Jack gasped as he moved toward an area of the creek where the water burbled over rocks. "My mom took me to a creek once before she got super sick. We played in it for hours. Wading, finding fish, crossing on rocks and logs. Living in the city after she died didn't give me many options for creek wading—not that Joseph would have taken me anyway." He picked up a leaf and placed it gently into the slow-moving water. When the leaf got caught in the current and sped toward the rocks, Jack grabbed my hand and squeezed. "Watch."

And I did. Not the leaf, but the heart wrenchingly beautiful look of awe on Jack's face as the little piece of green tumbled down the rocks and spun like a top in the swirling pool at the base of the tiny waterfall.

"Did you see it?" Jack's bright blue eyes twinkled with mirth.

With a quick nod to clear my head, hoping not to get caught staring at the beautiful man by my side instead of watching his little leaf boat, I smiled. "I did." I swallowed back emotions. I knew Jack didn't want my pity, but I couldn't quell the ache in my heart for him. "Hudson and I always loved playing in the creek. We sent hundreds of sticks and leaves down these little waterfalls. We had races, running along the banks to see whose boat would make it the farthest and fastest."

"Let me guess," Jack said with a soft smile, "you let Hudson win."

I shrugged. "Maybe. It wasn't like there was a prize. He was just a little kid, he liked to win."

Jack squeezed my hand again. "You were just a little kid too," he whispered. Stretching up on tiptoes, he feathered a kiss over my cheek. "You are a very good man, Henry Riggs."

I cleared my throat and ran a hand over my beard. "It's just what big brothers do."

Jack shook his head. "I didn't have siblings, so I'm not an expert, but I had an older cousin. I know for a fact he never would have let me win. Would've been more likely to push me in the creek, stomp on my boat, and smear mud all over my face. He delighted in seeing me cry."

Clenching my jaw, I swallowed down the rage. "You didn't deserve that. If I ever see that piece of shit, I'll be sure to make sure he knows just how good and perfect you are."

We stayed at the creek for a little longer while Jack sent a few more leaves and sticks racing through the water. When we headed to find Hudson, Jack reached for my hand again, and a soft current of electricity snapped between our bodies where our skin touched.

"Thank you," he said, the words barely a whisper on the soft breeze blowing through the orchard.

"For what?"

He brushed a thumb over my knuckles, and I thought I'd like to hold his hand for the rest of time. "For not making fun of me." Jack kept hold of my hand, but pressed his arm against mine and placed his other hand on the crook of my elbow.

"Why would I make fun of you?" I covered his hand on my elbow with my own, wondering how I could want so badly to wrap him up and protect him from the world.

"For my obsession with cake. For not knowing peaches have furry skin. For being so dumb about bees. For acting like a child when it comes to so many things."

I stopped in my tracks and gripped Jack's shoulders, moving him to face me. "Don't ever call yourself dumb. You're one of the smartest, bravest, most creative people I know. You lived through a traumatic childhood. Losing your mom at such a young age would have been painful enough, but the abuse and neglect you experienced during very formative years just added insult to injury."

Jack's eyes shimmered with tears, and his swallow was audible. "Sometimes it just feels like I missed out on so much, but then I feel like a complete fool when I find out bubble bees are real, and they aren't even called bubble bees."

I shook my head. "We can learn stuff together."

Jack sniffed. "I basically mauled you when you got home, and then sat on your lap like a damn toddler."

With his chin between my fingers, I lifted his face, so our eyes met. "There was nothing wrong with the way you greeted me." I shrugged. "Kinda liked coming home to find someone happy to see me." It wasn't even a lie. I never considered myself lonely, but having Jack waiting on me to get home stirred something deep in my gut I didn't even know had been simmering there. Brushing my thumb over his cheek, I whispered, "And cuddling on the couch is something we both enjoy. No worries there."

I'd cuddle his touch-starved body every damn day if that's what he needed.

Jack took a shuddery breath. "Like, I know I'm fucked up, but sometimes it's a punch to the face, and I wonder if anyone will ever even *want* to get involved with me."

"Anyone would be absurd not to," I mumbled despite my head screaming to retreat.

"What about you?" he asked, those bright blue eyes wide and filled with hopeful desire.

"Me?"

"Would you ever want to get involved with me?"

Danger! Danger!

A protest died on my lips when Jack snaked his arms around my neck and stretched up to press a kiss to my mouth. Gentle, tentative, and hopeful, his soft lips clung to mine, and something warm and wonderful woke inside me.

"Jack..." My brain insisted I needed to let him down gently. Tell him I wasn't the right person for him.

I was too old.

I didn't do relationships.

He deserved more than what I could offer.

But my heart? My heart did a little victory dance and shot down every single excuse I could come up with.

"Henry," Jack countered.

"I don't think—" I started, but Jack kissed me again, and I lost myself to the heady warmth of our lips tangled together and the flavor of him on my tongue

When Jack pulled away, he said, "I've never had a relationship—nothing real, nothing beyond a few disappointing hookups that left me empty and more alone than ever before—and I know I've got a shit ton of issues."

I gripped his chin and studied his face. "Are you drunk?"

Jack giggled. "No."

I sighed. "I feel like I should tell you this is a bad idea…"

"But?" His eyes sparkled with hope.

Cupping the back of his head, I pulled him into my chest, cradling his head against me. "But even though I've always sworn I don't do relationships—because I'm terrified of them—you've somehow worked your way into my heart, and I can't really come up with any valid reasons to tell you no."

"So, what does that mean?" His muffled words vibrated across my breastbone.

I groaned, clenching my eyes shut as I pressed a kiss to Jack's pretty blond hair. "I guess it means I just broke all kinds of boss and employee rules. Shit."

Jack giggled into my chest. "Nope. I haven't even made you any cakes. I'm not officially an employee yet."

"But you're going to be. What then?" This was bad, but I couldn't convince my heart of it.

"We have something going on before I become an

employee. There's nothing that says you can't hire someone you're involved with."

I pulled back and looked into those gorgeous blue eyes. "I don't have a lot of experience when it comes to relationships or sex."

Jack shrugged. "I'll take kisses and cuddles all day long before I worry about sex."

"Do you not like sex?"

"Eh," he said. "Sex can be good, I'm sure. I just need a connection before I can really get into it. Took me a few crappy hookups and big letdowns to figure some things out about myself, but that's the biggest thing for me."

"We're in the same boat then," I said. "We'll figure things out together."

Together.

Shit.

Jack and I were together.

I leaned down and feathered a kiss over Jack's lips. He tasted of peaches, and the way his soft lips clung to mine had a punch of unexpected desire swirling in my gut.

"Better find that brother of yours before he sees us making out in the orchard."

I chuckled and hugged him close and savored the way our bodies fit so perfectly like we were melting together. A wave of tender satisfaction washed over me. From the first day Jack walked into the Roadhouse, everything between us had been easy and right. It seemed like our connection taking a twisting turn toward something *more* was going to take the same easy route.

A tiny sliver of my head wanted to argue that this was a bad idea.

He's living with you.

He's going to work for you.

He's so much younger than you.

But a large chunk of me sighed and relaxed into the hug. Maybe it *was* a bad idea. Maybe I'd end up getting my heart broken because I gave in and didn't protect myself. As I breathed in the scent of my shampoo on Jack's hair, I realized I was willing to take that chance.

For the first time in my life, the potential benefits of getting involved fluttered in my heart, and I didn't hate the equally potential risk.

I'd take a chance for Jack.

I'd risk it for the man who'd shown up in town and captured my soul without even trying.

My heart erupted, tiny explosions of joy sparking in my chest as I took Jack's hand in mine and headed to introduce my brother to the most unexpectedly important man in my life.

Chapter 10
Jack

OH.

My.

God.

As I walked hand-in-hand with Henry, I wondered briefly if I was dreaming. Was the orchard covered in chemicals causing me to hallucinate?

Henry gave my hand a squeeze. Up ahead, three men could be seen as we walked toward a little cabin-like structure.

Nope. I wasn't dreaming.

I'd kissed Henry, and he'd kissed me back.

I wasn't sure if either of us had any clue what the heck we were doing, but it felt right to be clueless with Henry by my side.

"You ready for this?" Henry's words were gruff and laced with anxious concern.

"Is it going to be painful?" I asked, only somewhat joking.

"Mostly for me, probably," Henry groused. "I've never really introduced someone to my family before."

"Just tell them I'm a friend if that helps."

Henry gripped my hand tighter. "You *are* a friend, but I won't hide you. I don't lie to my family. Unless you're not ready to be introduced as..." He paused, cocked his head, and scratched his bead. "Someone I'm dating?"

The words took way too long to register in my head.

Someone he's dating?

What?

Who's he dating?

Oh.

Me.

He's dating me.

I swallowed thickly. A dream. It had to be a dream.

I'd wake up any second to find Joseph and Douglas laughing and making fun of me for thinking I'd ever find someone who'd accept me just as I was.

Instead, I shook my head. "No, I'm good with that. It's new for me, but I'm okay with it."

Henry gave a solid nod as if steeling himself for a battle and ducked his head to press a kiss to my cheek.

Like they had a beacon trained to find Henry in new and unfamiliar situations, all three men stopped and looked our way at that exact moment. They were silhouetted against the whitewash of the cabin, the dusk of the setting sun casting long shadows around them.

As we got closer, I could see they were stacking bushel baskets. The hose hooked to an outside spigot led me to believe they'd sprayed the baskets earlier—maybe to get rid of dust and cobwebs?

"Is it time to pick the peaches?" I asked Henry.

"Different sections of the orchard should be ready to pick at different times, but yeah, we've started picking."

Hudson sprayed his hands with the water hose and dried them on his faded blue jeans. "Hi, I'm Hudson, Henry's favorite little brother."

Henry snorted, and my preemptive bristles relaxed a bit. I wasn't sure why I thought Hudson might be rude or say something about Henry, but everything in me softened a bit at Hudson's words.

Taking his hand, I shook it, and said, "Nice to meet you. I'm Jack Garner."

Lance stepped forward. "I'm Lance Ingram. My family owns the Sweet and Creamy Dairy Palace."

I shook Lance's hand as well. "I like your ice cream." Pulling my shirt collar up, I tried to hide my embarrassment over such silly words.

But Lance beamed, and Hudson threw an arm around him and kissed his cheek. "Best ice cream around." Hudson gave me a wink. "We'll get you a t-shirt."

With my cheeks flaming, I thought about some of the shirts I'd seen for sale at the Roadhouse. The sayings on them were chock full of innuendo, and I figured they were popular.

I Love Sweet & Creamy DP

I Want My Juicy Peach Sweet & Creamy

My Juicy Peach Loves It Sweet & Creamy

DP'd at the Sweet & Creamy

DP My Juicy Peach

My Juicy Peach Got DP'd and Rode Hard at Riggs' Roadhouse

Sweet & Creamy – The Only Way I Want My Juicy Peach DP'd

While part of me couldn't help but wonder how far the pieces of Joseph's head would fly if he ever saw me wearing a shirt like that, I couldn't stop the warmth spreading through me at the fact that Hudson seemed to already be including me in the group.

Or maybe he just wanted someone as a walking billboard.

Henry and Hudson's dad grunted and elbowed Lance as he moved closer. "I'm Casey Joe. Don't listen to nothin' that traitor says," he growled, throwing a thumb over his shoulder toward Lance. "Henry and Hudson are my boys. The snake *used* to be my best friend."

"Dad…" Hudson warned.

Casey Joe held up his hands. "I'm joking, I'm joking." He narrowed his eyes at Lance before glancing back at me. "Mostly," he said with a smirk as he held out his hand.

"Nice to meet you." I shook his hand. "I was sorry to hear you were in the hospital. Are you feeling better?"

Casey Joe grunted. *"Thank you,* Jack." He glared at the other men. "It's nice when people are concerned, unlike these jackasses."

Hudson rolled his eyes. Lance coughed to cover up a "Bullshit." And Henry chuckled.

"Whatever, Dad," Henry said. "Maybe we'll start having a bit more sympathy when you follow the doctor's orders to get healthier."

Casey Joe grumbled something about rice cakes and water, pulled a Blow Pop from his pocket, ripped off the wrapper, and shoved it in his mouth. "Stopped smoking, didn't I? That's gotta be worth something."

"We're proud of you." Lance's words were genuine, but his best friend grunted and ignored the man.

"What brings you to town, Jack?" Hudson asked as if trying to steer things away from the awkward.

Before I could answer, Henry stepped closer and wrapped an arm around my waist. The instant spark of heat in my gut and the gooey way that protective gesture made my heart feel went straight to my head, giddy excitement over being able to call Henry *mine* almost making me dizzy.

Hudson's eyes grew wide and glittered with mirth as a shit-eatin' grin filled his face while he watched his brother, a mixture of glee and shock painting his features.

"Jack's stayin' with me and he's gonna be working at the Roadhouse." Henry's words were like gravel, daring anyone to say anything.

"The cake guy?" Hudson asked, his smile switching from teasing to actual happiness.

My cheeks heated, and I absently rubbed my shirt collar against my chin, but I nodded.

"Yeah, Jack's gonna be making cakes for us." The firm hold of Henry's hand against my side eased my anxiety.

"Sam was tellin' us how good you are," Lance said. "Glad to have you on board."

"Thanks." I wanted to tell them I wasn't officially hired just yet. Wanted to make sure they knew I was all about earning my place.

But Casey Joe interrupted my overthinking. "What you oughta do is fix up that extra space, been sittin' empty for so long."

I noticed Henry and Hudson's eyes meet and both men seemed to be thinking it through.

"That's not a bad idea," Henry said. "It's set up right. Kitchen area just needs an oven." He glanced down at me. "What do you think? You wanna do your cakes in Sam's kitchen? Or have your own space?"

Before I could answer, Casey Joe spoke up again. "Of course he'd rather have his own space. What kind of question is that?"

And then everyone looked at me.

I wanted to pull the collar of my shirt up over my eyes and hide away, but none of these men were being mean or hurtful. So, I leaned into Henry and said, "I'm really grateful to have a job and get to do what I love. Any space is fine by me."

"But if we set up that extra space with the right kind of oven, get you a good mixer, and put in some display cases, that would be a good place to bake and decorate, right?" Henry asked.

I could tell his mind was already going a million miles a minute. "It would," I started.

"But?" Henry smoothed down his beard, scowl lines marking his forehead.

Biting my lip, I continued, "It would be great, but I can make cakes anywhere. That stuff's expensive—"

Henry waved off my protest. "It's a business expense. If we do it up right, you'll be bringing in money to the Roadhouse."

Hudson grinned. "Might as well just let him do it. Once he gets something in his head, it's impossible to talk him out of it."

Casey Joe slapped Henry on the back. "We'll help with sprucing the place up." He turned to me. "What kind of cakes do you make?"

"Pretty much anything. Birthday cakes, wedding cakes, cakes for events. I really like to match cakes to certain foods and flavors."

"Sam said you were talking about cakes to go with Henry's drinks," Hudson said.

Henry eyed me. Was he hurt?

I shrugged. "Yeah, it's fun to pair up cakes with drinks or foods."

"That sounds really cool," Hudson said. "I'd love to try your combos."

God.

Was I really so starved for praise and positive attention that those simple words from Henry's brother could send me to Cloud 9?

"Keep your grubby paws to yourself," Henry groused which only made Hudson beam and Lance chuckle. "If anyone gets to try his cake, it's me."

Hudson and Lance nearly combusted, and Henry's scowl deepened.

Instead of feeling like I was the butt of someone's cruel joke, the atmosphere in the orchard with these men was one of family and camaraderie. Like for the first time since losing my mom I actually belonged. I had friends, and dare I say, *family*.

I leaned into Henry's side. "It's fun to think of the mix of flavors, textures, and colors to compliment meals and drinks." Glancing at Henry, I caught him studying me.

Again.

"What would you put with the Lemon Drop Martini?" he asked, his eyes never leaving mine like he was completely invested in my answer.

Swallowing, I pulled my collar up and rubbed it over my chin. "Probably a dark chocolate with sea salt. Maybe add in a ribbon of caramel."

"What about to pair with the Peach Sour?"

I held the collar of my shirt between my teeth while I recalled the flavor of the drink. "A spice cake—cinnamon, ginger, clove—with a rich, sweet vanilla bean frosting."

"Damn, can we get a flight of drinks and cake?" Lance asked. "That sounds delicious."

His words held a teasing quality, but Henry's eyes snagged on mine, and the whole group grew quiet.

"Could you pair pretty much any drink with cake?" Henry asked.

I nodded as ideas zipped through my head.

"Flights of cake and drinks," Hudson said. "That's perfect. We can make a little seating area on Jack's side too, for people who want to have their cake—"

"And drinks too," Lance finished, smiling broadly at Hudson. "That would be a perfect little section of the menu. *Have Your Cake and Cocktails Too.* Play on the famous saying, ya know?"

"Rotate drink and cake specials," Henry said.

"We could have a set of two or three cake and drink pairings that we always offer, a rotating specialty drink with a matched cake, and some sort of cake to pair with the dinner special each week," I rambled on, plans stampeding through my mind faster than I could process them.

"We're happy to provide all the orchard fresh peaches you might need for any of your cakes," Hudson said.

"And the Dairy Palace has the ice cream covered," Lance offered.

"What if you did a newsletter type thing?" Casey Joe raised his brows when we all looked his way. "What?" he asked around his Blow Pop. "Like people could sign up for a newsletter to get drink and cake recipes or some shit like that. Get 'em in with a coupon or announce sales or specials. People like that shit."

Henry glanced my way, and I couldn't help the giddy anticipation bubbling through me.

"Cake and cocktails?" I asked.

He grinned, and my insides melted. "Let's do this."

Chapter 11
Henry

"DAMN, TALK ABOUT *CAKE*," HUDSON DRAWLED AS Jack walked toward the little cabin with Lance for a bottle of water.

"Huh?" I asked, my eyes glued to Jack as he moved farther away. He was no longer walking with a sway, so I didn't think he was tipsy, but water would still be good for him.

"That ass. Definitely the definition of *cake*."

The backhand to his chest was probably a bit harder than necessary, but the gush of air from my brother's lungs was worth it.

"Fuck," Hudson groaned, but he chuckled. "Come on, you gotta know that kid's got an amazing ass."

Dad snorted and shook his head.

And I know just how fucking perfect he looks in tight pink underwear and my flannel shirt. And how good he feels cuddled on my lap.

"Doesn't mean I need you drooling over him," I grumbled. "You've got your own guy."

Dad rolled his eyes and grumbled something.

Hudson smirked, ignoring Dad's mini tantrum. "That I do." His face softened, and he cocked his head. "Guess you do now too, huh?"

A protest died on my lips when I recalled the taste of Jack on my tongue. "Yeah, I guess I do." I thought back to the conversation I'd had with Lance not too long ago. *When you know, you know.* Was that what this was with Jack? Was this what I'd wondered my whole life if I'd ever find? The elusive *one* who'd always seemed just beyond my reach? All I knew was the simmering heat in my belly wasn't something I'd experienced with anyone else, and the giddy anticipation of working with him, living with him, and figuring this shit out *with him* sparked something I hadn't ever experienced.

"Thought you always said you had to know someone before you felt something for them," Dad muttered, a new sucker between his lips.

"I do know him."

Hudson snorted. "*Know* him know him?"

Another backhand to his chest shut him up quickly. "He's been in town for a while. Been talking to him daily long before you went to the hospital. First by text, then face-to-face at the bar. We aren't strangers." Honestly, it felt like I knew Jack better than some of the folks in town I'd known my whole life. And I liked him a lot better than some of them too.

"You think it's smart to be living together, working

together, and getting together?" Hudson asked with a smirk, but a seriousness flashed in his eyes.

I shrugged. "He needed a place, I've got one. He needs a job, I can give him one."

"Bet that's not all you'll be givin' him." Hudson whooped when I launched a bushel basket at him.

"Don't be crude."

"Both you gettin' cozy with your guys, not sure there's any chance for me," Dad mumbled around his sucker.

"Huh?" Hudson asked with the same shock and confusion as I felt.

Dad hitched a shoulder. "Maybe you two have it all figured out."

For a brief moment, I thought Dad was being sarcastic or poking fun at Hudson and me being involved with men. But the way Dad stared off into the orchard, the fine lines around his eyes more prominent in the dusk, I realized he was serious.

"You boys think there's someone out there for everyone?" Dad asked.

Hudson nodded and I cleared my throat. "Yeah," I said.

"Sometimes I think there's more than one person for some people, while others truly only have the one. I think there are a lot of good matches for people, and some find the perfect match," Hudson said.

Dad hummed around the stick. "For the longest time, I thought your mom was the only one for me. Thought she ruined me. Well, she did ruin the me back then, but maybe that's not the me now." Dad was quiet for a moment before he continued. "But then I see Lance comin' back to town after his marriage not workin' out. And now he's gone and found himself his perfect match." Dad's words—as much as I knew they pained him to admit—were soft and slow, and for a moment I thought maybe he'd gotten into the cider. I cocked a brow at Hudson, and my brother just shrugged. "Maybe I shut myself off for too long." Dad gestured toward us with his sucker. "What I oughta do is be more open like the two of you. See who comes along."

"Dad, are you tryin' to tell us something?" Hudson asked, his eyes flicking back and forth between me and Dad.

"Ain't got nothin' to tell," Dad groused. "Just sayin' I'm tryin' to learn from my boys. Gotta be open to new things if I'm ever gonna find love again." He snorted at his own words. "Bunch of bullshit. Ain't gonna happen." He pushed himself off the stack of baskets he'd been leaning on and gave a wave as he started up the hill. "I'm tired. Goin' to bed."

"Dad," I called after him. "You okay?"

"I had a fuckin' heart attack, I need to rest." Dad raised a hand gripping the sucker over his head in a gesture of farewell.

Hudson and I watched him go.

"He been drinkin'?" I asked.

"Not a drop that I know of," Hudson said. "He's been with Lance and me pretty much all day."

"His medication making him loopy?"

"None of the warnings listed anything like that." Hudson wiped his hands on an old towel.

"Well, keep an eye on him. If he keeps goin' on like that we maybe oughta get him to the doctor."

"Will do."

Their voices reached us before Jack and Lance emerged from between the trees. "You come by the shop someday, you can build your own sundae. Any toppings, all the fixings."

Something crossed Jack's face—a look I couldn't quite decipher—but he smiled and nodded. "I usually just stick to plain vanilla, but I'll definitely take you up on the ice cream. Best I've ever tasted."

The four of us chatted for a bit longer, making plans for the renovation and upgrade to the extra space at the Roadhouse, and then said our goodbyes.

As Jack chugged his second bottle of water, I savored the tingly heat when our pinky fingers brushed together. Finally, determined to just bite the bullet even though I had no clue how to play it cool when it came to relationships of any type, I hooked our pinkies together.

"Do you not like ice cream sundaes?" I asked.

Jack shot me a look, and I shrugged.

He cleared his throat and tucked the empty water bottle in his back pocket. "Um, all the toppings and I have a bumpy past."

"Not a fan?"

With one hand tucked protectively in mine, Jack used his other hand to bring the collar of his shirt up to rub against his bottom lip. "For about three years in a row at school we were supposed to learn these lists of sight words. For every list we learned, we got to add a topping on the chart. At the end of the year, we had ice cream with whichever toppings we earned."

My gut churned. I didn't like where this story was going. I gave Jack's hand a squeeze.

"I sucked at reading. I eventually learned the words, but I was so much slower than most the class, so I never got the toppings. And the next year, I'd have to start at the lower lists, and I just never could get caught up." He chewed on his collar. "So, I got plain vanilla every year. I told people I didn't like toppings. Convinced myself I liked plain ice cream." A huff of humorless laughter escaped him. "Thing is, I spent so long eating plain ice cream, I really do prefer it to all the toppings. I love the taste of pure vanilla ice cream, and I don't want to miss out on that flavor by adding toppings." He wrinkled his nose. "But as a little kid, I sure wanted to earn all those toppings like the other kids. It's not like I have anything against ice cream sundaes, just some bad memories that go along with them."

"That's a sucky thing to have to go through," I said as we neared the Roadhouse.

"It is what it is," Jack said. "One good thing about it was Joseph paid very little attention to anything to do with my education—unless it was the school trying to get me extra help—so he either didn't find out about me never earning the toppings, or he just didn't care." He rubbed his arms in the cool breeze. "I was always so grateful he didn't know because he and Douglas would have made it into a huge thing for sure."

"Thank goodness for small blessings, I guess," I said as we made our way up the stairs to the apartment.

Jack leaned into me while I fiddled with the key in the

lock. "And now I'm in the perfect place with the best vanilla ice cream in the entire world."

"Everything works out in the end," I said.

Jack hummed. "I don't think I've ever really believed that."

I cocked my head.

"My mom died. I ended up with a terrible family. A large chunk of my life seemed to be just one bad dream after another, so thinking things were going to work out wasn't something my brain considered." He huffed a little laugh and brought the collar of his shirt to his lips, half with me and half lost in unpleasant memories. "Not until I hightailed it out of there and ended up here. For the longest time, I figured this was just a stopover until I was able to get somewhere else. What do I know about living in a small town?"

"But?" Maybe I was fishing. Maybe I wanted to hear that this town had proven it had something to offer him. Maybe I wanted to hear *I* was enough to make him stay. Selfish? Yes. But it was what my heart longed to hear.

Jack smiled. "But each day I stayed convinced me maybe I'd taken a leap of faith and landed exactly where I'm supposed to be. Can't say I've reached *the end*, but the whole *everything works out* part almost feels like it's a real thing."

With the door cracked open, I slipped a finger under Jack's chin and lifted his head so his eyes met mine. "You are one of the most resilient, positive people I've ever met." I brushed a kiss over his full lips. "It's something I've admired about you since we first met. I'll be sure to get you as many dishes of ice cream as you can stomach."

Jack grinned, his big blue eyes locked with mine, his full pink lip caught between his teeth. "I like when you kiss me," he whispered.

"Is that something new?" I wrapped an arm around his waist and hauled him inside, kicking the door shut behind me.

"Liking when you kiss me?" Jack asked. "I mean, we just started kissing today, but I've liked it from the first time."

I chuckled. "No, I mean is it new for you to like kissing?"

Jack paused and cocked his head. "Yeah, for sure. I've either had shitty kisses that led to shittier sex, or no kisses that led to the shittiest sex." He snaked his arms around my neck. "Kissing you feels right. Like it's full of promises rather than demands." He trailed his lips along my collarbone. "Like I know it's eventually going to lead to something breathtaking, but it doesn't feel like you're rushing me to get there."

I gripped his chin gently between my thumb and forefinger. "I will *never* force you into anything you don't want to do. I don't just fall into bed with people, so I wouldn't expect you to move any quicker than what you're comfortable with."

"Thank you," Jack whispered against my lips.

"You never have to thank me for respecting boundaries—"

"No, thank you for being the type of person who can help me savor the journey of getting there." He sucked my bottom lip into his mouth. "Don't get me wrong, I definitely want to have sex with you, I'd just rather explore along the way before we reach wham, bam, thank you, ma'am, and you throw me out like Roadhouse garbage."

I couldn't help the huff of laughter. "First," I murmured at his ear, loving the way he shivered in my arms. "The journey is sometimes the best part, at least in my experience. Second," I trailed my hands down his slim, muscular back and palmed his perfect ass, "wham, bam, thank you, ma'am isn't something I've ever been very good with, even if that was what you're looking for."

Jack shook his head. "It's not."

"And third," I pulled his hips flush against mine, Jack's tiny, needy whimpers filling the air, "I need you to know that going through relationships like yesterday's trash isn't something I can do. I will be very honest and tell you I haven't really had very many relationships, but the few I've had have meant something to me. They ended on good terms, and I appreciate what I learned from them. But if this is something you think will flame hot and then sputter and die quickly before we both say goodbye, I need you to know that's not how I work." I pressed him against the countertop in the kitchen.

"What does that mean?" Jack asked, his hot breath against my ear as he rutted his hard cock against my zipper.

"It means I'm in this for the long haul," I said, my words rough against his temple before I took his earlobe between my teeth. "I'm not proposing marriage or claiming we'll be together forever..."

"Forever sounds like a really nice place to be if you're

there." Jack's thick words penetrated my hormone-addled brain, and I couldn't help the groan as I held him close.

"I'm here," I whispered, lifting him onto the counter. Jack's spread legs were an invitation, and my body rejoiced at how perfectly we fit together.

"Even if we let things move slow?" Jack asked.

I nodded.

"What if I want to move faster?" Jack asked.

Sucking gently along his collarbone, I shrugged. "We move however slow or fast we want. There are no rules, just what feels right for us."

We made out for what seemed like an eternity. Soft, plump lips, warm, gentle caresses, rolling hips pressing together. We could have easily stripped down, jerked each other off, and called it a night, but that wasn't where our kisses led us.

When Jack's sleepy eyes stared up at me, his grin drunk on kisses and desire, I hugged him close. "You want to shower first?" I asked.

Jack nodded and slipped from the countertop, his dick rubbing against mine on the way down. "Tomorrow, I'm baking cakes for you."

I watched as he sleepily stumbled his way to the bathroom. When the water turned on, I grinned and shook my head. What the hell had I gotten myself into? A few months ago, I was single, not looking for any type of relationship, and perfectly content with the way the Roadhouse was running.

Then Jack walked into my life and turned everything upside down.

In the best way possible.

I couldn't imagine going back to life before I knew him.

How had I lived without him by my side?

And the Roadhouse clearly needed to add cakes to our cocktails. Not something that had been on my Bingo card, but thinking about starting the new venture with Jack had me excited about the business in a way I hadn't been in a long time.

Damn.

I was head over heels.

And my heart was at risk more than I'd allowed it to be since my mom left.

But I couldn't even summon the energy to care.

Because having Jack in my life was quickly proving to be the chunk of something I hadn't even known I'd been missing.

Chapter 12
Jack

"OH MY GOD," HENRY GROANED AROUND A forkful of cake. "That's amazing."

We'd been *together* for a bit. The first cakes I'd made for him had been a hit. Henry hired me on the spot—while grumbling good-naturedly about how it was a good thing he didn't employ an HR department since he'd already screwed up by kissing his newest employee—and our plan for adding to the business was full steam ahead. We'd spent weeks updating the Roadhouse addition with two top-of-the-line ovens, my choice of the very best mixers, exquisite baking pans, and gorgeous display cases.

Hudson, Lance, and Casey Joe had been huge helps in the updates. Turned out that Casey Joe was pretty darned good with graphics and designs—unbeknownst to his sons, he'd taken some online certification courses recently. "Don't have to tell you two everything," Casey Joe had drawled with an arched brow and a glance between his sons. "Not like you fill me in on all your secrets, is it?"

He'd shot a look at Lance but stopped short before giving me the stink eye. For some reason, Henry's dad liked me, and I wasn't going to question it.

So, Casey Joe created an adorable menu for my side of the Roadhouse. *Cake and Cocktails* had its own menu— Have Your Cake & Cocktails Too—but Henry also contacted his printer and had them update the Roadhouse menus to include the cake and cocktail flights in addition to the base cake options and rotating cakes. Since we'd be changing some flavors often, we opted to leave the menus fairly open, and we'd just post the rotations as we changed them.

Casey Joe had already set up a simple website that would be a one-stop-shop for the orchard, the Juicy Peach, the Roadhouse, Lance's ice cream parlor, and the newest addition of Cake and Cocktails. We all had access to the site, and CJ had given us a crash course on how to update the pertinent pieces as needed.

Plus, he'd set me up with a newsletter. It wasn't large yet, but I could send out cake and cocktail recipes to subscribers, in addition to keeping them updated on specials, new flavors, and events at the shop. I had a QR code near the display cases and register so people could sign up, and Henry was planning to push the newsletter on the Roadhouse side.

Casey Joe had talked me into starting an account on Instagram where I could post pictures of my cakes, our cake and cocktail flights, and anything else that might pull folks in. I had a decent little following already, and several had signed up for the newsletter and expressed interest in coming in to sample our goods.

I hadn't been so excited about something in...well, *ever*. Since my mom died, my life had been one bad dream after another. But Haven Grove had turned out to be exactly what the name implied—my safe place, my reset, my chance to step toward my future.

And having Henry by my side through all of it was the icing on the cake.

Baking for Henry had quickly turned into one of my favorite things to do. Honestly, spending time in the kitchen with Henry was like the world's most delicious foreplay, and I was definitely looking forward to hearing his groans of pleasure in the bedroom if they were anything like the noises he made when he sampled my cake.

So far, we'd kept to our original sleeping arrangements. I didn't mind the couch in the least, especially knowing I was safe and sound with Henry just down the hallway. Not gonna lie, though. Our make out sessions of late had me dreaming up all sorts of delicious ideas involving me in Henry's bed.

But I didn't want to assume anything.

Or pressure Henry into something he wasn't completely onboard with.

We'd been taking things at the perfect pace, and I knew we'd end up in the bedroom when it felt right for both of us.

Until then, we spent a lot of time cuddling on the couch, making out until we were both breathing heavily, and taking the occasional nap curled up together while a movie played if we weren't busy at the Roadhouse. When Henry wasn't with me, I enjoyed snuggling into the couch with one of his flannels engulfing me and plying my guy with cake just to hear his sexy sounds while he told me how fabulous I was.

I grinned and reached up to thumb a chunk of icing from his lip. When Henry caught my thumb between his teeth, I yelped with a giggle. His lips closed around my thumb, and his warm tongue swirled around the tip before Henry sucked gently.

With a knowing gleam in those honey brown eyes, he released my thumb while licking his lips. On some other guys, the whole scene would have been cringey and creepy, but with Henry, it just made me feel wanted.

And safe.

Deep in my soul, I knew I was always safe with Henry. Protective to a fault, Henry took care of those around him, and somehow, I'd lucked out to be one of those people in his inner circle. I had no doubt he'd go to battle for me without even blinking an eye.

As someone who hadn't felt safe in my own skin since my mom died, his caring, protective nature was the warm hug I'd desperately needed for so long. Henry was what I'd been missing—the reason so many crappy encounters with guys who wanted nothing more than a quick fuck had never led me to finding my person.

I'd just been waiting for Henry.

"That's the wedding cake flavor—white cake, white icing. Looks kinda plain, but it's a favorite," I said, pulling myself from my hormone-hazy thoughts and back to the task at hand. "Plus, I spruce it up with the decorations."

"I think I could eat the whole thing," Henry said, but he pushed the plate to the side. "But I don't wanna be too full for the other ones." He rubbed his hands together as he sat on a stool next to the counter in the extra kitchen. "What's next?"

"I wanted to do something with our peaches." When I realized what I'd said, my cheeks caught fire, and I immediately brought my shirt collar to my lips. "I mean—"

Henry grabbed me around the waist and yanked me close to stand between his spread legs. "*Our* peaches is perfect. *You* are perfect."

I snorted, but Henry gripped my chin and lifted my face so our eyes met.

"You are. Maybe not perfect as in no issues—hell, none of us are. But perfect in that you fit like you were always meant to be here." He brushed his lips over mine. "I love having you here—in my kitchen, in my apartment, in my life. Our peaches. Our business. Our home."

I knew my eyes were bugging out, and Henry must have noticed.

"Sorry, that's probably too much," he started.

I shook my head. "No. It's…" I smiled. "Perfect."

Henry smiled and pressed his forehead against mine. "Sometimes it's hard to believe this is all just so easy."

I cuddled into him, my lips pressing kisses along his jawline, the coarse hair of his beard tickling my lips.

"Tell me about this cake," Henry said, his whispered words gruff with that something special he seemed to save just for me.

"It's like a pineapple upside-down cake, but it's peach upside-down cake."

"I already love it," Henry said, nuzzling his nose against my ear.

"I'm beginning to think you pretty much love all cake," I said with a grin.

"I love *your* cake." Henry punctuated his words by placing big hands on my ass.

Was it wishful thinking to hope he meant the innuendo in exactly the way I wanted him to mean it?

"We'll pair it with a whiskey sour." I tried my best to keep the breathlessness out of the words, but I couldn't stop the slight whimper when Henry nipped at my ear lobe. "Henry..."

"Jack." Henry stood, hauling me against him, and we both groaned when our rock-hard cocks rubbed together. He swiped a glob of icing from his plate and thumbed it over my bottom lip before dipping his head to kiss me. The connection between us never failed to send me spiraling with its frenetic energy, protective warmth, and overwhelming sense of rightness.

The savory, sweet flavor of vanilla and almond extract exploded on my tongue, but the rich flavor of Henry teasing my tastebuds sent heat straight to my balls. Nothing in my past could have ever prepared me for how perfect I felt in Henry's arms.

When his big hand fluttered over my abdomen, the backs of his knuckles caressing up and down, I wanted to crawl into him and never leave. His fingers skimmed down to trace over my fly, and my hips thrust of their own accord.

Henry never broke the contact between the backs of his fingers and my denim-covered cock, but he lifted my chin, bringing my eyes to meet those honey brown orbs of his. "This okay?" A thrill shot through me, his gruff words making me feel wanted.

Not just sexually.

Wanted.

Desired.

Like I had a place in this world, a purpose, someone who would miss me if I disappeared.

It was a new feeling, an exciting feeling. And I wanted to curl into it, savor it, build memories and a future upon it.

I nodded my head.

"Jack, I need to hear the words. Can I touch you?"

Blinking slowly as my brain processed the question, I bit my lip and nodded again. When Henry leaned in and tongued what I guessed was icing from the corner of my mouth, I couldn't help the shiver that traveled through me.

"Tell me, Jack," Henry whispered.

"I...um..." I huffed through the annoyance and desire flooding through me. "I forgot the question."

Henry smiled against my lips. "Are you okay with my hand on your cock?"

The whimper was automatic. "Yes."

"Yes, what?"

"Touch me." When Henry cocked a brow, I amended, "Touch my cock."

Henry thumbed open the button of my jeans and gently worked the zipper down over my dick. "Say the word, and we stop. No questions."

I nodded, my head abuzz with the sensations. And

probably a little dizzy from lack of oxygen as I held my breath waiting for that first spark of fire when Henry's hand touched my cock.

He moved to trail a finger over the waistband of my underwear.

And chuckled.

Shit.

This wasn't a laughing matter.

What the hell.

I pulled back, ready to retreat within, but the bright gleam in Henry's eyes warmed my heart.

"I like 'em," he murmured, pressing kisses along my jawline.

The noise I made was only halfway intelligible as a question.

"The peaches. They're cute."

And then I realized what he was talking about.

I had on a pair of underwear Hudson had included in a stack of merch he'd given me. *"The underwear are a prototype. Let me know what you think; we might be selling them soon."*

Teal blue with a variety of peaches—whole, half, with the stone, without, dripping juice, covered in cream—the underwear I had on were a bikini style which was my favorite.

"Your brother gave them to me," I said, shifting my hips in search of more skin-on-skin contact.

"New rule I wasn't aware we needed," Henry grumbled. "No talking about my brother when anything sexual is happening. It's like a cold bucket of water."

A giggle escaped me. "Got it." His words from earlier

came back to me. "And if you want to stop, we can. Same goes for you; just say the word."

Henry shook his head, the scruff of his beard grazing my skin. "I'm good." He nuzzled into me. "So good," he whispered as one arm wrapped around my back and held me tight, and the other hand slipped gently under my peachy bikinis and engulfed my throbbing cock.

"Oh shit," I moaned. The heat and strength of his grip around me would have brought me to my knees if he hadn't been holding me close. No one had ever given any time or thought to foreplay with me before. Henry and I had been teasing each other for several long weeks, and the moment he finally touched me in such an intimate way, my balls threatened to unload right then and there.

When his thumb swiped over the drop of pre-cum beading on my slit, dueling urges exploded in my head. Throw my head back and lose myself in his touch or watch intently as he jacked me off.

In the end, I did both. My head thumped against the kitchen wall Henry had pushed me up against, and I thrust into his fist over and over. But the sound of his zipper lowering pulled me from my lust-induced haze. I glanced down in time to see Henry yank his flannel out of the way, tucking the flaps under his arm, and I stopped breathing for the second time that day when he shoved his boxers down under his balls and took his dick in hand.

Henry wasn't a fit, muscular god with washboard abs. He was broad and thick with an absolutely perfect dad bod. The very definition of a bear. And his big body surrounded mine, protecting me as he took both cocks in his big hand and slowly stroked us with a firm touch.

The cool press of the wall against my lower back where my shirt had ridden up took my breath away, but Henry's big hand splayed over the bare skin as his mouth dropped to mine. The press of his hand against my back, the slick heat of his tongue against mine, and the silky-smooth strokes of his fist around our shafts had my balls drawing up tight.

"Pull your shirt up," Henry demanded.

I yanked the hem of my shirt over my head and tossed it to the floor.

"Fuck," he growled. "I need a lot more time with you than a quick hand job in your kitchen."

"You can have all the time you want with me." I worked his buttons through their tiny slots until I could pull the flannel up and off. When Henry's shirt joined mine in a puddle of fabric, I leaned in and ran my tongue over first one nipple and then the other, loving the way Henry hissed.

I'd never been given the freedom to explore, either because the guy I was with just wanted to fuck me and leave or because I knew from the get-go I wasn't into him, and I had no desire to search his body for ways to turn him on.

But with Henry, I was free to touch, tease, and taste. He had the patience of a saint, and I knew he had a thing for me delving into new experiences. So, I sucked the tight bud of his nipple into my mouth and swirled my tongue around it as my hands roamed over Henry's broad shoulders.

Nipping at his pec, loving the way Henry groaned, I trailed kisses to his neck where I knew from weeks of making out that he enjoyed being kissed. Making my way to his mouth, I sucked his bottom lip between mine before Henry took over the kiss and owned my mouth like a starving man.

His fist around our cocks tightened and he jacked us faster. "Jack..." He pressed his forehead to mine, his ragged whisper joining the sound of our heavy breathing and the rough movement of skin against skin as he worked us both toward completion.

Losing myself in those honey brown eyes, I gave into the rhythm of his hand on me. With a cry of pleasure that honestly didn't belong anywhere in a kitchen, I let loose and shot my load over his fingers. My release on his hand sent Henry over the edge, and he erupted with a long, low grunt. The scent of our cum and sweat mingled between us as we caught our breath.

"Holy shit." Henry's words rushed out on a huff of air.

I chuckled, my face buried in his neck. "Yeah. That was..."

Suddenly, every harsh word Joseph and Douglas had ever thrown my way in their underhanded attacks came rushing in. My chest constricted and I struggled to take in a deep breath. Who was I to think a man as amazing as Henry would want to spend time with me? Teach me? Give me even a sliver of a chance?

The doubt swirled, hateful and frenzied, threatening to boil over.

"Perfect," he whispered, nuzzling the underside of my neck until his lips made their way to mine. "You are so fucking perfect."

"I'm not—"

"You're perfect for me and that's all that matters."

How could I argue with that? The dark shadows of my past retreated, shoved away by Henry's sweet words and the way he held me close. Like I belonged to him.

"I'm sticky and sweaty, and we definitely need to clean up before we do anything else with food."

"Good thing the health inspector already visited this month," Henry teased.

We got ourselves cleaned up in the staff bathroom before returning to my side of the Roadhouse to wrap up the cake tasting. Henry raved over my cake, heartily approved of the cocktails I wanted to match with each and helped me make notes for our first ever social media post.

The night I left Joseph's house—the night my plan was thrust into motion before I was completely ready—I never dreamed I'd find myself smack dab in the middle of a dream come true.

But there I was, with Henry by my side.

Chapter 13
Henry

I couldn't sleep.

Rolling from bed and padding down the hall to the kitchen, I glanced toward the couch where a Jack-sized lump slept. I'd asked him to share my bed, but he'd insisted he was fine on the couch, *"until sleeping in your bed is something we're both ready for."*

I respected his feelings on the matter, and I wasn't sure I'd truly been ready to have him sleeping curled next to me night after night a few weeks ago.

But now?

Well, now I was having a hard time not charging toward the couch, throwing him over my shoulder, and marching him to my bedroom. Not because I expected him to have sex with me right then and there—although, based on how heated our make-out sessions had gotten lately, I had a feeling we were both walking a very thin line on where we wanted our physical relationship to go in the near future. Honestly, I liked sex, but I'd be just as happy having Jack curled next to me while we slept.

I had a thing for *him*, not just for the sexy shit we might get up to.

Keeping the light off, I reached for a cup and filled it with water, hoping the water dispenser wouldn't wake Jake. At least I hadn't wanted ice.

Something had woken me earlier, and I hadn't been able to fall back to sleep.

Thoughts of the addition to the Roadhouse screamed through my head. I was excited about the new venture and looking forward to watching Jack come into his own with his cakes, the social media, and the newsletter.

Our idea likely wasn't *the only* one of its kind, but I didn't think many places near us were offering cake and cocktail flights. We'd keep the good folks of Haven Grove enticed and coming back for more, and hopefully, we'd be able to pull in customers from around the state—or farther—with our unique setup.

The whole cake and cocktail thing was a fun little gimmick. People loved flights of wine, beer, and cocktails. Hell, I'd seen places with flights of meats, cheeses, breads, coffees, and teas. Who wouldn't love a flight of the most delicious and gorgeous cakes I'd ever seen? We definitely had the potential to send our business through the roof with this new addition. And I loved the idea all the more because it involved Jack working right next to me and my family while he spread his wings and learned he was worth so much more than what those assholes convinced him of.

Speaking of family, Hudson and Lance had been as much help as I'd expected them to be.

Dad had actually surprised me with how much he'd helped.

He was a fan of Jack's—who wouldn't be?—and I think he wanted to see the younger man succeed as much as I did. Dad had his faults, but he'd always been there to quietly support his boys, and now it seemed like he'd gone and claimed Jack as one of his own.

Between Dad's emotional and physical health as of late, I worried about him. Whether he'd admit it or not, he was happy to have his best friend back in his life. And he was thrilled to see Hudson happy, even if his son's happiness coincided with Lance returning to town.

But Dad was lonely. He'd been heartbroken and lonely for as long as I could remember, but until recently, he hadn't seemed to want to remedy that.

Now though?

Well, he seemed a bit more open to the idea.

We just needed the right person to come along. Cantankerous, belligerent, and rough around the edges, Dad was a definite diamond in the rough. But I had a feeling when he finally let down his guard long enough for someone to get their foot in the door, he'd be someone's very last attempt at finding a forever type of love.

"Can't sleep?" Jack's rough whisper had me yelping and splashing water out of my cup in the dark kitchen.

He giggled sleepily.

"Sorry."

"What are you doing up?" I asked as he took the cup

from my hand and finished off my water. "Didn't mean to wake you."

"I couldn't stay asleep. I think my head is just buzzing with everything."

Jack placed the cup in the sink before moving into my arms.

Fuck.

Before Jack, I never considered myself lonely or longing for another person to share my life with. But then he showed up in Haven Grove, infiltrated my heart without so much as even trying, and now I couldn't imagine a moment of my life without him in it.

"I was thinking about business stuff too," I admitted. "I think it's all going to go great." I pressed a kiss to his head.

"I think we need a distraction," Jack murmured at my ear.

"What kind of distraction?" I asked, already on board with whatever he wanted to do. That was how it was with Jack. Wherever he went, whatever he did, I had no doubt I'd follow. Which was a slightly terrifying thought because I'd lived in Haven Grove my entire life. My family was here. My business was here. I didn't think Jack was planning to wave goodbye and drive off into the sunset anytime soon, but the fact I'd have very little hope of not packing my bag and following him right out of town was unsettling.

Not because it would be a terrible thing, just because this man had gripped my heart and owned me so fiercely in such a short amount of time.

"Maybe the kind that involves a bed and making use of

the fact we're both off in the morning," he said with a grin as he rocked his hips into me.

Without a second's hesitation, I bent and hefted him up, savoring the way his legs immediately wrapped around my waist. Careful not to bump him into the doorway, I left the dark kitchen and made my way down the hallway to my bedroom.

With my knees against the bed, I let Jack's smaller frame slide down my body until he sat on the mattress. He quickly stripped off the t-shirt he'd worn to bed and tossed it to the floor. In the dim glow from the security light outside my window, Jack's lean body gleamed, his hard cock straining against the fabric of his bikini briefs.

"Condoms and lube are in the drawer if we get to that point," I said, knowing it was best to have that conversation before desire clouded our judgement. "And I haven't been with anyone since my last negative test."

Jack bit his lip, his fingers dancing over his collarbone as if searching for his shirt to chew on. "I've always used condoms," he said. "And my tests have been negative," he rushed on.

"What do you want?" I asked him, tipping his chin so he brought his gaze to mine.

"Wanna taste you, make you come," he answered confidently. Then his bit his bottom lip. "And have you do that to me."

"And?" I pressed.

Jack's cheeks flamed.

"Jack, we talk about shit, or we don't do anything. We're not kids, and I'm not someone who is going to judge you or ridicule you for what you want. Ever."

Desire glowed in his eyes, and he swallowed hard. "I don't know when we'll be ready for anal," he started.

I waited.

"But if we get to that point, I want to do it without condoms," he rushed out. "If you're okay with that."

Leaning in to press a kiss to his lips, I smiled. "When we get to that point, I'm okay with that. I trust you; I trust *us.*"

Jack nodded, licking his lips as if to chase the flavor of our kiss. "What if we get to that point sooner rather than later?"

"I'm good with whatever we decide as long as we decide it together."

He chewed on his lip as he gazed at me. The desire and admiration in his eyes had my gut flip-flopping and my heart turning goopy in my chest. "Okay," he whispered.

Straightening up, I spread my arms and smiled down at him. "I'm yours. Do whatever you want."

Heat flared in Jack's eyes. He stood, bringing our bodies flush together, my cock pressing against his lower abdomen. In one quick movement, Jack spun us around. He shimmied out of his underwear—teasing me with just a glimpse of his pretty cock—before dropping to his knees in front of me. "Do you want to stand or sit?"

Knowing my knees wouldn't hold out once he got that pretty mouth on me, I dropped to the mattress.

Jack licked his lips before burying his face in my groin and breathing me in like I was a bouquet of fresh-cut flowers.

Fuck. He was gonna kill me.

"This okay?" His warm breath caressed my hard cock.

"Always," I choked out, the word a strangled prayer.

Jack teased his fingers along the waistband of my boxers as he leaned up to tongue over my navel and press kisses to the trail of hair on my belly. "Lift up," he directed, an adorable mix of innocence and confidence in his words.

With my weight on my hands, I leaned back and lifted my ass from the mattress, letting Jack slide my underwear down my legs. Spreading my legs for him, I threw my head back with a groan when Jack's hand wrapped around my leaking shaft, and those big blue eyes stared at me over my cockhead. Reaching for him, cupping his cheek in my palm, I thumbed over his full bottom lip. "You okay?"

Jack nodded. "Wanna do this, just not a lot of practice."

Fuck.

Why was that such a turn on? It wasn't like I was some Romeo with all the notches on my bedpost. I think I liked that Jack and I would mostly be learning together—at least learning about each other together.

"Take your time." I barely heard my own words. "Do whatever feels right."

Jack licked the pre-cum from my slit, never taking his eyes from me. When he spread his pretty lips and took me into his hot, wet mouth, I swore. At that exact moment, in the dim light of my bedroom, Jack Garner ruined me for anyone else in this lifetime or the next.

Like I was in a dream world, I watched as this beautiful man worshipped my cock. My grunts and growls of pleasure along with the way I ran my fingers through his golden blond locks spurred Jack on. He dropped his hands to my thick thighs as he bobbed his head up and down, those gorgeous lips gleaming with spit and pre-cum. The precious noises he made each time my cockhead hit the back of his throat sent a ferocious heat to my balls.

Doing my damnedest to keep from thrusting too hard into his pretty mouth, I let Jack set the pace. I'd never been a hard, fast, dirty lover, but Jack's lips stretched around my cock had my libido revving like the engine of my old truck.

Jack popped off my dick, saliva running down his chin. "Want you to come in my mouth. Wanna taste you."

Fuck.

Before I could say anything, Jack was back on my cock, his hands traveling over my belly, my back, and returning to run through the hair on my chest, his thumbs teasing over my nipples. I was a big boy—offensive lineman big— always had been. I'd never looked like Hudson, and I knew I never would. Between my broad shoulders, dad bod, and toeing the line of being the very definition of a bear with my hairy appearance, I'd always known Hudson got the looks, while I was his protective shadow of an older brother.

But watching Jack feast on my cock, feeling the heat of his hands all over my big, hairy body, it felt like I'd won the grand prize. Jack liked *me*. He liked me for the person I was, he enjoyed my body, and he'd picked *me* to spend his time with. I'd never once been jealous of my baby brother, but it sure was a boost to find myself in a position of more than just the big brother.

Somehow, and for whatever reason, the universe had smiled upon me and sent this beautiful, amazing man into my life, and I had no intention of questioning the why of it all.

When Jack's elbows pushed my legs farther apart, and his fingers teased over my balls, I knew immediately I was done for. Keeping myself propped up on one hand, the other gently cupped around the back of Jack's head with my fingers buried in his hair, I gave in to the urge to jerk my hips in short, tiny thrusts.

Jack's moan around my shaft sent me careening over the edge, and I grunted my hot release. Jack took everything I gave him, swallowing me down while he played with my balls.

"Come up here." The words held a mix of demand and begging.

Jack stood between my legs and wiped my release from his chin. "Was that okay?"

I snorted, wrapping my arms around his waist and pulling him close to bury my face in his flat, muscular belly. Jack groaned, and his hard cock likely smeared pre-cum on the underside of my beard, but that was a problem for later and nothing a little soap couldn't take care of. Pressing kisses to his torso, I breathed him in. "That was amazing," I murmured against his heated skin, tasting the saltiness of his sweat and the unique essence of Jack.

With my arms still wrapped tightly around him, I shifted to stretch out on the bed and brought him with me. Jack squawked and giggled when his long, sleek body landed on top of mine. Caressing my hands down his back, I cupped his firm ass. "Your turn."

Jack groaned and rocked his hips into me. "Please," he begged.

I rolled us to our sides, one hand coming up to grip the back of Jack's head as I brought my mouth to his. Our tongues danced together, a mix of peaceful post-orgasm haze and hot, lustful desire. When Jack rutted into my thigh, I broke away and trailed kisses down his neck, to his collarbone, stopping to tease his nipples—loving the sweet whimpers he gave me—tonguing his belly button, nipping at his hip bone, and finally reaching his leaking cock.

I swiped my tongue over his slit, savoring the first bitter, salty flavor of him before running my nose down the underside of his shaft and nuzzling into the dark brown curls at his base.

Jack rolled his hips seeking friction for his throbbing erection, his legs spreading wide for me. Caressing my hand over his inner thigh, the coarse blond hair tickling my palm, I moved to cup his balls.

"Tell me what you want." Hair crinkled under my lips as I spoke into the soft, sensitive spot where his upper leg met his groin. I knew what I wanted to do to him, but I had to know Jack was on board. Plus, hearing him tell me what he wanted was fucking hot as hell.

"Suck me," Jack begged.

"Anything else?"

He propped up on his elbows, blue eyes glowing with heated desire, his breathing heavy. "Like what?"

I shrugged, my nose nuzzling along his balls, and trailed my thumb to his crack. Nothing more, just the pad of my thumb tracing over him, but Jack gasped and nodded.

"Please, Henry."

"You have to say it, so I know we're on the same page."
I pressed a soft kiss to his balls.

"Want your fingers inside me," he pleaded. "Henry.
Please. Make me come."

Chuckling softly at the way he pouted his displeasure
when I moved away from him long enough to get the lube,
I returned quickly. Taking his cock in hand, I stroked
slowly, loving the way Jack writhed beneath me. Kissing
him while I jacked him was something I probably could
have done for hours, edging him, bringing him right to the
brink, backing off. Over and over. But right then and there,
I needed something different. *Jack* needed something
different.

I positioned myself to take his cock between my lips,
humming around his shaft when he cried out my name.
Tonguing the sensitive underside of his shaft, swirling
around his flared head, I savored the heated flavor of him
exploding on my tastebuds. "Give me some lube," I said,
blowing softly on Jack's spit-slick dick just to watch him
squirm.

He grabbed the bottle and doled out a couple pumps
onto my waiting fingers. Just as I started to check in with
him, Jack tossed the bottle to the mattress before guiding
my lubed-up hand toward his ass. Spreading his legs for
me, he said, "Henry, I swear to god, if you don't make me
come, I'm never making cake for you again."

His words surprised a huff of laughter from me, but I
bent to take him in my mouth and worked my slick fingers
between his ass cheeks.

"That's what I thought," Jack muttered, but his
breathy words were laced with desperate want. "Knew you

loved my cake—" He cut off with a soft whine when the tip of one finger swirled around his tight hole.

"Fuckin' right I love your cake," I growled, sure he caught the double entendre as I urged his legs farther apart before dropping back to suck his hard length between my lips.

Jack spread his legs for me, his fingers curling through my hair as his hips gave little thrusts with needy pants and whines. "Please, Henry. Give me more."

I pushed one finger deeper into his body.

"Oh fuck, that's good."

Knowing no one had ever taken their time with him hurt my heart, and I vowed to make every moment we were together something we both enjoyed. I'd been with other lovers, but none had ever touched my heart and owned my soul as quickly as Jack.

Sucking him harder, I added another finger, groaning when his tight muscle gripped my digits. "So fuckin' tight," I murmured against the warm wet skin of his dick. Just the thought of his perfect tight ass around my cock had me getting hard again.

With two fingers buried in his ass and his heavy shaft sliding in and out of my mouth, I crooked my fingers, looking for that sweet spot. Jack cried out and bucked his hips.

Found it.

"Oh shit," he panted, "oh holy shit. Henry..."

I curled my fingers again, loving the way he thrust wildly under me.

"Henry, oh fuck. I'm close. Please," he whined. "Please, Henry."

Loving the way Jack rambled my name, my fingers fucked in and out as I bobbed my head on his dick. With one last press of my fingers against that bundle of nerves, Jack tensed and cried out. His sweet release exploded from him and coated my tongue, his tight ring of muscle clenching around my fingers.

Easing from his body, I rolled to my side despite Jack's protest and grabby hands. Pulling out a tissue from the box on the bedside table, I quickly wiped lube from my hand before tossing it to the floor and pulling Jack into my arms. He cuddled into me with a satisfied sigh, pressing a kiss to my chest.

"You good?" I asked.

Jack hummed an affirmative, and I pulled the sheet up to cover us.

"That was really good," Jack whispered a few minutes later, his lips feathering over my pec before landing on a nipple. "No one's ever taken care of me like that."

My heart clenched. He deserved to be cared for, protected, loved.

Loved.

"I will *always* take care of you," I promised. It wasn't a sex-addled vow. I knew exactly what I was saying, and I meant every word. Maybe it was too early for me to declare my love for Jack, but that didn't mean the feelings weren't very, very real.

My heart knew.

Hell, I think my heart had known from the first moment I met him.

Jack snuggled closer. "As long as you let me take care of you."

Being taken care of wasn't something I was used to. Wasn't something I would have said I needed or wanted.

But ever since Jack came along, I'd found my heart and soul needing and wanting things I'd never let myself think about.

Maybe being taken care of by Jack wouldn't be such a bad thing.

I sighed into his silky blond hair, loving the way it tickled my nose and smelled of vanilla like he was my very own delicious piece of cake.

We drifted off to sleep wrapped together, limbs tangled, hearts beating as one.

Chapter 14
Jack

I woke when Henry shifted beside me. The room was still dark, and the clock showed we'd only slept about an hour. My bones were still mush from earlier, and I could have stayed curled into Henry's big, protective body forever.

"You want to shower?" Henry's sleepy words were warm against my head. "Get cleaned up before we sleep for real?"

Or get cleaned up before we get dirty again, I thought, and my cock perked up.

Like he heard my thoughts, Henry chuckled and pressed a kiss to my head. "Come on, we can save water."

When Henry rolled from the bed, I stayed tucked in the warm divot he'd left and admired his broad naked body. He wasn't lithe and smooth. He would never be a stick-thin, graceful runway model. But he was absolutely perfect in my eyes. Big and thick, like an immovable stone wall. Everything about Henry screamed protector. He was a safe place, a caretaker, and I knew he'd guard me with his life.

But what about my heart?

My heart was already happily entrenched into Henry's life, the town, our business. Maybe it was too soon. Maybe I'd let my heart drop anchor for the first man who'd shown me any attention or real affection.

The first man who hadn't seen me as a pretty face, an easy lay, a throwaway not worth investing any time in.

Maybe I'd end up heartbroken down the road.

But Henry made me feel alive for the first time since my mom died, and I wasn't going to give up on what we had just because we *might* not work out forever. I'd lived the majority of my life feeling worthless, unwanted, and alone. Leaving Joseph's house after what I'd heard him planning was the first step toward the rest of my life, and if that life included all the good I'd found since stepping off the bus in Haven Grove, I was one hundred percent here for it.

And even though Henry was the one deemed the caretaker by everyone who knew him, I had no doubt he could use someone to take care of him as well.

I was already completely committed to that role.

Once, while desperately trying to be happy selling cars for my uncle, I'd overheard a woman telling her friend, "You like taking care of people because it heals the part of you that needed someone to take care of you." The conversation had continued while they waited for Douglas to close the sale, and I went on to fumble through one of my usual awkward interactions.

I'd sold the car.

Barely.

But those words had stuck with me.

You like taking care of people because it heals the part of you that needed someone to care of you.

Damn.

That was Henry, through and through.

And it was me, if I was being honest.

I had the first handful of years with my mom. She was loving, kind, gentle, caring—everything you'd expect a mother to be. And then she was gone, and I went from being a kid who felt loved and protected to one who was constantly on edge, always looking over my shoulder, never able to trust the people who were tasked with taking care of me.

While I'd never been one to put a lot of trust in fate—I mean, she hadn't been all that kind to me up until now—I couldn't help but see all the ways Henry and I were perfectly matched and meant to be.

We'd found each other so we could take care of each other and heal the wounds of our past.

"You coming?" Henry poked his head around the doorway, true concern filling that beautiful face under his scruff.

Smiling, I gave him a nod and rolled from bed.

I'd go anywhere this man asked me to.

Our shower turned out to be equal parts steamy, soapy, and sensual. Before the water ran cold, I reached deep for my confidence and asked Henry if I could have some time to myself in the bathroom.

After a moment of confusion, Henry gave an understanding nod, kissed me soundly, and rinsed his face one last time before exiting the shower. Once he'd dried off and left me in the bathroom alone, I took some time to prepare for whatever intimate situation Henry and I might possibly find ourselves in. When the water hinted toward running cold, I turned off the shower and wrapped myself in a towel.

Once dried, I made my way to Henry's room. The sight of my gentle giant curled on his side, snoring softly, did funny things to me. I dropped my towel on the floor next to the bed and climbed in next to Henry. The way his big arm immediately reached for me and pulled me close meant more than any sexual situation we might have been moving to the back burner. With the blanket pulled up over our naked bodies, I snuggled into Henry's warmth and drifted off to sleep with visions of making scenes like this a permanent part of our life together.

I woke later with an aching dick, a delicious warmth wrapped around me, and a tug in my chest telling me I could quickly get used to waking up every day with Henry by my side.

With a cat-like stretch, I pressed my ass backwards and smiled when Henry's arm tightened around my waist. His warm, gruff words tickled my ear. "You need somethin'?"

The throbbing in my dick had already reached epic proportions when I grabbed Henry's hand and drew it down to cover my erection. "Could use some help with this."

He chuckled. "That so?" He lightly grazed his palm over my cock.

"Henry," I whined. "Please."

Henry's thick beard tickled my shoulder when he leaned in to kiss my neck. "What do you want?"

"Wanna feel you inside me."

"My fingers?" His words reverberated through me.

I shook my head.

"Words, Jack."

Huffing and wiggling my ass into him, I chewed on my bottom lip. "Want your dick. Want you to fuck me."

Henry's arms tightened around me. "Not sure I can do that."

I froze. Had I read the situation wrong? I'd thought for sure..."Oh," I started. "That's okay."

Henry chuckled. "No, I want to. I'm just saying I don't know that what I want to do to you can be called fucking."

My breath caught, and butterfly wings flapped into such a frenzy I was left lightheaded. "Oh." I swallowed. "Oh," I repeated as my brain realized what he was saying. "That's okay. It's all okay as long as we're together."

"Yeah?"

"Mmhm," I hummed. "Henry?"

He grunted, tracing my bottom lip with his thumb.

Without allowing myself to overthink it, I brought Henry's hand to my lips and pressed a kiss to his knuckles. "I love you." The words, whispered like a prayer, were the truest words I'd spoken since I said goodbye to my mom all those years ago. "You don't have to say any—"

Henry's large hand gripped my chin and turned my face to look at him over my shoulder. "The hell I don't," he whispered gruffly before capturing my mouth in a long, slow kiss. "Love you too," he murmured against my lips.

"Never really knew what love felt like until you walked into my life."

My heart soared, warmth oozing in my chest as I brought our mouths back together. Pouring my soul into the kiss, I rocked my ass against Henry until we parted, both of us breathless. "Want you inside me." My words barely a whisper as my lips feathered over his.

"You wanna be on top? Or like this? It's your call." Henry asked as he reached behind him blindly searching for the lube.

I knew straddling his waist and riding him would provide me with more control, but I loved the way Henry's big body pressed against my back, surrounding me with his heat, his protection, his love. "Just like this." Bending my left leg, I pressed it against the mattress. Before Henry, sex had always felt like searching. Searching for that missing piece, the euphoria, the escape. Searching for a man who would accept me for me. Someone who would enjoy spending an evening with me as much as he enjoyed getting his nut before ghosting me.

Searching for that elusive mix of camaraderie and intimacy.

A friendship built on trust, laughter, and genuine caring that meant as much, if not more than, the sexual relationship.

Searching, yet never finding what I'd been looking for.

Until Henry.

Don't get me wrong. The sex we'd had so far had been amazing, and I had no doubt what we were about to do would be just as spectacular. But Henry and I had something special and fulfilling—with or without sex.

Lying there in his arms, the warmth of his body wrapped around me, I knew my search was over.

The sound of Henry pumping lube into his hand filled the air, mixing with the swish of his big body against the sheets and the distant sound of an early morning train passing through town.

When one thick finger spread lube against my entrance, I whimpered and pressed my face into the mattress. Loving the slow intensity Henry applied to working me open while, at the same time, wanting to scream and beg him to give me his cock, I panted through first one finger and then another as Henry crooned words of encouragement in my ear.

"This feel okay?" he asked, ever the protector. No one had ever cared for my comfort the way Henry did.

"It's so good," I answered on a satisfied sigh. Truly I would have been completely content with anything Henry wanted to give me. Or not give me. Sex wasn't a deal breaker for me. I loved spending time with Henry, laughing with him, making out, cuddling on the couch.

"You want more? Or wanna stop here?"

"I'll take anything you want to give me," I said, meaning the words in the most literal terms along with the possible innuendo.

Henry kissed my neck. "You can stop me at any time."

"I know." I turned to catch his lips. "I trust you." I nuzzled my nose against his. "I love you."

The smile he gave me couldn't stay hidden behind his beard. It lit up his face, his eyes sparkling in the dim moonlight trickling into the room. "Love you." His gruff words were the perfect contrast to the gentle kisses he pressed to my eyelids, my cheeks, and my chin.

When I rolled my hips, trying to get some friction against my aching cock, Henry took his dick in hand and trailed his leaking cockhead up and down my ass, pressing against my opening, teasing the sensitive skin. "Push against me," he instructed.

The initial sting was expected, and it took my breath for a moment. After breathing through the brief flash of discomfort, I rolled my hips, groaning when Henry sank all the way into me. He wrapped an arm around my waist, pressing his chest to my back while gently pumping his hips. With my body molded around Henry like we'd been made for each other, we fell into an easy rhythm backed by the sensual sounds of skin against skin, heavy breathing, and soft whimpers.

The sensation of Henry's bare heat buried in my ass was more than I could have ever prepared myself for. Long before I was ready for things to end, my balls drew up tight, and I lost the rhythm as my body sought release.

Henry trailed his big, warm hand down my torso and took my throbbing dick in his fist. Thumbing over my slit, he stroked my cock. "You feel so fucking good," he murmured in my ear. "So hot and tight. Wanna feel you come, feel this tight little ass on my dick."

I whimpered, thrusting hard and fast into his grip. "Please, Henry."

"Mmm," he hummed before taking my earlobe between his teeth. "Tell me what you want, Jack. You wanna come for me?"

I threw my head back with a low groan. "Henry. Please.

Wanna come so bad. So close. Wanna feel your cum in my ass."

"That's it," Henry crooned. "That's a good boy. Come for me."

His words sent me over the edge, and my release exploded over his fist. As I rode out my own orgasm, Henry grunted and took my hand in his while burying his face in my neck. "Fuck, Jack," he growled, his searing hot cum exploding deep within me. "Fuck."

Henry held me close, our pulsing bodies coated in sweat as we came down from our shared high. When a soft current of air coaxed goosebumps from my skin, Henry slipped from my ass and quickly pulled the sheet over us.

The bed was a mess. The scent of sex hung on the air. And we'd definitely need another shower before work. But Henry's arms around me, his chest heaving in tandem with mine, our hearts thudding erratically was the most sated, content, and protected I'd ever felt.

Nothing before Henry had ever been so right.

So perfect.

So unbelievably scary.

So exciting and fulfilling.

"You okay?" Henry whispered at my temple.

"Never been so okay."

His smile pressed into my hair. "I know this is new," he started. "And I know you're young with a long future ahead of you."

I tensed, fearing an ending before things even really got started.

"But," Henry continued, "I need you to know that sex

for the sake of sex isn't my thing. I would *never* hold you back, but this isn't just some quick and easy thing for me. I'm in this for as long as you want me."

"What if I want you forever?"

"Then forever is what you get."

Tears stung my eyes as I turned in Henry's arms and cuddled into his broad, hairy chest. "Best plan ever."

Chapter 15
Henry

"OH MY GOD." JACK COVERED HIS PINK CHEEKS with his hands and groaned while the guys laughed. "How do I fix it?"

We were gathered at the end of the bar toward the end of the lunch rush at the Roadhouse. The five of us eating together had become a semi-regular thing as of late.

Couldn't say it bothered me.

Not one bit.

"Fix it?" Dad groused. "Are you kidding? It's perfect."

Hudson laughed, and Lance shrugged with a huge grin.

Jack looked my way, and all I could do was put an arm around him and press a kiss to his head. "Might be good for business."

"What if people think—"

"Fuck 'em."

Jack paused when Dad cut him off and then tried again. "I just don't want anyone being offended."

"I don't think anyone is offended," Lance said. "I heard folks laughing about it at the shop today."

Jack's eyes grew wide.

"In a good way," Lance assured.

"It's all people could talk about at the store." Hudson slapped Jack on the back.

"It's fuckin' damn good marketing, and I wish we'd been smart enough to think of it on purpose," Dad said, a hint of pride and a heap of support in his words for Jack. The two had hit it off almost immediately once Jack realized Dad's bark was worse than his bite.

Jack coming to town had been almost as good for Dad as it had been for me. In addition to sneaking in those graphic design classes, he'd also taken a few online courses about the basics of marketing. Two of the most important men in my life were now spending hours a day together, and it was the sweetest thing in the world to watch.

For Jack, their relationship gave him the father figure he'd never had. That was a position I had very little interest in fulfilling for him since, well...yeah.

For Dad, it gave him a bit of a redo. He hadn't been a *bad* dad to Hudson and me, just drowning in his own emotional shit for so many years. But now, he got to revisit teaching someone how to change a flat tire, check and change the oil, drive a stick shift, and build a good fire. Those were all things I could have taught Jack—not gonna lie, I was maybe a tiny bit jealous of Dad's time with him—but I knew they were both getting something good from each other, so I let Dad take the reins.

The two of them had been working their asses off for

the last few weeks. Amid their father son bonding, they were also up to their ears in ideas and planning for Cake and Cocktails.

Photo shoots.

Who knew Casey Joe Riggs was such a great shot with a smart phone? I couldn't help but think it was partly because Jack was a great subject, and his cakes were gorgeous too.

Social media posts.

Setting up online ads.

Building up newsletter subscribers.

We'd all agreed to help each other build up our social media presence—a rising tide lifts all boats, that type of thing—and Dad and Jack had set a goal of one thousand Instagram followers before they sent out the first Cake and Cocktails newsletter.

Two days earlier, the 'gram had taken a leap in followers and even rolled over to 1,001 thanks to a bus of senior citizens who'd stopped in, went wild for our cakes and cocktails, and spent several minutes figuring out how to scan QR codes, follow, and even share the account with their friends and families. The pictures they all took with the cake and cocktail flights were amazing, and the whole group got a kick out of tagging our Instagram account.

Thanks to our cake-loving octogenarians embracing technology, the first Cake and Cocktails newsletter had gone out to just under five hundred subscribers. While we'd found it fairly easy to get followers, it took a bit more effort to get people to sign up for a newsletter.

Unless you accidentally reeled them in.

Our subscriber numbers and social media followers

had jumped exponentially thanks to a very convenient cut off point in the subject line.

Even before publication, the newsletter had quickly and easily become known as Cake and Cocktails, and each edition would include photos, recipes, deals, and links to interesting articles about cake baking, decorating, history, and even some fun facts about cakes and cocktails.

The reason the first edition had everyone talking, as we'd quickly found out, was because the subject line of "Cake and Cocktails: Where You Can Have Your Cake and Cocktails Too" had been truncated by the newsletter service to show only "Cake and Cock..."

I was on the same page as Dad. It was a great way to get people talking, sharing, and looking forward to the newsletter. Plus, the more interest the newsletter stirred up, the better our chances of getting people to visit not only our social media, but also the actual Cake and Cocktails portion of the Roadhouse.

"If they're offended, they can unsubscribe." I gave Jack a squeeze. "We should celebrate."

"We're heading to the city this weekend," Lance said. "Come with us."

"Double date." Hudson elbowed me with a grin.

Lance glanced at Dad, but his best friend only grunted. "Don't even think about asking me to go with you. No way you're getting me to be the fifth wheel, and y'all know I don't belong anywhere near the city." Dad nodded toward Jack's addition to the Roadhouse. "Come on, let's get those pictures taken. People went gaga over the one of you decorating that big ol' tiered bastard the other day, I want a few more of those to schedule." Dad glanced at me.

"We're changing the oil in your truck this afternoon, don't plan on going anywhere."

Jack gave me his soft smile, rubbing the collar of his shirt over his bottom lip. The pretty blush on his cheeks when I sent a wink his way had me wishing we could escape upstairs for the rest of the day.

But no such luck. The lunch rush had slammed us, and I had plenty to clean up plus paperwork. As we'd done for the last several weeks since officially opening Cake and Cocktails, Jack baked and decorated in the morning. Then he manned the cake counter during brunch and lunch hours. He did a soft closing for the late afternoon hours which meant he'd pop in to sell cake if he was around, or I'd help if someone was desperate for a slice right then and there. Jack was back behind the counter for dinner and late-night cake cravings. He usually worked in ingredient prep, extra baking or decorating, and administrative type stuff between the dinner rush and the late-night customers.

Occasionally, if we hadn't purposely scheduled a day off together, we'd grab those afternoon hours and retreat to the apartment for a nap. And by *nap* I meant we eventually took a quick snooze after whatever other activities we found ourselves wrapped up in.

But more often than not, Dad usually had plans for Jack's afternoon hours, and I couldn't even be mad about it.

"Wouldn't dream of it," I told Dad with an eye roll. "Even if I wanted to go somewhere, I've got way too much to do here. Deliveries coming in, a leaky dishwasher to look at, and payroll to take care of."

"Oh!" Jack brightened. "Can you make sure the delivery has the extra order of cake flour."

I wrapped an arm around his shoulders and pulled him close. "Yep. And I already confirmed your decorating bits are in there too."

Jack stared up at me, those sparkling blue eyes making me feel like the luckiest man in the universe. "Thank you," he whispered before pressing a kiss to my lips. "Love you," he murmured.

Dad made a gagging noise.

Lance laughed.

And Hudson cooed. "Awww, so fucking adorable."

"So adorable I might puke," Dad grumbled. "Come on, let's get out of here before all the lovey-dovey stuff rubs off on me."

Hudson and I exchanged a knowing look, and Lance's tiny grin confirmed what the three of us were thinking. Dad had a crappy past when it came to love, but he'd been healing a lot lately. He didn't *like* that Hudson and Lance had gotten together and kept it secret, but even he couldn't deny they were good for each other. And Jack coming to town had been a really good thing for Dad. Seeing what Jack and I had found together maybe had Dad making goofy jokes about love rubbing off on him, but I had a feeling his heart was ready to try again.

The fact Dad had always been so accepting of his queer sons—plus the comments he'd made lately regarding finding *someone* to love instead of automatically pigeonholing himself into finding a woman to love—made me think Dad had slowly been discovering things about himself. Maybe things he hadn't been ready to uncover way back when. Or maybe he was taking the *not a fixed point on the spectrum* approach to figuring himself out.

Whichever it was—and even though he didn't seem completely comfortable with sharing with us yet—Dad had definitely been doing some deep-dive soul searching as of late.

And damn if that didn't make me proud as hell of him.

Sure, he was a bit later to the game when it came to figuring shit out about himself, but everyone was on their own timeline, doing things at their own pace.

Maybe Dad would end up with a lovely woman. Or maybe he'd end up with a guy. Or maybe gender wasn't something Dad was concerned about these days. But my gut told me Casey Joe Riggs was ready to love again, and the person he found would be the perfect mix of accepting, challenging, and completely devoted.

And Dad deserved every single bit of love the universe wanted to send his way.

"Those two really hit it off, huh?" Sam nodded through the dining room to where Dad and Jack laughed over posing the perfect pictures and what they could write to bring in followers and hopefully turn them into customers.

I shook my head with a grin. "Sure did. They're good for each other."

Sam smirked. "They are, and he's good for you."

There was no reason to deny it. Haven Grove was a tiny town. The moment Jack and I had been seen holding hands in the Juicy Peach, our secret had been out. It wasn't like we'd been trying to keep anything a secret. Not really. We just hadn't been in any rush to bring the town into our personal lives. But the fact we worked together, lived together, and were now running one of the most popular new businesses in town meant there wasn't a lot of room for privacy.

Most of the townsfolk had taken our relationship in stride. The Riggs family was well-liked and highly-respected in Haven Grove, and many of the people in town had known Hudson and I since we were babies. Even if some people weren't a hundred percent on board with our same-sex relationships, very few folks in town were rude enough to say anything about it.

Just as the thought flitted through my head, fate brought one of those people right to my door. Sam's eyes narrowed as Haven Grove's very own fire and brimstone preacher walked through the door.

"Got a mess to clean up in the back," Sam said. Under his breath, he continued, "I'll let you deal with this mess out here."

Steeling myself for what was sure to be an unsettling conversation, I finished wiping down a table before turning to greet the man. "Brother Larry," I said, holding out my hand. I maybe didn't care for the man, but I had no reason to be rude.

Not yet.

"What brings you in today?" I refused to say it was good to see the man. If he'd lowered himself to coming into the Roadhouse, he definitely wasn't there on a friendly visit.

"Does the shepherd need a reason to check in on his flock?" Larry Holmes ran a hand over his thick wave of red hair as if to check it was still shellacked into submission.

It was.

"Well, you've made it pretty clear in the past that you wanted nothing to do with my place of business." I kept my voice calm, grateful Dad and Jack had left through the side door. Probably already elbow deep in their oil changing fun.

Woulda rather sipped a piping cup of motor oil if it meant not talking to Brother Larry. The preacher had never been my favorite person, and I sensed the oncoming conversation wasn't going to change my mind.

His nervous chuckle jiggled his thick jowls. "There's that Henry Riggs grumpiness."

I crossed my arms over my chest and stared him down.

Larry ducked his head in mock sheepishness. "I will admit I find it off-putting that so many good people deem it necessary to eat amongst such sin."

I huffed and rolled my eyes. "It's a restaurant, man, not a den of iniquity."

"You'll excuse me if I don't find my God calling me to take part in what goes on here." Larry glanced around the nearly empty dining room as if he'd smelled something foul. "As a man of God, I do have a responsibility to rescue those of my flock who wander and find themselves in danger."

"Yeah, the fresh-baked pretzels almost did poor ol' Delores in last week," I deadpanned.

"The grumpy routine is only cute for so long." Larry's

admonishment sent fire to my gut. He was going to see anger rather than grumpiness pretty soon.

"Then get to your point so you don't have to deal with it." A throbbing beat at my temple, likely from the heavy grinding my molars were taking.

Larry's nostrils flared. "Many of my flock have been tempted by the devil himself—surrounding themselves with drink and," he waved a hand around the bar in a vague gesture I took to mean his insinuation of depravity, "it's my calling to keep them safe."

"I thought it was your calling to love others the way Jesus instructed," I drawled, finding a lot more enjoyment in trying to rattle Brother Larry than I would have expected. "Isn't that Rule Number One? Love one another? Did I miss the rule about judging, shaming, and manipulating your *flock*?"

Don't get me wrong. I never wanted anybody in town to find themselves in an addiction or anything similar because of the drinks I served at the Roadhouse. But, as usual, Brother Larry had taken the high and mighty road.

With steam threatening to pour from his ears, the preacher straightened the sleeves of his button-up and gritted his teeth as he spoke. "The way I care for my parishioners is of no business of yours."

When he started to say more, I cut him off. "Anyway, I'm actually glad you stopped by." I hadn't decided until that exact moment if I was going to confront the preacher about his grandson making a mess of my trash, but his attitude had pissed me off.

Brother Larry cocked a brow. "Is that so?"

"Haven't had too much trouble lately," I started, "but a

while back, my trash was getting torn into on the regular. Thought it was an animal for a while, but it was too neatly picked through before being tossed about."

He stared at me blankly.

"A witness pointed out Randy and Pete as the trash bandits. Wanted to make sure you were aware. Not only because they were making a mess on my property, but also because it's not safe to be digging through trash, especially with possibly spoiled food."

Larry's cheeks caught fire. "Randy wouldn't dare dig through trash. That Sanders boy is on a dangerous track from what I can see—"

"Both boys were identified as being the culprits digging through my trash. Vandalizing my property. On multiple occasions."

He looked as if he wanted to argue, but I crossed my arms over my chest and took a tiny step closer. Larry snapped his mouth closed, easing back a smidge. "Seems to me that a little mess is the least of your problems. Boys like to have a bit of fun; I don't really think a bit of trash is a sin."

I cocked my head, thinking of all the ways I could have responded to that. "If the vandalization of my property—which is something I could easily press charges against—is the least of my problems, maybe you'd care to fill me in on what the worst of my problems are?"

Larry took a deep breath and closed his eyes, looking toward the ceiling as if hoping to make contact with a higher power before continuing. "I've heard about the new business you've got going on."

"Cake and Cocktails? Surely you don't have anything against cake."

"Enticing my flock with sugary sweets, encouraging gluttony, trapping them in the grip of alcohol." Larry paused to wipe spittle from his lips with his ever-present hanky. "And now you and that *boy* you've got shacked up with you have gone and sent out pornography to the innocent and unsuspecting members of my congregation." His voice had risen as he spoke, and he dabbed at sweat on his brow.

For a moment, I thought he was joking. When he didn't find my huff of laugher amusing, I rolled my eyes. "Are you serious right now?"

"The eternal damnation of my flock is something I take very seriously, son."

"Don't call me son," I warned. "I've seen you at Glazed Buns having coffee and a cinnamon roll. You can't tell me you don't eat sugary treats."

"Of course not," Larry said. "Our fine coffee shop doesn't serve alcohol, and it most definitely isn't an establishment that would send out godless profanity to their customers—good people who were only subscribing out of the goodness of their hearts."

I ran a hand through my beard. "Give me a moment, preacher. I want to recap what I'm hearing to make sure I've got it right." I displayed one finger. "One, it's okay for your grandson to vandalize my property. If it were just Pete Sanders, you might hold a different opinion, but Randy Holmes is above reproach because Grandpa has an in with the big guy. Gotcha." Ignoring Larry's sputtered excuses, I added another finger. "Two, you are against both of my establishments because we offer the people in town food, spirits, and...let me check my notes...ah, yes, *sugar*."

Larry puffed out a breath, the fleshy part of his neck jiggling.

Before he could say a word, I went on, adding a third finger. "Three, you find a simple newsletter worthy of being labeled sinful." I waved my fingers in the air. "Is that the gist of it?"

"Now see here," Larry started. "You and I both know alcohol is the very basis of so many sins. And, and," he sputtered, "and gluttony is one of the worst."

I nodded. "I agree that alcohol can be a huge issue for a lot of people." My mind traveled to all the trouble Uncle Billy got in because his drinking became a real problem. "The good thing about the Roadhouse is we serve water, tea, and soft drinks as well. No one is forced to drink alcohol of any type. And we cut folks off if it seems like it's going to become a problem." Plus, everyone in our small town was well-aware of those who either couldn't handle their liquor or who struggled with dependency. "I'm not in the business of supporting drunk driving or alcoholism."

"Well, I—"

"As for the cake," I barreled on. "I don't really know what to tell you. If I saw you making such a fuss at the bakery or the Dairy Palace, I'd think you're truly puttin' up such a fight because you're worried about your flock's eternal damnation if they stuff themselves silly on sweets." I crossed my arms over my chest again. "But it seems like you only have a problem with Jack's new business, which leads me to believe you truly only have a problem with Jack—either because he's gay or because he's involved with me."

Larry's cheeks pinked, and a thin sheen of sweat broke out on his brow. "Now, you know, God teaches us to hate the sin, love the sinner—"

"That's a bunch of bullshit and you know it," I bit out, stabbing a finger in his direction. I'd pretty much ignored Larry Holmes the majority of my adult life—he just wasn't worth the trouble of getting worked up. But the moment the man insinuated Jack was a problem—what we'd started building together was a sin—all bets were off, and I was bound and determined to defend Jack.

"That doesn't erase the fact that you've moved in a man half your age to live in depravity right above a public restaurant, *and* he's sending out pornography to the good folks of Haven Grove." Larry's face was so red, his face so sweaty, and his lips so spitty, I truly worried for a moment he'd keel over right in front of me.

"Jack is twenty-five which is clearly not even close to half my age. While it's none of your business, a ten-year age gap isn't much—"

Larry snorted. "I guess your brother definitely wins in *that* contest."

It's wrong to punch a man of God.

It's wrong to punch a man of God.

I took a deep breath and unclenched my fist.

Larry's eyes grew wide, and he glanced nervously where I shook out the tension in my right hand.

"Jack living with me is none of your business either. Maybe be a bit more concerned about your grandson digging through trash and a little less worried about what your *flock* is doing in the privacy of their own homes." I cocked my head. "Unless you get off on thinking about the sex lives of your sheep?"

A deep blue vein threatened to throb its way out from under Larry's pale, sweaty skin. "Don't be vulgar."

I shrugged. "Just seems like you're very interested in what Jack and I are doing in the privacy of our own home."

"My main concern is the newsletter. Cease and desist, and I'll let this go."

I threw my head back and laughed. "Cease and desist?" Wiping at the tears in my eyes, I worked to calm myself. "First off, no." I took a step closer to Larry. "Second, no way in hell." One more small step, loving the way he inched away from me. "And third, *fuck* no." When Larry hit the wall, his eyes bulging, and a drop of sweat trickling down his ruddy cheek, I couldn't help but grin wickedly. "Oh, and thanks to this little show, you better believe we'll be sending out *Cake and Cock...* newsletters every time we get a chance."

"I'll go to the city council," Larry threatened.

"Feel free. Let me know which meeting, so I can let the elder Sanders know his boy is out rummaging through trash with Randy." I rubbed my beard as if mulling it over. "I'm sure the rest of the council members would love to hear the story of how two of your very own flock found themselves digging in trash."

"You can't send out such profanity—" Spittle flew with the few words he got out before I interrupted again.

"And if I remember correctly, Randy and Pete are both interested in making Varsity this year, isn't that right?"

Tapping a finger against my chin, I waited for the moment when my words sank in. "Quite a few of the boys' teachers and coaches visit the Roadhouse a couple times a week." I leaned in and whispered, "And they *love* our cake. Would hate for them to get wind of two of their potential players vandalizing private property. I'm sure they'd wonder what the world was coming to when the good *shepherd* of Haven Grove can't even control his own sheep."

"But, but—"

I jabbed a finger into Larry's shoulder. "No. This is where it ends. You don't like the Riggs family? You don't like me? Fine. Don't want to give us your business? Totally your choice. Don't want to drink alcohol? Your prerogative. Don't want cake? Perfectly fine. Don't like the newsletter? Unsubscribe. Block us for all I care." I poked at him again. "But don't you ever come in here on your high horse and insinuate that my business or my relationship is a sin unless you plan on listing your own."

Larry side-stepped me, shouldering past me with a grunt. "I remember when you and your brother were little boys. So much potential. Such a shame Casey Joe succumbed to the ways of the devil."

I snorted. "Excuse me?"

"Divorce is a sin. Your Jezebel mother brought shame on herself, her boys, her marriage, and this town." Larry puffed his chest as if gearing up for a sermon. "If your father had turned to the church—"

"Turned to the church? Turned to the people who shut him out when he and Mom got pregnant before they were married? That's rich."

Larry waved away my words. "Casey Joe and his sons

needed God, but he was too prideful to lay down his sins. And look what happened."

"Get out."

"Son—"

"Don't call me son." The metallic taste of blood coated my tongue as I bit the inside of my jaw. "Don't come back. Keep your kid away from my property."

Larry narrowed his eyes, a sneer painting his fleshy face. "That *boy* is trouble. He's been the catalyst to all the problems. Like you were just waiting on him to show up and lead you astray."

My teeth would soon be tiny piles of shards and rubble if the man kept talking. "Leave Jack out of this."

Larry reached into his back pocket and pulled out a Bible. "I'd like to pray over you both. Bring Jack in. Let us ask God in to save your souls."

"Get out."

"Son—"

The punch landed on the corner of Larry's eye, my knuckles glancing off his cheekbone.

And it felt damn good.

Larry yelped, fell back against the wall, and wailed in pain. "You son-of-a-bitch," he roared, but it was muffled by his hand cradling his face.

"Naughty words, preacher. Guess we're all just sinners at heart, huh?" I grabbed his elbow and shoved him toward the door. "Don't come back here."

"You'll regret this," Larry growled.

"Not as much as you'll regret if you say another damn word about Jack." I took a step toward Larry, satisfaction washing over me when he stumbled away quickly. "Have the day you deserve, Preacher."

I waited until the door swung closed behind him before running both hands over my face with a strangled noise, part frustration and part anger.

A slow clap echoed through the bar behind me, and I turned to see Sam grinning broadly as he applauded. "Was that as satisfying as it looked?"

Snorting, I glanced at my hand. "Hell, yeah." I flexed my fingers. "Hurt like a bitch though."

"That man is a walking hemorrhoid," Sam said. "He deserved it." He scooped some ice into a bar towel and handed it to me. "Here, keep this on it for a while." His gaze strayed to where Larry had exited. "Think anything will come of that?"

I grunted before hissing when I placed the ice on my knuckles. "Maybe? Probably? Fuck, I don't know. He's pissed, but I don't think there's a lot he can do about a randomly placed cut-off on a word in a subject line. No one is forced to sign up for the newsletter. We've followed all the necessary steps to make sure the newsletter is compliant—people have to confirm they wanted to sign up, they can unsubscribe at any time, all the shit. It's legit."

Sam scratched his goatee. "Probably not a whole lot he *can* do, but I doubt that keeps him from blabbing his story all over town and doing his best to cause you and Jack some problems. I'll keep an ear out."

"Thanks. You're probably right, he's likely not going to let it go easily."

"You'll probably be the subject of his next few sermons."

I snorted. "Guess if my ears are burnin' on Sunday, I'll know why."

Sam smirked. "'Course, probably quite a few who will be wantin' your autograph once they figure out who gave the good shepherd that shiner."

We laughed. Part of me figured Larry would badmouth me, warn the town of my sinful and violent ways, and then move on to protecting his flock from something else. But a tiny part of me wondered if I'd just whacked a hornet's nest.

Chapter 16
Jack

"You thirsty?" Casey Joe asked.

I wiped a bit of sweat from my brow as I leaned against Henry's truck. While I hoped to never need the skill of changing a tire, I was grateful to Casey Joe for teaching me.

Henry would have happily taught me anything I needed to know, but I got the feeling he was glad to let his dad step in. It was pretty obvious—and so dang cute— Henry enjoyed watching his dad revisit his parenting years with me. From what I could gather, Henry and Hudson hadn't been neglected or anything growing up—outside of their mom leaving them—but it seemed like maybe Lance had been the glue holding them all together while Casey Joe licked his wounds.

Casey and I had already done the oil before we moved to the tires. Checking and changing the oil wasn't nearly as difficult as I had imagined. The fact I could now do something Joseph and Douglas had likely never even attempted filled me with a sense of pride I hadn't expected.

"Yeah," I said. The weather was pleasant, but we'd been working for a bit, and water sounded really good.

"I'll grab us something." Casey Joe wiped the smears of dirt and grease from his hands with the shop towel we'd slung over the edge of the truck bed. "You want anything to eat?"

"Nah, I'm good."

The sun warmed my face even as the breeze cooled me. It was a gorgeous day in Haven Grove, and I couldn't help feeling like the luckiest guy in the world for ending up in this place and with these people.

Casey Joe was more of a father figure to me than my sperm donor or uncle had ever been. I knew the guy had a rough past, and he'd been dealing with healing from that and some medical issues lately, but the way he'd taken me in and treated me like I was one of his boys meant the world to me.

Hudson was definitely the brother I never had. My cousin could have treated me like a brother, but he chose to act like I was worse than shit on the bottom of his three-hundred-dollar sneakers. I couldn't imagine a world where Douglas Hill was upset his pissant cousin had up and disappeared.

Henry's brother, on the other hand, had easily accepted me into their little family group, and acted like I was the baby brother he'd always wanted. Hell, he'd taken to texting me funny memes and asking me to come help him in the orchard when I was available.

Feeling like I belonged was a feeling I hadn't experienced in a very long time, and it would take some getting used to, but I would have been lying if I said I didn't enjoy it.

Immensely.

Lance was the uncle I only wished Joseph would have been. The age gap between Hudson and Lance wasn't even something I noticed because they fit together so well; they had a healthy, loving relationship—the type I'd never really experienced growing up—and I wanted the same thing. Lance and Hudson were solid.

The only real tension in that area was between Lance and Casey Joe, but it was easy to see the best friends would eventually work their way back to where they used to be—there was just too much history between them. And both men were just too good deep down to let their friendship wither and die over something that clearly brought Lance and Hudson so much joy.

Casey Joe loved his family. He might not have liked the way Hudson and Lance found their happiness, but Casey wouldn't begrudge his son and his best friend the joy of finding their other half...even if it took him a while to adjust to the fact their other halves were each other.

And then there was Henry.

Henry Riggs had this reputation for being a grump, but people who really knew him understood he wasn't truly grumpy. He was quiet. He kept to himself. He took a while to get to know people, and even then, he didn't do a lot of superficial friendships.

But Henry had a heart of gold. A person just had to be

lucky enough to see the other side of him to get beyond the grump rep.

Henry was a big teddy bear, my fierce protector, a knight in shining armor, and my closest friend all rolled into one. Sometimes, it was weird to think about the fact he was also *kinda* my boss, but we worked so well together, it hardly ever even crossed my mind. Henry insisted we were colleagues, not boss and employee— although, we'd already agreed to see where the thing between us went even knowing the original plan was for me to work for him. The fact we came up with Cake and Cocktails, and I was pretty much running it separately from anything Henry did was a bonus.

"It's not like you're on my payroll," Henry'd said. *"The money you're bringing in on your side of things is a lot more than I would have been able to pay you. You work* with *me, not* for *me."*

What he said made sense, but he'd done so much for me, it was hard not to think of how much I owed him. Even if he'd never let me pay him back. That much, I knew.

Footsteps on the gravel pulled me out of my head.

"That was—"

The man standing near me was *not* Casey Joe.

I'd seen the preacher around town enough to recognize his overly gelled red hair—his grandson was one of Henry's trash bandits and would likely look just like his grandpa when he aged.

Larry Holmes's cheek was bright red. The swollen, split skin had to be throbbing. He jabbed a finger in my direction. "You," he hissed. "Showed up in town and jumped right into the thick of things, didn't you, son?"

Swallowing thickly, I stood up straight. I was taller than the preacher, but he definitely outweighed me by several pounds. I could outrun him if needed, I was sure of that. "Afternoon, Mr. Holmes."

He snorted, running a knuckle over his swollen cheek. "It's Brother Larry." When I didn't correct myself, he sneered and went on. "Henry is too kind to tell you, but I'm a man of God, and I'll always tell the truth."

My heart clenched. I didn't like him bringing Henry into the conversation.

"I know your type." His lip curled. "Coming into town, acting like you belong here, getting your greedy little hands into one of our own."

Oh god. Was that what the town thought of me? Everyone had been pretty friendly ever since I arrived, and the whole town seemed to love Cake and Cocktails—I'd been super busy with flights and orders ever since we opened, and reviews online were positive.

"I'm not sure what you mean," I croaked out.

"The Riggs family will forever be saddled with the shame and humiliation of their family drama all those years ago," Larry said. "The last thing they need is your type showing up and making a mockery of their business, running their good name in the ground again."

Wrapping one arm around myself, I brought the other to my collar, pulling it to my lips. Larry reminded me of my uncle, and I couldn't help wishing Casey Joe would come back with our waters. Or that Henry would come check on me.

Instead, the preacher went on.

"You've been an embarrassment since the day you

showed up. A vagabond. Mooching from Henry, taking every bit of hospitality he and this town could give you. And the worst part is Henry's too good of a man to turn you away. So, he just lets you make the Riggs family name look like trash. He lets you ruin his future, any chance he has at a normal life." Larry took a step toward me, the movement sending me retreating backward. I clenched my teeth, hissing against the pain of my shoulder banging into the truck's side mirror. "If you care for that man at all, you'll take your trashy, sinful ways out of his life, out of Haven Grove, and never look back. Henry Riggs deserves more than another round of humiliation because he's been duped by you."

Too stunned to speak—and too much in my head with memories of Joseph and Douglas backing me into a corner like a helpless, injured animal—my breath burned in my chest as Brother Larry hefted his bulk toward the front of the truck. With a purposeful bump of his elbow against my shoulder, disguised as a hand protecting his busted cheek, the preacher pounded a fist on the hood of Henry's truck. "Think about it, son. We all know the saying, 'If you love someone, set them free.' Don't let Henry suffer again simply because he was unable to resist the wiles of a pretty little sinner like yourself."

And then he was gone, rounding the corner just moments before Casey Joe moseyed up with four bottles of water. Henry's dad eyed me, handing me one of the cold waters.

"You okay? Look like you saw a ghost."

Should I tell Casey what the preacher had said? I knew Henry's dad would go from zero to pissed in point-five-seconds. The man had no filter, and he was ferocious when it came to those he called his own. But he'd recently had a heart attack, and I knew Henry worried about his dad's overall health.

No. Best not to get him worked up.

It wasn't like Casey Joe beating the crap out of Larry would solve anything other than making us both feel a little better.

Plus, if I told Casey Joe, he'd tell Henry.

And I wasn't sure I was ready to tell Henry.

Partly because it didn't matter and partly because I wasn't sure how to bring it up. Plus, what even needed to be done about it? Did I want Henry going after the preacher to defend my honor?

No. Best to just let it go.

But Larry's words steamrolled through my head, a scalding heat bubbling just under the surface of my skin.

Was I really ruining the Riggs family name? Did all of Haven Grove think I'd come to town just to get my hooks in some unsuspecting citizen? Would Henry be better off in the long run if I left and did a redo of setting up a new life?

I knew without a shadow of a doubt that Henry would let me keep the Cake and Cocktails name, social media, and newsletter. No questions asked. I had a hunch he'd even let me keep the pairings of his cocktails with my cakes.

Henry was the type of man to let me walk away if he thought it would be the best thing for me. He'd send me on my way with a hug, a kiss, and best wishes, and then he'd step back and suffer in silence. Tuck in on himself, lick the reopened wounds of his heart, and probably find someone else to take care of when what he really needed was someone to take care of him.

Nah, I'd just tuck the preacher's visit in my back pocket unless things changed.

Chapter 17
Henry

"YOU OKAY?" MY HAND ON HIS THIGH DID LITTLE to stop the bouncing of Jack's knee as we rode into the city in the extended cab of Lance's truck. Signs of his anxiety were easy to spot when you knew him.

Jack took a deep breath and nodded, the collar of his sweatshirt pinched between his fingers as he rubbed it on his chin. "Yeah, sorry." He bent slightly to stare out the window as the truck edged into the downtown area. "I know it's not the same city, but the skywalkers remind me of where I used to live."

"The what now?" Curiosity laced Hudson's words.

"Skywalkers?" Jack repeated, his gaze bouncing from Hudson to Lance to me. "The big buildings?"

I traced my thumb in circles on the back of his neck and tucked him closer to me.

"What?" Jack asked.

"Umm…"

Jack's cheeks flamed, and he buried his face in my shoulder. "Oh god, is this another bubble bee thing?"

"A what what?" Hudson asked.

Jack groaned. "Nothing. I'm so ridiculous."

I chuckled and kissed the top of his head. "You're not ridiculous. It's cute."

"It's not cute. I'm a fucking grown-ass man, and I don't even know the real words for everyday things."

"I like the words you have for things," I said. "Tell me how skywalkers came about."

Jack groaned again. "I used to be scared of the buildings when Mom would take me into the city. I've always called them skywalkers." He sobered. "I guess she didn't correct me. She died before I learned the right word."

I pulled him close. "I'm sorry."

"It's weird how the buildings have so much connected to them in my mind. I'm fascinated by them now that I'm older, but I still get a vaguely threatening vibe from them because they remind me of living with Joseph and Douglas." He glanced out the window. "I'm sure I should know this, but what are they really called?"

Shooting a warning look at Hudson, I said, "They're usually called skyscrapers."

Jack studied the buildings. "Yeah, that makes sense; I'm sure I've even heard that word before." He sighed. "I wonder why Mom didn't correct me."

I nuzzled his temple. "Probably because she adored you, thought skywalkers was cute, and didn't want to stifle your creativity."

Jack huffed. "I remember drawing pictures of the buildings walking through the city. She hung them on the fridge."

"Skywalkers is a lot more fun," Hudson said. "Speaking of, we're in that one right there." He pointed to a medium-sized silver and glass building that housed the hotel we'd be staying at for the weekend.

Grateful for my brother's charming way of taking the spotlight off Jack, I pressed another kiss to his head before nuzzling his ear and whispering, "I love you."

Jack sighed and cuddled into me. "I love you. Thank you for not making me feel any more ignorant than I already do."

"Don't. We all have shit in our past and things that make us unique. I love you for you, and that includes everything about you." I dropped a kiss on his cheek, his nose, and then his mouth. "Let's have a good weekend, huh?"

Jack smiled. "Yeah. A good weekend sounds perfect."

Lance maneuvered the truck off the interstate and took a right toward downtown. "You know the song 'Every Time I Close My Eyes' by Babyface?" When the three of us gave him a blank look, Lance sighed. "Tell me you're the oldest one in the friend group without telling me," he muttered.

Hudson reached over and patted Lance's knee. "It's okay, babe. Your experience is part of your appeal." My brother laughed and pressed up against the window to escape Lance's far-reaching arm.

"*Anyway,*" Lance grumbled. "The song has a line in it

that says *Every time I think of it, I pinch myself*, but for the longest time—like, I'm not even going to admit how old I was when I figured it out—I thought it said *I piss myself.*" He shook his head, laughing at himself. "Why in the world I thought those lyrics even made sense, I'll never know."

Hudson leaned over and rested his head on Lance's shoulder. "Oh my god, that's adorable—even if also hilarious. Let's not forget about my ill-fated understanding of the term *jailbait.*"

Jack giggled which told me he'd definitely heard the story.

Hudson pretended to scowl at Jack over his shoulder which sent Jack into a another fit of giggles. When he finally got himself under control, Hudson went on. "You think skywalkers is bad? How about me calling them Rice Christmas Treats until I was in like eighth grade and some kid made fun of me for it?"

A wad of emotion knotted in my chest. "In your defense, we only got those around Christmas time when the bakery had them, so it made sense."

Hudson's eyes softened. "Thanks. Speaking of, we should definitely make some Rice *Krispie* Treats, don't even have to wait until Christmas time." He turned to catch Jack's eye. "See? We all have our own mess ups."

"Yeah, well, how about me thinking those big ol' bees were just in movies, *and* that they were called bubble bees because they have bubble butts?" Jack groaned and held his head in his hands. A giggle escaped him when Hudson's mouth dropped open like a fish, and his eyes blinked rapidly as if trying to decide whether Jack was serious.

"But like," Hudson started, a sparkle in his eyes, "they *do* have little bubble butts."

"Right?" Excitement coursed through Jack as he wriggled upright, and I'd forever be grateful to my baby brother for giving Jack the friendship he so desperately needed.

"They're totally bubble bees from now on," Hudson declared, and Jack whooped.

"Yes!"

"I'll even give you skywalkers if you want," Hudson said. "It's cute as fuck."

Jack's cheeks pinked.

"What about you, Henry?" Lance asked, his twinkling eyes catching me in the rear-view mirror.

I grumbled under my breath. Lance knew very well I had a couple words and phrases I'd mixed up as a kid, and some of them had lasted well into adulthood.

"What was that?" Lance asked, a good-natured smirk filling his face and letting me know if I didn't spill an embarrassing story soon, he'd do it for me.

Jack bit his lip, a giggle escaping as he watched me in anticipation.

"Fine," I growled. "For the longest time, I said *from the gecko* instead of *from the get-go.*"

"Awww," Jack cooed. "That's cute."

Hudson chuckled. "Tell him about the drier sheep."

I reached up and flicked my brother's ear, laughing when he yelped.

"Come on, I had bubble bees and skywalkers," Jack said. "At least give me your two."

Leaning in and nuzzling Jack's ear, I whispered, "Only because I love you."

Jack shivered against me and turned those gorgeous blue eyes my way, trust and joy dancing across his features. "I love you too," he murmured against my lips.

Running a hand over my beard, I cleared my throat. "I used to call drier sheets *drier sheep*. But I played the long game, and they eventually came out with those wool drier balls, so I like to think I was just ahead of my time." I couldn't help busting into laughter with the rest of the gang as Lance turned the truck onto the street in front of our hotel.

We were all still grinning ear-to-ear when Lance parked on the first level of the parking garage connected to our hotel. Climbing from the truck, we all stretched despite the drive taking just under an hour.

Once we had our bags hoisted on our shoulders, Hudson glanced at the bank of elevators and the stairs. "Last ones to the top buy dinner," he said before grabbing Lance's hand and yanking him toward the stairs.

Jack stood, gaping like a fish, until I tugged him toward the stairs. "Come on, we can't let them win."

I swore Lance and Hudson slowed way down until Jack caught on to the game, but then we were racing neck-and-neck up the stairs to the walkway on the third floor. By the time we burst through the door, all four of us were breathing like we'd run a marathon, and Jack's eyes sparkled like a kid on Christmas morning.

Lance glanced at the empty enclosed walkway that

stretched over the busy city street below before taking Hudson's overnight bag and hefting it over his neck. "Jump on," he instructed Hudson. "Let's see if we can get drinks from them too."

Hudson's evil grin spurred me into action, and I yanked Jack's bag from him, threw it over my shoulder and gave him my back while my brother climbed onto Lance's back. "Come on, piggyback. I'm not buying them dinner *and* drinks."

Jack was quicker this time after watching Hudson take his position, and we were barreling down the empty walkway only half a pace behind Lance and Hudson within no time. Jack's laughter echoed through the narrow corridor, his arms and legs wrapped tightly around me.

Hudson's long legs were what eventually did them in, and he and Lance nearly toppled to the ground just before we reached the doorway into the hotel.

"No fair," Hudson yelled, laughter lacing his words. "Ouch!" He and Lance cracked up, peals of laughter filling the air as they leaned against the glass wall.

"Damn you and your long legs," Lance grumbled as he shifted the bags and accepted a kiss from Hudson.

When I eased Jack from my back and turned to give him a high five, the shine of threatening tears caught me off guard. "Hey," I murmured, stepping close and cupping his cheek. "What's wrong?"

He shook his head and huffed. "Nothing."

"Then what is it?"

Jack sniffled and used his sleeve to dash away the tears. "This." He gestured between the four of us.

"We wouldn't have been fuckin' around if there'd been

people in the walkway—at least not as much," I said, feeling bad if he'd thought we were out of line.

"No," Jack said. "Nothing like that. All my life, I've wanted a brother or friends to do this kind of shit with. Started thinking it was one of those fictional things you only saw on movies or read about in books." He tucked his face into my neck when I pulled him close and rubbed his back. "But then I met you guys, and I found the family I've wanted for so long."

Fuck.

This man.

Shredding my heart day after day with all the shit he lived through.

Then putting it back together piece by piece with his zest for life and huge heart.

I ran my hand up and down his back and pressed a kiss to his head. "You've got us forever, like it or not."

Jack looked up at me, something clouding his face for a moment. "What if what we have doesn't work out?"

Shaking my head, I nuzzled my nose to his. "Nothin' doin'. You've got me forever. If *you* choose to walk away, that's a different story. If we decide we're better off as just friends, that's something we'll work out together. But losing me because what we've got here doesn't work for me anymore? Not a chance." I tipped his chin and brought my lips down to his in a butterfly kiss. "We're your family now. Don't ever forget that."

Tears shimmered in Jack's eyes once again, but he nodded and smiled.

We eventually made our way up to the eleventh floor

where we found our adjoining rooms. Lance had made the reservations, and when I'd asked why we didn't just share a room, Hudson had piped up and said, "Don't know about you, but I'd rather not listen to my brother having sex."

Lance's cheeks had burned bright pink, but he'd smiled. "That." He pointed to Hudson. "And the fact I figured maybe Jack would be more comfortable rooming with just you rather than all four of us sharing a room."

Hudson had wrapped his arms around Lance's neck. "And he doesn't want you to have front row seats to him boning your baby brother."

So, the adjoining room was a nice gesture, and we had an amazing view of the city as a bonus. Hudson had already opened the doors between our rooms, and the four of us found ourselves lounging on the balcony. We towered over the streets and some of the buildings, but several of the others stood tall, shadowing us in the late afternoon sun.

"The show is at eight," Lance said while scrolling through his phone. "I made our reservation for five-thirty, so we'll have plenty of time to enjoy dinner and not have to rush."

Jack's knee had returned to its bouncing, and he worried his bottom lip between his teeth.

"You okay?"

He nodded. "Yeah, just nervous I'm not going to be dressed as nice as you guys."

Hudson reached over and slapped Jack on the thigh, giving a rough squeeze that had Jack yelping. "No way," my brother said. "I helped you pick it out, I wouldn't underdress you. Plus, neither the show or restaurant are black tie."

Lance shook his head. "Not at all. I'd say both lean much more toward the casual side if anything. You'll look great, but we'll see people in jeans and T-shirts all the way to tuxes and evening gowns."

Jack relaxed slightly, leaning into me with sigh.

The four of us relaxed for a bit before Hudson stood and stretched. "I wanna shower before we head to dinner." His pointed look directed at Lance didn't go unnoticed, but I was pretty sure my brother didn't care.

Lance stood with a grin. "I'll, um, come check the water pressure."

Hudson wrinkled his nose. "What? That was so lame."

I snorted, and Jack giggled as we watched the two of them disappear into their room. When the bathroom door slammed shut, I pulled Jack close. "You want to get ready? Nap? Sit here for a while longer?"

Jack snuggled into me. "Yes."

I kissed the top of his head. "We have time for sitting here and then getting ready or taking a power nap before we get ready."

He sighed. "I think a power nap without the nap." Jack stood and reached for me, pulling me up from my seat.

"How can you power nap without the—"

Jack snaked his arms around me and pressed kisses along my jaw. "I want the bed, but no sleeping." He nipped at the sensitive skin of my neck. "Want a reason to need to clean up before we leave."

"Oh," I murmured, my arms full of Jack as I maneuvered us through the balcony door. "Good plan."

When my legs bumped into the king-sized bed, Jack slid down my body, his thick cock brushing against my own. Deep groans reverberated from our chests, heat blooming between us as Jack pressed his forehead to the hollow of my neck. His breath caught, a shudder running through his body.

Tipping his chin up so I could see his eyes, I feathered my thumbs over his cheeks. "What's wrong?"

Jack shook his head. "Nothing. I don't think anything in my life has felt this right since before my mom died." He leaned into my palm, closing his eyes as if savoring my touch. "You, your home, your family—" Jack cut himself off, his voice cracking.

"*Our* home." I kissed his forehead. "*Our* family." Kisses to his eyelids. "*Our* business." A soft press of lips to his pretty pink mouth. "Us. You and me, Jack. I wasn't looking, but that's only because I didn't know how badly I needed you in my life."

Tears spilled down Jack's cheeks. "My mom dying was the worst thing that ever happened to me. My uncle was the added insult to injury." He took a deep shuddering breath. "But if those things both brought me to you, I'll believe in silver linings and fate forever."

Hugging him close, loving the way our bodies melted into each other, I let him just be silent with his thoughts for a moment. When I finally spoke, my words rasped thickly in my throat. "I'd give anything for you to have your mom back, even if it meant us never meeting."

Jack pulled back, a tiny scowl on his pretty face.

Cupping his cheek, I nuzzled our noses together. "Not because I don't want what we've found, but I hate the way your mom's death hurt you. Hate that you had to live with those assholes. As much as I love you, I'd give you up in a heartbeat if it meant you got to have your mom back."

He shook his head, eyes shiny with tears. "You have no idea the number of times I've tried to bargain a way to get her back. The pain never goes away, but it's not as sharp and all-consuming as it once was." A pained look crossed his face. "The memories of her aren't as sharp either. I think that's what I hate the most." Jack closed his eyes and leaned into my touch, moisture sparkling on his lashes. "She would have loved you."

I cocked my head and raised a brow. "Yeah?"

He nodded. "Yeah. I was her world. I don't say that to brag, it's just the truth. She made sure everything revolved around me. I wasn't spoiled, but I was loved beyond measure, and she spent every moment available making sure I knew how loved I was." Jack's fingers curled into my beard, lightly scratching. "And I know she's thrilled I found you. You're the most protective, caring man I've ever met." His thumb traced over my bottom lip, his voice catching when he spoke. "I wish you could have met her."

Gathering Jack close again, savoring the simultaneous beat of our hearts between us, I rocked him back and forth. "I would have loved to meet her. But I got to meet you, and I think you're a pretty damn good extension of her. Bright, creative, talented—I have a feeling you took after her."

"That may be the nicest thing anyone has ever said to me," Jack said, tears rolling again. "Being a reflection of my mom would be the highlight of my life."

"She was the best person in your life, and now you're taking after her."

A soft smile dance on Jack's lips. "You're the best person in my life now."

"I'd never try to replace her," I started, but Jack put his finger to my lips.

"Not replacing, just joining her. No one could ever take her place, and I never thought anyone could stand beside her, but then I met you." Tears dampened his lips as our mouths met in a slow, sensual kiss. Heat and longing poured between us until Jack broke away and hooked his thumbs in the waistband of my pants.

The cool air of the hotel room hit my skin as he pulled everything down to my ankles. When he pushed me to sit on the edge of the bed, I quickly kicked the clothing to the side and spread my legs.

The wet heat of Jack's mouth and his hands caressing up and down my thighs nearly did me in before we even got started. With the sweet suction of his mouth around me, I shoved the fingers of one hand into his hair and gripped his shoulder with the other. "Oh god, Jack." The gruff words sounded desperate even to my lust-addled brain, but I couldn't have cared less. That was what this beautiful man did to me. He owned me, heart and soul.

When he swallowed me down after several long moments of worshipping my cock, I lost any semblance of control, and unloaded in his throat with a groan I had no doubt could be heard next door if they weren't busy doing the same thing we were.

Jack looked up at me, his lips spread, and his mouth stuffed with my cock, his eyes glassy like he was drunk on my release. When he smiled, and my cum dribbled from the corner of his mouth, I'd never moved so damn fast in my life.

Yanking him to stand, I kissed him hard and deep, savoring the taste of me on his tongue as I shoved his pants down. Breaking away to tear his shirt over his head, I stripped my own off and climbed onto the bed with my back against the headboard.

"Straddle me," I demanded, a palm to my chest and one hand reaching for him.

Desire flared in Jack's eyes as he knee-walked his way up my body, his legs spread to accommodate my broadness, his gorgeous cock leaking and bobbing enticingly. When he reached the perfect spot, I gripped his ass cheeks and pulled him forward the last couple inches until his cockhead bounced against my lips.

"Hold on to the headboard and give me that cock," I murmured before spreading my lips and teasing his slit with my tongue.

Jack whimpered and took hold of his dick, smearing precum over my lips before sliding into my greedy mouth. He groaned the most precious of groans and reached for the headboard, adjusting his hips so his thrusts fucked perfectly between my lips.

His rhythm only faltered once when I released his ass long enough to slip a finger into his mouth. When it was good and wet, I returned to his ass and spread his spit over his hole.

"Oh shit. Oh god, Henry." Jack rolled his hips, pressing forward to sink deep into my mouth, and retreating backward, his ass seeking the pressure of my teasing finger. When I slipped the tip into his tight pucker, Jack cried out and squeezed around me.

Groaning around his cock, loving the way the vibrations made him shiver, I pressed into him deeper. We needed more than spit, and I wanted him under me when I made love to him, but I greedily sucked him down and worked him open. We'd get off, have some fun in the shower, and then have something to look forward to after dinner and the show.

Moving to caress the sensitive spot behind his balls, I swirled my tongue around his cockhead, and let Jack use my mouth in whatever way he wanted. Pressing gently on his taint, I moaned around Jack's shaft when he whimpered and pumped his hips harder and faster.

When Jack locked his arms and tensed above me, his cock pulsed his sweet release onto my tongue, and I greedily swallowed down his load as his whimpered cry echoed through the room. With a final gentle thrust of his hips, Jack slipped from my mouth and collapsed onto my chest, both of us spent and content.

A handful of heavy-breathing-moments later, Hudson pounded on the connecting door. "Get ready! We have to leave soon."

Jack chuckled into my neck, our bodies slick with quickly-drying sweat as the cool air pebbled our skin. "I guess we took too long, no time to enjoy our shower."

I ran my hands down his back and over the perfect curve of his gorgeous ass while glancing at the clock. "We can shower together to save time. All we have to do is get dressed."

Jack scrambled from the bed and raced toward the bathroom.

By the time I joined him, the hot water was steaming up the bathroom, and Jack had climbed into the luxurious stream. I stood mesmerized for several moments, taking in his lithe body on display behind the frosted glass.

When he reached out a hand for me, I broke from my trance and stepped into the shower stall behind him. Jack turned and stepped into my arms. "Thank you for this weekend," he murmured against my mouth. "I didn't realize I needed it."

Our tongues mated as our bodies melted together and hot water sluiced over our skin. Breaking the kiss, I cupped the back of his head. "We both did." I kissed him again. "I love you."

Jack's eyes flamed. "I love you."

Instead of pressing our cocks together or giving me another filthy kiss, Jack wrapped his arms around me and rested his face in my neck in a full body embrace. "The sex is nice, but I love you just as much without it." Sighing, he tucked himself tighter against me. "Just wanted to make sure you know that."

I chuckled against his wet hair. "The sex *is* nice." His giggle lit up my insides like a Christmas tree. "But I agree. I love you for you, with or without the sex."

Jack pulled away and looked at me. "Do you think most people feel that way? Love someone sex or no sex? Or do most people feel like the sex is the most important part?"

I gave his question some thought before shrugging. "I

think there's probably as many answers to that question as there are people. Everyone's a bit different."

He nodded. "Guess we're lucky we feel the same."

Lifting his chin with my finger, I brushed a wet kiss over his lips. "We're definitely lucky." Before the kiss could go any further, Hudson pounded on the door again, and we laughed.

With a quick wash and rinse of bodies and hair, we finished our shower and dried off. There was no way we were both fitting at the sink, so I slapped Jack's ass, loving the way his yelp dissolved into giggles. "You go get dressed. I'll use the sink, then we'll switch."

He hurried from the bathroom while I set to work brushing my teeth, combing my hair, and putting on deodorant. A few moments later, I exited the bathroom only to find Jack sitting on the bed looking sad and defeated.

"Hey, what's wrong?" I asked, tossing my towel over the back of the desk chair and pulling on a pair of boxers.

Jack, dressed in dark gray slacks, black dress socks, and a black dress shirt, flipped a silk necktie through the air. "I don't even know how to tie a tie."

The defeat in his words tugged at my heart. I slipped into a pair of black dress pants, pulled on a pair of socks, and held out my hand for Jack.

He sighed and let me yank him to a standing position.

"I feel like such a loser. The few times I had to wear a tie in college, I had a clip on because I didn't know anyone well enough to feel comfortable asking them for help."

I lifted his chin and pressed a kiss to his lips. "It's no

problem. I'll teach you. You've got me—hell, you've got all of us—and we can always help."

"It just sucks to have to be the one always needing someone to teach me things." His eyes widened. "Not that I don't appreciate you all taking the time to teach me, I do."

Kissing him again, I took the tie from his hand. "I know you do. And we appreciate you teaching us all about cake. Having you around has helped Dad more than you know. No one should feel bad about not knowing something; we're all lucky to have each other to learn from." I slipped the tie around his neck and pulled him close. "Now, come here."

We ended up in front of the mirror, my hands guiding Jack's as he practiced tying the tie several times. When he finally gave up with a huff, I tied it for him and whispered in his ear, "You'll get it. Nothing wrong with needing practice. You bake cakes perfectly the first time?"

He sighed and leaned into me. "No."

"There ya go." I kissed his cheek. "Practice makes perfect."

Jack's shiny purple tie picked up the bits of purple in my tie's paisley design. We didn't *match*, but we definitely complemented each other. By the time we were slipping into our dress shoes—Jack's a sleek pair of black ankle boots and mine a bit stockier pair of black boots to complement the heavier weight of my pants—Hudson was about to knock down the door.

"Damn man," I said when I unlocked our side of the door. "Chill out."

Hudson rushed in, taking in Jack and me with a

whistle. "I thought maybe Jack needed help, but I see you both got yourselves put together perfectly. Damn, we look *good*."

Lance insisted on a picture to send to Dad, but I had a feeling he wanted it for himself as well. Hell, who was I kidding, I wanted a copy for me too.

The four of us made our way to the elevator ready for our night out on the town. Friendship and love sparking hot and bright between us. And yeah, maybe a few tears. At least on my part.

Chapter 18
Jack

WHEN THE GUYS HAD SAID WE WERE HEADING TO the city for some big fancy double-date, part of me freaked out because of the memories I had of another city not so very long ago.

My gut churned when any thoughts of Joseph or Douglas appeared in the shadows of my mind. It was amazing being on my own and away from them, but that didn't mean the trauma they saddled me with for all those years didn't come slinking back to haunt me from time to time.

Okay, probably more often than that.

But I should have known Henry and the guys would help me make new memories in a new city.

Not gonna lie, it did *suck* to constantly realize I had a few childish words stuck in my head, didn't know how to tie a damn tie, and had no real family to my name. But Henry was right when he said Mom probably thought my words were cute, so she let me keep them.

It's not like she planned to die and leave me using the wrong words.

And in all actuality, the words weren't really that big of a deal.

The tie thing was a simple fix, it was just a blow to my ego to have to admit I didn't know how to do something so many people took for granted. But having Henry and his family—*my* family—there to ease the discomfort and teach me new things at every turn was what I'd been missing since losing my mom.

As the four of us made our way through the silver and glass lobby of the hotel, I caught a glimpse of us in the mirrored wall.

Lance and Hudson looked fantastic in their dark dress pants that clung to them in all the right places. What? Henry was the guy for me, but that didn't mean I couldn't appreciate how hot my friends were.

Lance wore a maroon dress shirt with a rose and silver tie which perfectly complemented Hudson's deep rose shirt and his black and maroon tie.

I'd been worried I'd be under dressed, but Hudson had been right when he said he picked out something for me to wear that would look perfect with the three of them. While I wore charcoal gray slacks and a black shirt with a royal purple silk tie, Henry wore black pants, a charcoal gray button-up shirt with a silver paisley tie that had enough purple in it to blend with mine perfectly.

While I wasn't *short*, I was the shortest of the four of us, but we looked really good together. A group of friends ready for a nice night out together.

Truly, something I never thought I'd have. The tight

squeeze of forever grateful took hold in my chest. Walking away was always my plan, but the timing and ending up in Haven Grove couldn't have gone better. I used to think it was silly when I'd hear the phrase, "Everything happens for a reason." Honestly, it pissed me off when I heard it about my mom's death, but after that, it just made me roll my eyes.

Until I stepped off that bus in Haven Grove.

Henry gave my hand a squeeze as we made our way down the sidewalk. His eyes scanned me, checking me over, making sure I was okay. Always there, always protecting. I gave his hand a return squeeze and smiled. How this broad, gruff teddy bear had wedged his way so far into my heart and soul I honestly could barely recall what life was like without him, I'd never know. But I'd also never question it because the connection we'd found together was nothing short of magical.

The four of us fell into easy conversation as we walked toward the restaurant. Chatting about the orchard, the ice cream parlor, the general store, the restaurant, and our newest cake and cocktails business venture as we told stories about townsfolk and funny things we'd heard or saw in Haven Grove.

Right then was the perfect time for me to bring up Brother Larry. We were too far away for the guys to get a wild hair up their asses to go teach him a lesson, even if I kinda wanted them to do just that.

Only *kinda*.

For the most part, I wanted to forget about the preacher's visit.

Even though it nagged at me constantly, and my gut told me I needed to let Henry know what Larry had said.

But I let the conversation move on to Henry's dad because that was easier than mentioning the preacher had threatened me.

Supposedly on Henry's behalf—and that was the part bothering me the most.

Why did Brother Larry want me out of Haven Grove and Henry's life? What was in it for him? Why did he care? Was it simply homophobic behavior? Or was there something more?

The guys were talking about Casey Joe, so I pushed the thought away and joined the conversation.

Everyone who'd known Casey Joe for their entire lives expressed he seemed different these days, but they couldn't quite put their finger on it. All of us agreed we didn't want any more medical scares with the Riggs family patriarch. His heart attack had been one of those situations that was bad but could have been much worse. The biggest issue at this point was that Casey Joe was doing *better*, but he was still only half-assing most everything the doctor had instructed him to do.

By silent agreement, I knew the four of us would be pushing him a bit harder in the coming weeks and months. Henry and Hudson had already lost a mother, they didn't need to deal with losing their father too. Plus, Casey Joe had quickly become one of my favorite buddies, and I'd be crushed if I lost him.

I asked about certain buildings as we walked, and the three of them filled me in on businesses, locations, and important parts of the city. While they didn't come to the city often, I could tell they enjoyed visiting. My heart gave a little leap at the thought of making trips to the city part of what the four of us did together.

"I picked this place," Lance started as we approached the unassuming eatery, "because it's super casual, and the food is amazing."

Sighing inwardly because I was both starving *and* concerned I'd look like a fool at some fancy-schmancy restaurant, I gave Lance a quick smile. He likely didn't realize how anxious I'd been about dinner, but his choice made things a lot easier for me.

Henry's big, warm hand on the small of my back calmed me even more, and we made our way to the host stand. One overly cheery person took our name and handed us off to another overly cheery person who showed us to our table in the back corner of the restaurant.

Again, I wasn't sure if Lance and the guys had purposely made things easy on me, or if my good friend fate was just shining on me right then, but I was grateful we weren't at one of the tables out in the middle of everyone.

Dinner was absolutely amazing, and I hadn't laughed so hard in my entire life.

Thanks to the casual atmosphere, I didn't feel the least bit pressured about using the right fork or worried about ordering the wrong thing because I couldn't read the language on the menu. And Lance's plan of eating early had worked out perfectly so we weren't rushed to get to the show.

The guys laughed at me when I ordered a Lemon Drop

Martini despite the fact the place served a couple drinks made with peach syrup from the Juicy Peach.

"What?" I asked when they all ordered peach drinks, and I asked for the lemon concoction.

"Isn't it like sacrilege to order lemon when you live and work in Peach City, USA?" Hudson asked.

I shrugged. "I like lemon drops."

"What's wrong with my peaches?" Hudson asked, a pout on his pretty face.

Giggling, I patted his shoulder. "Nothing is *wrong* with your peaches—or your peach," I teased, and we both leaned into each other laughing until tears threatened the corners of my eyes. "I'm just a lemon guy, I guess."

Henry gave my thigh a squeeze, and I knew he was perfectly happy with me getting any drink I wanted as long as it made me happy.

Sigh.

This man.

He made me happier than I'd ever allowed myself to dream of being.

The food was amazing, and I was impressed with Lance's idea that we all get a different dish and the share when our meals arrived. We all ended up with a soup, salad, and four small portions of our shared entrees. Maybe it was purposeful, or maybe it just worked out that way, but Lance, Hudson, and Henry all ordered meals I'd never had before, so the sharing gave me a chance to discover new foods.

I started to feel self-conscious that I hadn't had the somewhat ordinary meals, but Henry's hand on my leg reminded me that I hadn't had a normal childhood after

Mom died. Any feelings about what I'd missed out on needed to be directed toward Joseph and Douglas rather than pointed inward.

My stomach was near bursting, but it was my heart that really threatened to explode. One night out with these three men had given me more love, support—a true sense of belonging—than all the years I'd been stuck with Joseph and Douglas.

I knew it wasn't my mom's choice to have me suffer for all those years, but I couldn't help but think she was excitedly cheering me on from the other side now that I'd finally escaped.

If only I'd left sooner. Maybe if I'd overheard their shit before that night, I would have gotten out of there quicker.

No.

The night I left was just right because it led me to Haven Grove and Henry.

A shiver shot through me as I recalled the conversation I'd accidentally eavesdropped on.

"You okay?" Henry asked.

I am now, I thought, but I gave him a real smile and nodded. "Perfect. Thank you for tonight." Joseph and Douglas were out of my life for good, and I'd spend the next however many months and years forgetting all the shit they put me through.

When our bubbly waitperson came back to check on us and asked, "Who's thinking about the D word?" I was extremely proud of myself for not choking on my drink. Hudson bumped his knee into mine, and Henry put his hand on my thigh, but the four of us kept our composure.

Mostly.

Lance smoothly interjected for the table. "I can assure you that we are *all* most definitely thinking about the D word, Mia."

Her eyes lit up.

"However, we have a show to get to, so we're going to have to get the D word a bit later," Lance continued.

Mia deflated. "Oh, shoot! We have the best cannoli. The cream is made fresh right here in the kitchen. Really, it's to die for. You should come back after the show and try some!" She truly was the very definition of effervescent.

"Coming back for cream-filling sounds like something I could definitely get behind," Hudson said, his grin a mixture of wicked and sincere while his knee dug into mine. "Maybe we'll see you later."

Mia beamed and left the check on the table.

Henry grabbed the check just as Lance swooped in to pick it up.

"Back off," Henry groused from behind an amused smirk. "You set all of this up *and* got tickets for the show. Least you can do is let me get dinner."

Hudson nodded. "Let him get dinner."

Henry shot a look at his brother. "Maybe you should get dinner."

Hudson just grinned. "Nah, I'm good. Thanks for buying."

Henry just grumbled something and put his card in the bill folder while tossing a glance at Lance. "You better make him pay for gas or something, or his spoiled ass will think he gets everything for free."

"Oh, I'll be sure to pay him back tonight," Hudson drawled, and then threw his head back and laughed when Lance's cheeks pinked.

Henry groaned, but he wasn't quite able to hide his smile. "You," he pointed at his brother, "are a menace." He looked at Lance. "And I'm pretty sure you're at least partly to blame."

Lance's brows shot up. "Me? What did *I* do?"

All I could do was sit there and watch the exchange with a goofy smile and all the warm fuzzies in my heart for these men.

My friends.

I had actual, honest to goodness *friends*.

Back in college, I'd been too...well, too *everything* to put a lot of effort into any relationships. I wanted friends, but it was hard to tell if anyone was actually genuine or if they were just along for the ride—homework help, designated driver, someone to cover a shift, that type of shit.

And intimate relationships were even harder. So many people were only interested in fuck and run type connections—like anti-connections—and that was *so* not me.

What I'd found with Henry and the guys was exactly what I'd been missing all those years. Closeness, fondness, joking around, truly knowing each other, laughing together, spending time building and celebrating what we had. I knew I was the new addition, but Hudson and Lance were pretty new as a couple too, so the four of us could grow our connections together.

By the time Mia returned with Henry's card, and he

signed the receipt, we had the perfect amount of time to walk to the theater. The cool night air nipped at my cheeks, and Henry took my hand.

From the opposite side, Hudson hooked his arm in mine. "Have you seen this one?" he asked, pointing at the marquee with the show's name in lights.

I shook my head, suddenly nervous.

"It's one of my very favorites," Hudson said. "I mean, I have a lot of favorites, but I love this one. What about you?"

I shook my head again. "I've listened to a lot of Broadway musical songs, but I've never actually seen one." I frowned. "Actually, that's not true, I've seen some that were released to be streamed, but I've never been to a theater to watch a live show."

For the tiniest fraction of a moment, I thought Hudson was going to laugh at me. Instead, he tightened his hold on my arm. "Oh my god, that's perfect. I'm so glad you get to pop your cherry with this one, *and* we get to be here with you."

"No one is popping anyone's cherry," Henry grumbled, his hand on mine tightening while Hudson chuckled.

And just like that, we headed into the theater. No one laughing at me for all I'd never done. No one calling me names or threatening me. Just friends happy we were all spending time together doing something we loved.

Well, I guess I didn't *know* I loved watching musical theater productions, but I definitely adored the music I'd listened to, and I'd been enthralled with the few productions I'd been able to watch on streaming services. And I was with three of my favorite people, so I had no doubt I'd leave the show being able to say I loved attending musical theater productions.

Hudson made sure we got our playbills and took the proper selfies and group pictures with them before we hit the restrooms and found our seats. Since no photographs were allowed in the theater, we made our way back out to the lobby to snap pictures in front of the promo images.

"Anyone want drinks before it starts?" Hudson asked. "I'll buy." His charming wink made me smile.

"I'll take a—"

"Lemon drop," they all said in unison before I even had time to glance at the menu.

For a split second, I thought about changing my order, but tasting lemon drops in every location had somehow become my *thing*, so I just shrugged. "Yeah, I'll take a lemon drop."

Henry threw his arm around me and kissed my temple. "I love you and your lemon obsession, even if it's a blow to my ego."

I giggled. "It's not like I'm saying I don't like *you* or even peaches. I just like lemon drops best."

"Good thing," Henry whispered in my ear. "Because I like *you* best."

Hudson returned with our drinks.

I took a sip, enjoying the sweet tartness on my tongue before biting my lip and batting my lashes at Henry. "I guess if I *had* to choose, I'd pick you over lemon drops," I teased.

Henry grinned and kissed my cheek. "Thank fuck for that." The deep words rumbled through me, and I shuddered.

This man was my everything.

We sipped our drinks and milled around the lobby. The theater was fairly old, but it had been refurbished and updated. Everything was crisp and clean, and I was seriously already daydreaming about the future shows we'd come to watch.

A large poster caught my eye with the next season's top shows. Three I'd heard of, one I loved, and two new-to-me titles. Maybe we'd be able to come to some of them if tickets weren't too expensive, and if the dates fit with our work schedules.

A thought flashed through my mind. Maybe someday Cake and Cocktails would be doing well enough I could treat my friends to season tickets to the theater. Based on how well we'd been doing since opening, I had high hopes it wasn't a far-off dream.

When people began making their way toward their seats, we joined the flow. Our location was absolutely perfect, Lance had done a great job choosing our seats. Nestled into a comfy chair with Henry on my left—we let him have the aisle seat so he could at least stretch out one leg—and Hudson to my right with Lance on the other side of him, I thumbed through the playbill until the lights dimmed.

And then I lost myself to the show.

Chapter 19
Henry

LANCE CAUGHT MY EYE OVER HUDSON AND JACK'S heads, a soft smile tugging at the corner of his mouth. Jack had been going a mile a minute since the show ended. The lights had come up, he'd blinked as if he'd been in another world, and then the non-stop chatter had started.

Hudson loved it because he loved talking about his favorite theater shows.

Lance loved watching them rehash the entire show.

And I just loved seeing Jack happy, loved, and protected.

I could love and protect him just fine on my own—and I would, every second of every day—but it meant the absolute world to me that my brother, my dad, and my friend loved Jack like family. Between the four of us, we could give him something he hadn't had since his mom passed away.

The night air had a bite, but the brisk walk between

the tall buildings kept us fairly comfortable. Jack's sweet voice danced on the cool breeze as he recalled one of his favorite songs from the second act.

Lance lifted his chin toward a little bakery, and I knew Hudson and Jack would both be perfectly satisfied to grab coffee and pie as our nightcap, but I wasn't in the mood for dessert.

I shook my head, and Lance nodded in agreement while mouthing, "The D word."

With a chuckle, I steered Jack toward the crosswalk. Grabbing a shower and cuddling in bed with Jack was all the dessert I had on my mind.

Okay, fine. Maybe I wasn't completely against exploring the various facets of the *D word*.

We made our way through the silver and glass hotel lobby, Jack and Hudson still going on and on about the show. When we stepped off the elevator and stopped in front of our rooms, Jack paused, glanced around, and blinked. His big blue eyes took in the hallway before landing on me. "I didn't know we were here," he mumbled.

Lance and I laughed. Hudson let himself be pulled into Lance's side. And Jack's forehead wrinkled with a tiny frown. "No, but seriously, I thought we'd stop somewhere for drinks or something. I didn't realize we walked all the way back here."

"We'll get breakfast in the morning before we head out," I promised.

As I swiped the keycard, Hudson pulled Jack into a hug. "I'm so glad you loved it. I have a new musical buddy."

"Hey," Lance grumbled with a grin. "What am I? Chopped liver?"

Jack squeezed Hudson back before letting him go and hugging Lance. "We can all geek out over theater together." His gorgeous blue eyes met mine. "Oh my god, we're theater kids. There was a group of theater kids in high school, but Joseph would have shit himself if I'd ever asked to join theater."

I took his hand and brought it to my mouth for a kiss. "Being theater kids sounds perfect."

"I always wanted to be a theater kid," Hudson said with a broad grin. "I was into musicals in high school, but we didn't have a big enough theater department to make it happen."

We said our goodnights and made our way into our separate rooms.

Just as I pulled Jack into my arms, a knock sounded at the connecting door.

"Go away," I growled over Jack's giggle.

Another knock.

"I swear to god, Hudson," I muttered as I took a step toward the door and flung it open.

My brother, who must have started stripping before the door even closed behind him, stood there in his boxer briefs with a toothbrush hanging out of his mouth. Grinning, wiping away toothpaste, he said, "Don't forget to get your fill of the D word."

With a hard hand to his chest, I shoved him and shut the door. His laughter was almost as loud as Jack's as I locked the door. "How did he undress and get his toothbrush so fast?"

Jack giggled and fell over on the bed.

"Do you want to watch a movie? Go to sleep?" I asked as I kicked off my shoes and removed my tie while he continued laughing. "Or just lay there and laugh yourself silly?"

Jack propped himself up on his elbows and watched me. All silliness gone, heat blazed in his eyes, his lip caught between his teeth. "Can I shower first?"

All I could do was nod. He rose from the bed, his eyes never leaving mine, and slowly worked every piece of clothing from his body until he stood there in front of me with just a pair of neon purple bikini underwear.

With a deep breath, I spoke barely above a whisper, "You have about ten seconds to get that pretty little ass into the bathroom before I throw you on this bed, shower or no shower."

Jack's eyes went wide, and he turned with a yelp of laughter while grabbing his bag. The bathroom door clicked shut a moment later.

While the shower ran, I fished lube from my bag and placed it on the bedside table. I turned down the bed, turned off the lights, clicked the television on, and set it on mute. Busying myself hanging up our shirts and pants, I tidied up until Jack called for me.

Worried something was wrong, I cracked open the bathroom door. "You okay?"

"Just lonely," he teased, his blond hair plastered to his forehead and a big grin on his face.

Grateful he'd had whatever private time he needed, and there was still enough hot water, I stripped off my underwear and climbed in with him.

The wet heat of his body against mine went straight to my cock. "You just miss me, or did you have something in mind?"

Jack's mouth met mine in a needy kiss, the taste of him as potent as the sweetest cocktail. "This shower is a lot bigger than the one at home," he murmured against my lips.

Home.

I loved when he let himself lean into that confidence. Let himself think of Haven Grove and our apartment as home.

"True." My big hands traveled from his shoulders to his pecs, down his torso to his lower back, and ended the journey with a handful of his perfect ass.

When Jack turned in my arms and pressed his chest against the tiles, my eyes landed on the travel-sized bottle of lube he'd smuggled into the shower.

"We could have some fun in here before we go to bed." The fiery glance he gave me over his shoulder just about did me in.

But more than the lust and desire burning bright between us, the trust and soul-deep intimacy we shared melted me to the core. This man who had been mistreated, unloved, and lonely for so long had given me his heart. Handed it right over for safe keeping because he trusted me. And in return, he'd stolen mine—just plucked it right from my chest. He owned my heart, owned my soul.

Owned me, from here to eternity if he'd have me.

So, it wasn't just sex. Wasn't just fun in the shower— although, I planned to take full advantage of the space. It was the fact the universe had somehow seen fit to drop this gorgeous sweetheart of a man smack dab in the middle of my midwestern postage stamp of a town. And Jack had found his way to me. Why me? How was I so lucky? I didn't know. All I knew was that I hadn't been looking for love—really and truly, I'd come to accept that I likely wasn't going to mesh well with most people when it came to anything outside of acquaintances and the occasional friendship beyond my family—and then *BAM!*

There he was.

Jack.

A friend I hadn't known I needed.

The perfect filling for a Jack-shaped hole in my heart I didn't even know existed.

Jack was my person, plain and simple.

With the steamy air billowing around us, I pressed my chest to his back and nibbled along his jawline, my hands gripping his pecs before traveling down his stomach. "Tell me what you want."

Jack whimpered and rolled his hips so his ass rubbed against my cock. "Anything. Please, Henry. I just want you touching me."

First, with soft kisses to the back of his neck and each shoulder, I trailed my lips down his spine as I dropped to my knees. Nuzzling my nose into the little divot just above his ass, I couldn't help the smile when Jack whimpered and thrust his ass in my face. We'd learned a lot about each other over the time we'd spent together since he came to town, and one of the things I knew best about Jack was that he loved to be rimmed. And he knew I absolutely loved to bury my face in his ass and feast on him.

By the time I'd teased and tongued his hole open, Jack's knees kept nearly buckling, and his whimpers told me he could come with just my tongue in his ass.

While I'd enjoyed making that happen a time or two, I wasn't ready for our shower fun to be over just yet. I stood, grabbed the lube, and pressed my body to Jack's. "What do you want?"

He grunted in frustration. "You inside me. Please, Henry. Make me come."

"In here or in bed?" I flipped the cap on the lube and coated my cock.

"Yes. Here. Bent over the sink. In the bed. All of it."

Shit.

Who was I to argue?

With the head of my cock pressing slowly and gently against his entrance, I eased in inch by inch. The tight heat of Jack's body hugged me, and I worked my way into his body. After several long, slow thrusts in which the angle wasn't quite right, knees banged the tile wall, hands fought to find purchase *anywhere*, and skin prickled with goosebumps on the side not getting the hot water, we quickly realized shower sex wasn't nearly as fabulous as porn made it out to be. We gave it a shot, but Jack giggled as the water turned cooler. "Maybe we mark shower sex off our bucket list? Guess we're not missing much with a tiny shower at home."

We stepped out of the shower and dried with big, fluffy towels. When Jack flipped off the bright overhead light and wiped the condensation from the mirror, my dick perked right back up and took notice.

Jack's beautiful blue eyes caught mine in the mirror, and he chewed on the edge of his towel. Never taking his eyes from mine and keeping the towel between his hips and the solid edge of the sink counter, Jack bent at the waist and propped himself on his elbows.

With his ass spread open for me in gorgeous invitation, I quickly grabbed the lube to reapply. Gripping his shoulders, never taking my eyes from his intense gaze in the mirror, I lined up and slid back into him.

Like coming home.

The way his body opened for me, molded itself to my dick, and held me tight was absolute perfection.

But the love and trust in Jack's eyes as he stared back at me in the mirror was the truest form of intimacy. Open and bare, we clung to each other. Right then and there, in that sensual moment in the hotel bathroom, and through the trials and pain of our pasts, we held tight, journeying toward our future.

Together.

Jack pushed up on his hands and my arms automatically went around him, bringing his back to my chest and burying my face in his neck as I thrust in and out of his tight heat.

"Wait," he panted. "Stop."

I froze. "What?"

"I want to be in bed with you. Want to feel you on top of me, see your face when you come in me." His hands gripped my forearms.

Gently, I turned his face and brought our mouths

together in a slow, needy kiss. "I love you so damn much," I murmured against his lips.

"Love you too," Jack whispered.

We made our way to the bed, and Jack stretched out on one side of the mattress. I chuckled and joined him, knowing he was leaving the other side of the bed for sleeping when we made an inevitable wet spot.

"What?" He blinked at me, those big blue eyes *trying* to look innocent. "No reason to mess up the entire bed just yet." Then he spread his legs, wrapped his arms around my neck, and kissed me with so much love and trust I thought my heart might explode.

Adjusting his hips so my still-slick cock pressed against his hole once again, I eased into Jack's body, loving every single whimper and groan he gave me. With his legs wrapped around my waist and my arms anchored under his body, hands gripping his shoulders, I pulled out almost all the way before sinking back in.

Over and over, his tight ring of muscle stretched open for me, our sweaty skin slapped together, and Jack cried out each time I slid deep enough to press my balls against him. The clean scent of soap mixed with sweat and lube, a potent mixture that teased my senses.

Jack held me tight against him, his face buried in my neck as I slowly thrust into him again and again. "Henry," he gasped. "Oh shit, Henry. Oh my god, I'm so close."

With my arms under his shoulders, I brought my hands up to cup the sides of his face and pressed my forehead to his. "Come for me," I demanded, surging deeper into his body to elicit a moan of wrecked pleasure. "That's it, Jack. Let go, baby. Give it to me."

On a final thrust, Jack came apart in my arms, his warm release pooling between our bodies as I held him close. As wave after wave of his orgasm washed over Jack, his body gripping me tightly, I gave myself over to the ecstasy and exploded deep inside him.

When we finally came down from our high, Jack's cum smeared between us, I eased from him slowly. Losing that most intimate of connections had both of us wincing and shivering, so I kissed him and quickly made my way to the bathroom for a washcloth.

Once we were both semi cleaned up, I gathered Jack in my arms and pulled the blankets over us.

Just as I thought we'd both slip into a well-loved, sated sleep, Jack whispered, "Can I ask you something?" His soft lips feathered over my chest with each word.

"You know you can. Always."

He took a deep breath and shifted so we were face to face. "Am I making things hard on you? Like in Haven Grove and with your business?"

Like a swift sucker punch to the solar plexus, his question knocked me for a loop. "What? No." I huffed out a breath and tried to take in another. "What?" I repeated. "I don't understand what you mean."

Jack's eyes sparkled with tears in the dim light from the muted television, and he shook his head. "Like, would it be better for you and the Riggs family if I wasn't around?"

I propped up on an elbow and cupped his face. "Where is this coming from? Do you want to leave? Is something bothering you?"

Jack sat up, facing me with his legs crossed. "If things

were bad because I was there, would you tell me? Would you ask me to leave?"

I sat up and faced him. "I would never ask you to leave." Some silent part of my heart set off an alarm. Is this Jack wanting to leave? Does he feel like he has to stay? "I'd never force you to stay either. You are free to make whatever choices you want, I hope you know that."

A tear streamed down Jack's face. "But if I was making things worse for you, would you tell me?"

I reached for his hands. "Babe, what's wrong? Why these questions? Did something happen?"

"Would you tell me to leave?" Jack persisted.

"No, never."

"Even if me being there was a problem for you?"

"You aren't a problem. You're the best thing that's ever happened to me." I cupped his chin and lifted his face, so our eyes met. "But if there's something bothering you, you have to let me know. If you need to leave, I'd never hold you back."

"Do you want me to stay?"

I cocked my head. "What? Of course, I want you to stay." That alarm sounded again. "But I won't *ask* you to stay if it means keeping you from something else, something better." Brushing a thumb over his cheek, I asked, "Where is this coming from?"

Jack took a shuddery breath. "I'm sorry, I should have told you sooner, but I knew you'd get angry, and I thought I could just keep it tucked away. But his words just keep eating at me, and I keep worrying that he's right. What if I am making things hard for you? Taking away business? Messing things up for the Riggs family name."

A fiery ball of anger torched through my chest. "He who? What who said?" I worked hard to keep the words as neutral as possible. Who the hell would have told Jack he was a problem for me?

The answer punched me in the face even before I finished thinking the question.

Fucking Larry.

"Brother Larry," Jack started, but he paused when his voice cracked. He took another deep breath. "He said I was making things bad for you and the whole Riggs family; I was ruining you, and I needed to do the right thing for you by just leaving town."

My blood boiled, and a tightness clutched my chest. That fucking self-righteous piece of shit prick.

"When was this?" I asked, trying my best to keep the low growl from my voice.

Jack shrugged. "That day your dad and I were working on the truck."

Working to keep my jaw relaxed so as not to grind my teeth into smithereens, I breathed deeply through my nose for a three count. "Did he also tell you that I punched him in his damn face that day?"

Jack's eyes went wide. "What? That was you?" A hysterical giggle burbled from him. "Oh my god, I wondered why his cheek was so swollen and red. He was pissed about that."

"Good. Serves him right coming into *my* business, *our* business, and trying to tell us what the hell we can and can't do in the name of his parishioner's virtue."

I didn't think it was possible, but Jack's eyes grew even wider. "What? What do you mean? What did he say?"

Shit.

Jack squeezed my hands in his. "Henry, what did he say?"

I sighed. "He said we were causing the good people of Haven Grove to sin and sending out porn."

Jack wrinkled his nose. "Wait, what?"

"Encouraging alcohol consumption by pairing it with cake, enticing people to sin."

The frown on Jack's face—that cute little scowl line between his brows—was so damn adorable I nearly forgot I was pissed. "But that's ridiculous."

"Mmhm."

"And porn? What porn?"

I rolled my eyes. "He's mad about the newsletter showing up in most inboxes saying *Cake and Cock…*"

Jack's mouth formed a little O. "I told you we should have fixed that."

Shaking my head, I leaned in to kiss him. "There's nothing to fix. People either unsubscribe if they don't like it, or they get a laugh out of it, or they don't even notice it. It's something that gets people interested, and interested people are more likely to come see what we're about." I nuzzled my nose against his. "Plus, now that I know Larry is mad about it, I feel like we can't change it just on principle."

Jack chewed on his bottom lip but nodded. He let me pull him into my arms and ease us back down to the mattress. When he'd tucked himself into my chest, he spoke. "You really wouldn't ask me to stay?" There was a hint of challenge and a lot of uncertainty in his words.

"There's a big difference between *wanting* and *asking*. I

want you to stay in Haven Grove. *Want* you to be by my side for anything and everything for as long as we're given." I kissed the top of his head. "But I won't ever *ask* you to stay. It's not fair to you. I'll never stand in your way. If at any time you feel like there's something more out there for you, I'll step aside and let you go."

"That's kinda sweet and kinda sad."

I smiled and ran my hand up and down his back. "Haven Grove is my home, and I want you to share that home with me forever. But I won't ever make you stay. Forcing someone to stay somewhere they don't want to be only leads to regret and heartbreak."

Jack made a little noise and pressed a kiss to my neck. "So, even if I want to be asked to stay?"

I shook my head again. "Brat," I teased, and he giggled. "No, I won't ask. I'll show you how much I love you every single day. I'll make living in Haven Grove something you'll hopefully never want to leave. But I'll never put me before you and ask you to stay if there's something more in life you want to experience."

Jack sighed. "I love you. You're too good for me, but I'm never letting you go." He pulled back and kissed my chin. "And if there's anything in life I want to experience, I'll ask you to take me there. We'll travel, we'll explore, and we'll always come home." He sealed his words with a press of his lips to mine. "Together."

With that, we drifted off to sleep.

Jack's giggle woke me some time later, and I groggily checked the clock.

Middle of the night.

Then a sound caught my attention, and Jack giggled again as he wiggled his ass against my cock.

What's a guy to do when he wakes up to a horny boyfriend in his bed and his very vocal brother having sex in the next room? Obviously, I had no choice but to drown out Hudson and Lance.

Jack was completely on-board and eager to help me out.

As Lance drove us the last few miles toward Haven Grove, Jack's head resting against me while I hugged him close, I couldn't help the smile teasing my lips.

The trip to the city had been spectacular. Sure, the sex had been amazing, as it always was with Jack. He and I clicked like we'd been perfectly designed for each other. Being with him sexually was one of those things that just made sense after years and years of never really finding the right connection.

But more than the sex, the time away spent with Jack and our friends had been so meaningful. Getting to know my brother as an adult was something I hadn't known I needed to do more of. Hudson would always be my little brother, but hanging out with him, seeing him happy and in love, it healed a little corner of my heart I hadn't realized was still hurting for those two little boys who lost their momma all those years ago.

Reconnecting with Lance warmed my soul. That man had been one of the only reasons the Riggs family hadn't collapsed and blown away like blossoms off peach trees way back then. But it was good getting to see Lance be his true self, and watching him be so head over heels for Hudson was a smile-inducing mixture of kinda strange but mostly heartwarming.

And being right by Jack's side as he flourished with new experiences, new friends, and a safe place to be himself was quite possibly the most rewarding moment of my life. Even if we'd just been exploring the city as friends, I still would have felt like a proud parent watching Jack blossom. But knowing we were there together because we'd connected on a deeper level than I ever had with anyone in my life meant that the entire trip to the city had been humbling, exciting, and left me with such a warm, contented feeling I was still floating as we neared Haven Grove.

Breakfast that morning had been just one more example of things I hadn't known I was missing in my life. Gathering around the table with a simple meal of coffee, juice, bacon, and eggs as the four of us laughed, teased, and made plans for future happenings with our family and businesses had warm, comforting hands gently wrapping around my heart. The simple act of a meal with friends—the people I called family—was the soul hug my heart had been desperately seeking for so many years.

Once we'd unloaded the truck and said our goodbyes—although, we were meeting up for dinner with Dad to talk business—Lance and Hudson headed off to catch up on the work they'd missed, and Jack and I tossed our bags on the couch before taking the stairs right back down to the Roadhouse.

A harried Sam met us with a look that told me he was both relieved to see us and irked we'd been gone.

"Shit," I muttered. "That bad?"

Sam huffed. "It's not been good. Just made it through the lunch rush. Sent Kayla home throwing up. I need four more pairs of hands if I'm ever gonna to get caught up in the kitchen. The register is one hundred percent off—probably over but could be under. We need more of almost everything, and the truck won't be here until right around dinnertime because it got a flat tire." He ran a hand over his face. "Your buddy Larry has been spewing shit all around town trying to convince people to boycott us." Sam threw a towel my way. "I've had to piss since this morning. I'm taking a break."

As he headed toward the restroom, he pointed at Jack.

"Your cakes are pretty much wiped out. People love those damn things. Better get to baking because all I've heard since you've been gone is Jack's cake this, and Jack's cake that."

Jack's cheeks pinked and he pulled the collar of his shirt up to rub it over his chin—I never wanted to change the quirky things that made Jack *Jack*, but I'd noticed with a happy heart that he'd slowly and surely been easing away from the deeply engrained trauma response.

Sam just shook his head with a good-natured smile and headed for his break.

I pulled Jack close and kissed the side of his head. "I'm a fan of Jack's *cake* too," I murmured.

His giggle was exactly what I needed. Jack turned his head and looked up at me. "I need to get a bunch of ingredients if the order didn't come in. Can I borrow the truck to head up the road to the store? If I time it right, I can at least have something ready for the dinner rush, and still get everything else mostly restocked for tomorrow."

Nuzzling my nose against his before brushing my lips over his pretty mouth, I closed my eyes and breathed him in deeply. "Wish I could drive you."

Jack accepted another kiss and whimpered a bit when we finally broke apart. "I do a pretty good job with the stick shift now." I huffed out a laugh when he snickered at the innuendo. "Sam will have your head if you leave him again. I'll hurry." He batted his eyelashes. "Please?"

I nodded toward the hook where my truck keys hung. "Do *not* hurry. Be careful."

"Yes, Daddy," Jack teased.

I swatted him on the ass as he scurried away.

And then I turned to tackle the mess that had accumulated while we'd been off gallivanting in the city.

Two hours later, I had the register balanced. The kitchen was cleaned up and reorganized. And I'd helped Sam prepare as much as possible for the dinner rush.

I took a break and checked my phone.

No texts from Jack.

I calculated what time he left, how long it would take him to get to the big discount store, shop for ingredients, and get back home.

He could have been back by now.

But he also could have run into traffic, had trouble finding what he was looking for, been lollygagging in the store. Anything, really.

After all, he hadn't done a lot of solo shopping trips. I

needed to just let him have some freedom and be on his own a bit.

Or maybe something was wrong. He could have had car trouble —a flat, overheated, anything. Maybe he was tired and fell asleep. Did he check the gas before he left?

I tapped the screen to call Jack.

No answer.

I texted him. The message was delivered, but he didn't read it.

A coil of worry and fear wound itself up tightly in my belly.

Maybe he was driving and couldn't answer. I didn't want him texting and driving.

Yeah, he was likely just being a safe driver.

Or maybe something was wrong.

I called my dad.

"What's up?" Dad said in way of greeting.

"Are you home?"

"No, heading back from running some errands. Need something?"

"Jack ran up the road to the store to get some ingredients because our truck didn't show up on time. He should have been back by now—he also might just be taking his time. But he's not answering calls or texts."

"I'll come by once I'm back in town. He in your truck?"

"Yeah," I said, the dread in my gut building with each second.

"I'll keep an eye out. Might have just stopped to talk to Lance or Hudson."

"Maybe," I said, not really believing the words. Jack would have answered if he was with Lance or Hudson.

"Try to stay calm. I'll be there in a bit." Dad disconnected the call.

Stay calm.

Yeah, right.

But the delivery truck pulled up out back, and I had no choice but to recruit Sam to help me bring in the inventory so we could get finished in time for the dinner rush.

Every beat of my heart, every moment Jack didn't text back or call, brought bright-hot bombs of fear exploding in my chest.

Chapter 20
Jack

THE AIR HAD A DISTINCTLY CRISP FALL FEEL TO it as it whipped through my hair. With the window of Henry's truck cracked slightly, my groceries tucked safely in the back, and the radio playing the classic rock station Henry favored, I was as free as the bird in the song floating through the speakers.

Outside of hopping on that bus to take me far away from Joseph's house months ago, I hadn't really experienced a lot of freedom. Joseph and Douglas had always been breathing down my neck at home and work. Douglas seemed to be everywhere when I was in high school, and too many people knew my uncle and cousin to make it feel like I was truly on my own during college. Joseph reminded me all the time that he had plenty of minions willing to do his bidding and reporting my every move to him.

So, driving myself to and from the grocery store had me riding high as I thought about the lemon pound cake I planned to bake and pair with dinner. Plus, the three new cakes I'd been toying with, the pictures and recipes I wanted to include in the next newsletter, and the social media posts Casey and I had been talking about were all tumbling around in my head. But not in a bad, overwhelming way, just in a way that had me excited about the turn my life had taken recently.

Maybe that was why it took me a moment to realize the gun-metal gray Jeep I'd seen in the parking lot at the store was the same one that had been behind me on the highway and was now behind me on the narrow country road heading toward Haven Grove.

So what, Jack? Lots of people from Haven Grove drive up the highway to do their grocery shopping at the discount store just like you did today. It could be anyone from anywhere.

That was true. It totally could.

But Haven Grove was a small town where pretty much everyone knew everybody else. Which meant, like it or not, most people were all up in each other's business. And *that* meant we all would have heard about a fancy new vehicle like the one behind me.

No one in town drove a dark gray Jeep.

No one in town drove a vehicle as shiny new as the one currently following me.

The only Jeep in Haven Grove was a complete junker the owner used for parts.

The person behind me wasn't from Haven Grove.

Stop it. You're freaking out. Don't ruin your first little independent outing with conspiracy theories. The Jeep could be anyone from anywhere. Maybe they were heading to Haven Grove to pick peaches. Heck, maybe they'd heard of Cake and Cocktails and wanted to get a flight of cake paired with fun drinks. Proof of advertising at work.

Or maybe someone was trying to scare me.

Larry had made it clear he wanted me out of town. Did he send someone to follow me? Creep me out? Send me packing?

Did Randy and Pete get in trouble for messing with the trash, and now they were out to get revenge? But how would they have known it was me who saw them and told Henry?

Did they hear about Larry's visit to Henry and put two and two together?

But that didn't explain the Jeep. If two teens from a tiny town were going to seek revenge on a narrow, dusty ol' gravel road, wouldn't they be in a beater truck rather than a brand-new Jeep?

Glancing in my rearview mirror, I realized all my thinking had done was given the Jeep a chance to speed up and close the distance between us.

I pressed hard on the accelerator, but I immediately didn't like the way the truck felt under me when she reached a certain speed on the gravel so, I eased up a bit.

The Jeep did not.

Not even slightly.

In fact, I was pretty sure he gunned it.

I screamed when the first force of impact slammed into me. Absolutely unprepared for how violently I was thrown forward, I said a tiny prayer of thanks for the seatbelt.

When the Jeep smashed into me a second time, my brain remotely registered the slicing pain in my neck being from the seatbelt, but my focus was more on keeping the truck on the road. I didn't have a lot of experience driving on gravel, and the rocks beneath my tires made it hard to keep a grip on the road.

For a split second, the truck's tires left the gravel road, tugging toward the ditch. With another shriek, I yanked the wheel, screaming again when that move shot the truck to the far side of the road, the back end fishtailing on the loose rocks.

Dust billowed around both vehicles, and my view in the side and rearview mirrors was greatly diminished. For a hopeful moment, I thought the Jeep had backed off. But then the gray beast emerged from the cloud of dust and pulled up almost even with me. The grinding of metal on metal sent dread straight to my gut, but all my focus was on keeping the truck on the road.

When I shot a quick glance at my side mirror, a cold-hearted sneer shone through the dust and brought every single moment of my haunted past colliding with my present. Just as my brain tried to wrap around how or why he was in Haven Grove, the Jeep swerved to the left and then side-swiped the truck with a hideous screech of metal.

My head shot violently to one side before whipping back to bounce off the window, pain reverberating through my skull. Knowing I had no way to outmaneuver him, I let off the gas hoping the Jeep would sail past me.

Instead, it collided with the truck again, this time ramming me off the road. The last I saw of the Jeep, it sat in a cloud of dust just off the road as the truck bounced and rumbled down a steep incline toward a ditch. For a split second, I held onto hope that the impact would be gentle as the truck seemed to slow. But it hit something big, and all hope sped out the window as the hunk of metal tipped over and somersaulted the rest of the way down the bank.

Thankfully, my head busted against the glass once more, and I was blissfully unaware of the final impact by the time the truck came to a violent stop.

"Fuuuuck," I moaned when I came to later. Minutes? Hours? I had no idea.

My head throbbed.

My body ached like I'd been run over by a semitruck.

But nothing hurt like I was severely injured.

Blood trickled down my temple, stinging as it got into my eye, and dripped from my chin. *Don't freak out, Jack. Head wounds bleed a lot.*

Doing a quick scan, I moved my extremities. No screaming pain.

What if nothing hurts because you can't feel it?

No, I could feel each arm, leg, finger, and toe. Everything hurt, but nothing was breathtaking in its pain.

Taking a deep breath, I winced as pain sliced through my neck and chest. The seatbelt had definitely saved me, but also left its mark. But again, nothing so bad as to have me passing out from the pain.

My biggest problem seemed to be I was strapped into the truck at a very weird angle with no way to extricate myself.

Yes, I had a head wound. Possibly a concussion.

Yes, I was bumped and bruised, but nothing seemed broken.

How in the hell was I supposed to get myself out of the truck and out of the ditch?

Shit.

Did I even want to know where the Jeep was or where *he* was?

Fuck.

I wrecked Henry's truck.

Henry.

He'd be worried.

I got dizzy trying to locate my phone hanging in the odd position. No way to call for help.

Shit, shit, fuck.

The throbbing in my head intensified. Still didn't think anything was broken, but the adrenaline seemed to be wearing off, and my body screamed in pain.

Would Henry come looking for me?

Was the Jeep up there waiting on me?

Double fuck.

Did I smell gas?

I didn't know how long I hung there. Between the blood rushing in my ears, the pain lancing through my body with each breath, and the throbbing in my head, I wasn't sure if I heard vehicles passing on the road above me or not.

I closed my eyes for a moment, knowing it was probably best to stay awake, but unable to fight the waves of exhaustion washing over me. When I woke again, it was definitely darker, and I swore I heard someone calling my name.

Then the sound of twigs and sawgrass under feet

reached me, and a face filled my line of sight. A familiar face.

Relief washed over me. I'd be okay now.

But it was too hard to keep my eyes open.

I'd just sleep for a couple minutes.

The blaring of something very loud woke me.

My alarm clock? A fire alarm?

Ah, siren.

Lots of voices.

Bright lights in my eyes.

I told them not to drop me just moments before the seatbelt let loose and thrust me into waiting arms, then a hard bed.

Something around my neck.

A collar? That was weird.

I thought I answered questions. I tried, at least.

My head might have exploded when they finally got me free of the truck.

And maybe all my bones were broken because each and every movement hurt, but I appreciated their effort as they hefted me up the bank.

"Jack?" The voice was close to my ear. "You hang in there, okay? Gonna get you to the hospital."

"Henry." The murmured name was all I could muster.

"Yep, he'll be there. Promise you that."

They bounced me like a little kid stuck on a trampoline —Douglas used to do that to me all the time—and my world went upside down. Moaning in pain, I squinted my eyes against bright lights surrounding me.

"Fuck, man." The voice grumbled. "How about you be a little careful and don't add any more injuries."

A deep voice answered, but I didn't catch the words.

My hard bed stopped rocking and rolling.

Voices. Far enough away I couldn't make out what was being said, but close enough I could tell they weren't happy.

"Sorry, family only." The words were clearer now.

"He's my son-in-law."

A pause.

A grunt.

Then someone took my hand.

A door slammed.

And we took off.

An ambulance.

I cracked an eye against the pain and bright lights.

Casey Joe sat next to me holding my hand.

"Son-in-law, huh?" I managed between dry, cracked lips.

He winked and gave me a conspiratorial smirk. "Shhh, don't make me look like a liar. Just go with it."

I smiled the best I could and slipped back into the haze of pain and exhaustion. Yeah, I'd definitely like to be Casey Joe's son-in-law someday. Maybe if Henry wasn't too mad about his truck.

A noise bubbled up from my chest. I thought it was a giggle, but it might have been a groan of pain when something cold and wet touched my face.

Probably wiping the blood to check my head.

"We're going to start an IV to get some fluids in you," a voice said.

How many people were in the ambulance?

Another something cold scratched against my arm and I tried to jerk away, but Casey Joe held tight to my hand.

"You're going to feel a pinch, maybe a cold sensation."

Holy fuck. A pinch, my ass. That hurt like hell.

Shit.

Wait. What was I thinking about?

Henry.

Henry's truck.

Damn. I wrecked Henry's truck.

He was gonna be pissed.

My throat clenched, but then I pictured his gentle smile and soft eyes.

Nah, Henry wasn't going to be pissed at me. He loved me just as much as I loved him. I smiled.

Then I sobered. Henry loved me, and he was going to be worried.

Shit.

So worried.

"Henry," I tried to say, fear and worry catching in my throat.

Damn, I was a mess.

"Shhh, it's okay," Casey Joe said. "He's on his way to the hospital. He'll meet us there."

"But dinner," I mumbled. I wasn't sure what time it was, but I knew we'd been planning for dinner rush.

"Sam's got it covered. Hudson and Lance are going to help, then they'll come see you." Casey Joe patted my hand. "It's all good. Everyone just wants you to get better."

Again, I thought something like a hysterical giggle

escaped my lips, but it sounded closer to a panicked moan. "Not everyone."

The leering sneer I'd seen through the Jeep window came back to me. A face I'd hoped to never see again. How had he found me? Granted, I hadn't done much to cover my tracks once I got to Haven Grove, but I'd been careful when jumping on that bus.

Shit.

A wave of nausea washed over me.

Could they make me go back?

There was no way I could after what I'd heard that night.

I was out of their hair, why would they even want me back? I was useless to them. They could have just let me stay gone. So, why track me down?

Between the pain, the wailing of the siren, and the rocking of the ambulance, I lost myself to the foggy pain. When I became aware again, Casey's hand was gone, and a million fingers and tools poked and prodded all over my body.

"Casey Joe," I mumbled. "Henry."

"We'll get your family in to see you as soon as we know you're not in immediate danger." The voice was calm and confident. I liked her. She'd take good care of me.

Over the next few—was it minutes? Hours? Shit, it seemed like weeks—the ER staff ran me through a bajillion tests, asked me the same damn questions five thousand times, and made everything hurt worse than it did when I was hanging in the truck.

But finally, the lights dimmed, an extra blanket was

wrapped around me, and a curtain screeched on its metal bar.

"Jack, I'm Doctor Barnes. You're a lucky young man."

I tried to smile or huff out a laugh, but nothing seemed to be working the way I wanted it to.

Lucky. Yeah.

"I'm sure the bumps and bruises tell a different story right now," the doctor continued—my eyes weren't super focused, but the glimpse I got of him made me think of Santa with scruff instead of a long beard, "but you could have been hurt a lot worse. No broken bones, no internal injuries, and the concussion is very minor. Your family has been invited in to see you. I'll check back in a bit and determine if you should be admitted or if you're able to go home."

"Go home," I mumbled. "Please."

Dr. Barnes chuckled. "I had a feeling you'd say that. We'll see how things go, but I think we can probably make that happen."

The metal rings of the curtain jingled, and then a new voice spoke. "Good evening, dear, I'm Donna, your nurse for the time being. We've got fluids running through your IV. You got a dose of the good stuff once we'd checked your head, so you should be feeling pretty footloose and fancy free. You're perfectly fine to sleep if you feel like it. I'll bring some ice and water; would you like any juice or crackers?"

"Juice and crackers," I answered. "Gonna just sleep."

"You do that. I'll be back. Your family should be making their way here any moment. You had quite the fan club in the waiting room, but only a couple can come see you at a time."

When my tiny space fell silent, I shifted on the gurney and gave myself over to the exhaustion. Every single inch of my body ached, but I couldn't help the warm fuzzies in my chest. Donna said a fan club had come to see me. I hadn't had anyone give two shits about me since my mom died. While I'd rather not be in the hospital, it meant the world to me that I had friends and family who cared enough to be there with me.

I drifted off to sleep knowing the next face I'd see would be Henry's.

The man I was hopelessly, head-over-heels in love with.

It was time I filled him in on the night I left Joseph's.

And even though he was going to be pissed, he needed to know why I'd wrecked his truck. I was in this for the long-haul, and that meant no secrets.

Chapter 21
Henry

IF I NEVER SAW THE INSIDE OF A HOSPITAL again, it would be too soon.

My heart had been in my throat for hours. Not hearing from Jack and wondering where he was had me imagining the worst. My head throbbed as adrenaline continued to course through my veins at top speed. When Dad called to let me know he'd found Jack, relief washed over me.

Until he told me Jack had been in a wreck and was at the hospital.

I didn't recall a single moment of the drive to the hospital—as scary as that was. Thank god for Sam, Hudson, and Lance—and for the good people of Haven Grove understanding why the Roadhouse was closing early.

My chest squeezed with the memory of bringing Dad to the hospital not so very long ago as I charged through the ER doors to get to Jack. This time, Dad met me and took me to a different waiting room.

"They're letting us wait here until they're ready for us to see him."

"Tell me everything," I demanded, my words rough and raw as I ran a shaky hand over my beard.

Dad put his hand on my shoulder and pushed me toward a chair. "He was awake and talking a bit when they brought him in. Nothing was visibly broken. He had a nasty gash on his head."

None of this was new, Dad had already told me pretty much everything. But my mind wasn't functioning right, and it helped to have something to focus on when all I really wanted was to slam through every inch of the hospital until I found Jack. "What the fuck happened?" I stared at the geometric pattern on the floor, not really seeing the shapes or colors, but focusing on *something* so I didn't lose my damn mind.

Dad shrugged. "Can't rightly say. He was on his way back from what I can tell. Maybe some loose gravel. Could have been speeding, I guess. But that doesn't sound much like Jack." He cracked his neck. "Truck might be totaled, not quite sure."

I squeezed my eyes shut, this next part was the hardest to stomach.

"He was stuck upside down when I found him. Truck was flipped in the ditch, and he was hanging there. Seatbelt probably saved his life."

A wrecked sob tore from my chest.

Fuck.

How long had Jack been stuck in that ditch? Hurt, scared, alone.

"Hey," Dad said, his words gruff with what was

probably unshed tears. "He couldn't have been there very long, not based on when you said he left and when he should have been getting back home. If I had to guess, I came up on him pretty soon after it happened."

I wasn't sure how Dad knew what I was thinking. And honestly, I wasn't even confident that his mathing would add up if I really took a look at it. But it helped to think Jack wasn't hanging there for too long.

The door we'd entered earlier swung open, and Sam, Lance, and Hudson came barreling in behind a hospital volunteer. Hugs were given all around, and Dad launched into the details again, but I didn't have the energy to listen to the specifics for a third time. My mind wandered as Dad filled the guys in, and a fist gripped my heart. Seriously, it took everything in me not to climb out of my skin and start busting down doors.

When someone who looked official finally came through another door, I jumped to my feet.

"With Jack Garner?" she asked.

"Yeah," I croaked. "Yeah, that's us. He's my partner."

Something crossed her face, and she cocked a brow. "I was under the impression his father-in-law was here?"

Dad cleared his throat. "That's me. Jack is married to my son, Henry." He gestured toward me, and I'd never been so grateful for my dad in my entire life. "Can we see him?"

She glanced between us. "You're Henry? That's who he's been asking for."

"Henry Riggs. He's okay?"

"Two of you can go back at a time. He's awake and doing well. Probably going to be sleepy from the medication, and he's pretty banged up." She gestured toward Lance, Sam, and Hudson. "Gentlemen, you can take turns as these two finish up."

Lance nodded. "Tell him we're here. One of you come fill us in."

The nurse led us through the door and toward a long line of cubicles with their openings covered by curtains, and a whoosh of chilly, antiseptic-laden air wafted over us. When we reached A4, she held the curtain back for us, and I nearly sprinted through to get to Jack.

The tiny make-shift room was dim, and Jack looked small and pitiful in the bed. An angry gash on his temple had been stitched together, most of the dried blood cleaned up from around the wound, but enough evidence left behind that I knew he'd want to wash it away once he was home.

My guess was they'd cut his clothes off since he appeared to be swimming in a hospital gown under two heavy blankets. A machine beeped next to him, and a bag of something hung from a hook with a tube leading to his arm.

Dad and I immediately parted ways, me going to one side of the bed with a singular focus of getting closer to Jack, Dad taking up a guard dog position on the other. The moment I dropped into the chair and took Jack's hand in mine, his eyes fluttered open.

He tried to say something. Swallowed, licked his lips, and tried again. Finally, he murmured my name barely above a whisper.

"Hey," I said, my lips against the back of his hand.

A tear formed and threatened to spill from the corner

of Jack's eye, and I'd never been so pissed and grateful in my life. Pissed that he was upset and hurt, grateful that it hadn't been worse.

So damn grateful.

"Shhh," I said. "It's okay."

Jack shuddered, a sob escaping his lips as the tear cascaded down his cheek.

Without a moment's consideration for anything other than Jack, I shifted from the chair to the edge of his bed before gathering him in my arms as gently as possible. Luckily, the IV was on the other side, and the other items were stuck to his chest pretty tightly.

Dad grabbed the call-button thingy just before it tumbled to the ground, but my focus was completely on Jack. Pressing soft kisses to his forehead, careful to avoid the gash, I whispered, "Shhh, it's okay. I love you." Then with a whoosh of breath, I finally let it all go and hefted out a sob. "Fuck, Jack. I was so damn scared."

Jack gave a half laugh, half sob into my chest. "You and me both. I'm so sorry about your truck. I was scared no one would find me, and I was so worried because I knew you'd be worried."

"I don't give a damn about the truck."

Dad cleared his throat and placed a hand on Jack's shoulder. "Don't you worry about that truck. We'll either build her back to shape or use her for scrap and fix up a different truck. You being okay is all that matters."

Jack sniffled and nodded into my chest. "I tried to keep it on the road. Glad I was wearing my seatbelt. Hanging upside down wasn't fun, but I think it kept me from the worst of it."

I held him for several heartbeats, just listening to him breathe and feeling him in my arms, almost like I needed to have him pressed against me to believe he was here and okay. I hadn't lost him.

Fuck.

It could have turned out so much worse.

Dad patted Jack's shoulder again. "I'm gonna tell the guys what's going on and let them come back to see you." He leaned down and brushed a kiss to the side of Jack's head, and my heart clenched knowing just how much my dad loved this man of mine.

Jack winced as he reached for Dad's hand. "Thank you for finding me and not leaving me alone."

Dad nodded. "Nowhere else I would have been. It's what we do for family." The curtain fluttered back into position as he exited the cubicle.

"I'm sorry I wasn't the one to find you," I started.

Jack pressed a finger to my lips. "Shhhh, there's no reason for you to be sorry. I had your truck. You were wrapped up with the deliveries and dinner. It makes sense that Casey Joe would have been the one to find me." His big blue eyes had lost some of their sparkle behind the haze of medication, but he smiled up at me. "Plus, don't tell me you weren't the one who sent him out looking."

I smiled and nuzzled my nose against his. "Yeah, okay. You wanna tell me what happened?"

Before he could answer, the curtain jangled, and Sam stuck his head into Jack's little room. "Hey there, man." The three of us talked a bit before Sam gave Jack a fist bump and left with a promise to send in Lance.

Lance came in looking as worried as Dad had, but

talking to Jack seemed to ease his biggest concerns, and he told Jack he'd bring him some ice cream as soon as we had him settled on the couch at home.

"I won't need to be on the couch for too long," Jack started, but snapped his mouth shut as soon as I shot him a look. "I mean—"

"I'm sure what you mean, oh love of mine," I growled in his ear as we waited on Hudson to come visit, "is that you'll definitely take the doctor's orders seriously, and you'll follow his discharge instructions to a T. If that means resting for several days, that's what you'll do. Right?"

Jack huffed. "Yes. If it means getting out of here and not having to stay overnight, I'll do whatever they tell me to do."

"Sounds kinky," Hudson said with a huge grin as he flung the curtain to the side.

Because the bed was most definitely not made for someone my size to share it with another full-grown man, I eased from the mattress and took a seat, never letting go of Jack's hand.

"Hey, baby brother," Hudson said with complete sincerity. "You had us worried." He touched his own forehead and nodded toward Jack. "Gonna have a sexy scar."

Jack snorted. "Whatever."

"Seriously, man. Guys go for scars. Especially older guys. They like to take care of us like we're injured baby birds." Hudson's eyes twinkled, and he struggled to keep the smile hidden.

I grabbed a plastic bedpan and tossed it at his head, all

of us laughing as Hudson yelped and dodged the projectile.

A nurse popped her head in and eyed us. "Can I get anyone anything?" Clearly annoyed with the noise we'd been making, she quickly made sure we knew she wasn't down with any shenanigans.

Once she'd left, after giving us a particularly evil eye, Hudson ducked his head. "Oops, guess I better leave so you guys don't get in trouble." He leaned down to hug Jack before standing next to my chair and hauling my head against his stomach. "Love you. Let me know if you need anything. I can't make cakes, but I can help however else you need me to."

As Hudson gave one last wave and headed out, Jack's phone buzzed from somewhere behind my chair.

Then it buzzed again.

"Is that yours?" Jack asked, his words heavy with exhaustion.

"Nope, must be yours. Dad said he grabbed it from the truck. Said he hoped your wallet was in your pocket, but your phone had landed up on the dash." I stood and rifled through the cabinet behind my chair. A hospital bag contained Jack's socks, shoes, and jeans along with his phone and wallet. His shirt didn't seem to have made it through the accident unscathed.

As his phone buzzed again, I grabbed it and put the bag back in the small cabinet before handing the device to him.

Jack stared at the screen, frowned, then tapped in his unlock code. "Damn face messed up more than I thought, I guess," he muttered.

"Huh?"

But just when he started to repeat himself, Jack's face transformed from annoyed and exhausted to ghostly white and panicked.

"Jack?" I asked, moving quickly to his side. "What's wrong?"

He shook his head and squeezed his eyes shut, despair washing over him. "Fuck."

"Babe, what is it? Let me help." I settled myself back on his mattress and placed my hand on his thigh.

"How did he find me?" A sad hiccup escaped Jack as he wiped away what appeared to be a tear of mostly frustration. "I mean, it's not like I tried to stay hidden in Haven Grove, but I thought I'd done a good job of throwing them off my track when I left."

Dread and fury swirled in my gut. "Who? What's going on?" But deep down, I knew.

Jack handed me his phone and covered his eyes with his hand, a heavy, shuddery breath seeping between his lips. "Douglas was the one who ran me off the road."

Fiery red bloomed in my vision. Jack's words and the words on his phone screen blurred together. "What? That fucker is here? He wrecked you?"

Jack nodded and gestured toward the phone. "He messaged me on Instagram—him or Joseph. It's not like I kept the Cake and Cocktails account private. I mean, that kinda defeats the purpose of a business account." He shut his eyes, scrunching up his face. "Damn it. Why didn't I think to block them?"

"Did you know they had an account?"

He shook his head. "I guess I knew they had an

account, but I don't think that one is old. Probably made a new one."

I glanced at the screen and ran a hand over my forehead. "I say we take screenshots of this and then block the account. You don't need to be dealing with this shit."

"But what's he even mean?" Jack nodded toward the phone in my hand. "Give us back what you stole, and we'll be even."

I hadn't even seen the words at first, but I took time to read them. "Did you take something when you left?"

Jack shook his head miserably. "I didn't have time. Even if I'd wanted to steal from them, I left pretty quickly."

I ran my hand up and down his thigh. "You wanna tell me about it?"

He leaned back on the inclined mattress with a sigh. "Not really, but it's probably for the best."

Quickly screenshotting the message, I saved the photo to Jack's phone and then emailed it to myself. "You okay with me blocking this account?"

Jack nodded. "Yeah. It won't make them stop, but maybe it will give me some time."

I blocked the account and handed the phone back to Jack just as Dad walked through the curtain. "We need to call the police and let them know about the wreck."

"What about the police?" he asked.

Jack ran a hand over tired eyes. "I know who wrecked me. It was Douglas."

"You're sure?" Dad asked, fury in his eyes.

"I'd recognize him anywhere. He lives in my nightmares."

I gave Dad a nod, and he left. I knew he'd get the authorities so they could take a statement from Jack. Not gonna lie, I wasn't going to be upset if he went searching for Douglas and beat his ass.

But that wasn't what Jack needed to be thinking about right then.

"Okay, tell me about the night you left."

Chapter 22
Jack

THERE WAS NO REASON I'D KEPT THAT NIGHT from Henry other than I didn't want to relive it. If I didn't talk about it, I could pretend like it didn't happen.

My head hurt, and I wanted to sleep for a week, but Henry's gentle touch and patient words gave me strength. "Some of this you might already know, I can't really remember what I've told you so far."

"That's fine. Just tell me what you think I need to know."

I gritted my teeth together and launched into my story. "So, Joseph owns Hill's Autos. He planned on Douglas taking it over and me working for him. I never liked working there, but he insisted I work for the family business. That's why he made me get a business degree. But I was a really bad car salesman," I said with a huff. "Like, the worst."

"That's because you're amazing at baking," Henry said with an encouraging pat to my leg.

"The night I left, I overheard something I definitely wasn't supposed to." I took a deep breath. I'd done my best not to think about it, but I needed to fill Henry in. It was important that he knew. "I'd forgotten my phone, so I went back to grab it, and I heard Joseph and Douglas talking in Joseph's office when I left mine." Swallowing thickly, I opened my mouth and replayed the entire conversation.

"Douglas was saying, 'He sucks. He couldn't sell a car if a person walked in and said they were there to buy the most expensive car on the lot.'

"Joseph laughed, but not like he found it funny. 'I spent a shit ton of money getting him that business degree. We need to keep him around at least until he earns out.'

"Douglas was whiny when he said, 'Can't he have a desk job? Like something pointless? Be your assistant?'

"Joseph snorted. 'Maybe I'll make him your assistant. You know we can't have him near the finances.'

"Douglas had scoffed. 'He's got shit for brains. Reads like a child, and numbers aren't much better. Unless it's on a damn recipe card for cake, he's not gonna notice it.'

"'Well, once he's earned back what I spent on his college, I don't care what happens to him,' Joseph said. 'In fact, the life insurance would be a nice little bonus. Maybe he'll have a terrible accident.'"

Tears streamed down my cheeks as I finished. "They were laughing their asses off when I grabbed my phone and ran out of the building." I cried harder when Henry leaned in to pull me into a hug. "As soon as I got home, I shoved everything I could into an old suitcase, filled my backpack, and took the car they let me drive. It was an electric car, so I knew it wouldn't get me far, but it was charged. I thought maybe it would give me a head start since they'd think I was just out—I went to the library a lot. They hardly ever checked in on me when it really counted, so I figured they wouldn't really notice I was gone until the next day." I nuzzled into Henry's chest, wiping my tears on his shirt and breathing him in.

At that point, the curtain was pulled aside, and Casey Joe walked in with two uniformed county officers. They introduced themselves as Officer James and Officer Smathe.

"I think you better start over. Tell them everything you just told me," Henry suggested softly.

So, I did.

The officers listened intently and took notes.

When I got to the point of leaving, I took a sip of water. Henry taking my hand in his helped boost me.

"So, I drove to a spot where I knew I could charge the car. It got me about fifty miles out of town. I slept for a while as the car charged. Then I drove until I reached the next city, charged the car, and drove some more. By the time I'd left all the skywalkers behind—" I snapped my mouth shut and looked at Henry as my cheeks heated. "I mean, once I'd left the city, I drove to where my map said there was a bus station. I stopped and withdrew almost every cent from my account. As soon as I had all the cash, I destroyed the card. I drove past the bus station until I found an old barn. I parked the car behind it and covered it with this big tarp. I knew they'd be able to track it, but I planned on being long gone." I stopped to take another drink while the officers scribbled furiously. "I walked to the bus station and told the ticket guy I wanted to get at least five hundred miles away. He pointed to a few spots on a map, I told him to give me the one that cost the least but got me the farthest. Within five minutes, I had a ticket. I washed up in the bathroom, bought a hotdog from the little concession stand, and stocked up on water and crackers from a vending machine."

My nurse came in, checked my stitches, took my temperature, clicked away at the keyboard, and told me she was going to start my paperwork to go home.

I nearly cried again.

"So, I settled in on the bus. I slept a lot of the way. We stopped once, and I got off the bus to stretch, buy some more crackers and water, and get some fresh air. I lucked out on the second half of the trip because the seat next to me was empty, so I stretched out and slept some more. I guess I was tired from the anxiety or something. When the bus stopped again, I purposely left my phone turned on and stuck it between the seats. I hoped it would look like I was somewhere completely different if Joseph tracked it." I shrugged. "When I climbed off the bus, I saw the sign for Haven Grove, and that was where I decided to go."

Everyone was quiet while the officers wrote notes. Henry gave my hand a squeeze, and I wondered if he was as grateful as I was that I'd decided to head to Haven Grove.

Smathe finished writing first. "Okay, can you tell us about the wreck?"

I nodded. "Yeah. I drove Henry's truck up the road to

get some groceries. Our truck delivery was going to be late, and I needed ingredients for that evening's cakes."

Henry interjected. "I run the Riggs Roadhouse. Jack just started running Cake and Cocktails there."

James smiled. "I've heard of your place. My wife's been begging me to take her there."

Smathe chuckled. "We've gotten a good laugh out of the newsletter emails. Good marketing."

Despite the throbbing in my head and the exhaustion blanketing me, I couldn't help the smile. "Give me a few days, and I'll be back good as new. Come in and say hi. First cocktail and cake combo is on the house." The warmth of Henry's hand on my leg, and the excitement of hearing these guys had heard of my business were enough for me to continue the story.

"So, as I was driving home from getting the supplies, I noticed a gun-metal gray Jeep behind me. At first, it didn't register, but then I realized it was the same Jeep I'd seen in the parking lot at the store. I tried to tell myself it was just a coincidence that it was behind me. Maybe it was someone from Haven Grove, right?" I shook my head just as Henry chuckled. "But one thing I've learned about living in a small town is that everyone is all up in everyone else's business, so I would have known if someone in our town had a pretty, fancy new Jeep. Then he got closer and closer. The first time he bumped into me I got slammed around pretty good. I kinda lost my bearings for a bit. I slowed down hoping he'd go around me, but then I saw his face in my mirror. It was Douglas. He was grinning like he was having the time of his life. I knew he was going to try to kill me after what I'd heard them talk about. He slammed into me again and I went flying down the embankment into that ditch." I shrugged. "Then Casey Joe found me," I said with a nod toward Henry's dad.

Henry and Casey both cursed under their breath.

James and Smathe hurriedly finished their notes.

Smathe showed me photos of some Jeeps until I pointed to the one that looked most like what Douglas was driving. James tapped around on his phone until he found photos of Joseph and Douglas for me to identify. He confirmed their address.

They asked a few more questions and then they handed the three of us their cards. After promising they'd be in touch and telling us to be on the lookout for anything strange in Haven Grove—and to report anything we might notice directly to them—the officers left.

Before the curtain had even stopped fluttering, Donna came bustling in. "Who's ready to head home?"

I groaned. It was supposed to sound excited, but it just came out pathetic.

"He means *yes*," Henry translated for me with a big smile.

Donna chuckled. "Perfect. I'm going to print out your papers and get your prescriptions. You get dressed." She glanced at Casey Joe. "Can you bring your vehicle around to Door Two on the south side of the building? We'll bring him out there."

Within half an hour, I was dressed in most of my clothes—minus my shirt which I think they'd cut off me. I was swimming in Henry's t-shirt, but it was better than nothing, and he'd just buttoned up his flannel.

Donna told me if I didn't ride in the wheelchair I could

stay an extra day, so I flopped down with as much attitude as my tired, achy body could muster and let her wheel me toward Casey Joe's truck.

I was asleep against Henry's shoulder before Casey Joe pulled onto the highway.

Henry gently shook me awake when we reached the apartment. "Come on, babe. Let's get you upstairs. Dad's going to go get your medicine."

"No," I protested. "It's okay, I don't need it." I wasn't completely aware of what was going on, but I knew it was late, and I didn't want Casey Joe to have to go back up the road to the 24-hour pharmacy.

"It's not a problem," Casey Joe said. "I'll be back in a jiffy. You'll be wanting those pain meds through the night —even if it's only some strong Tylenol."

I didn't have the energy to argue, so I grunted before Henry hefted me into his arms and headed up the stairs.

Once we were through the door, he placed me gently on the couch. "I'm going to get the shower started. You need to wash off before you sleep. Don't move."

I think my only answer was a snore.

The next time I cracked my eyes open, the sun was streaming through the window, and I was cuddled under a cover in bed. Blinking myself awake, I tried to recall how I got into bed. Fuzzy images of Henry helping me shower while keeping the stitches mostly dry trudged through my sleepy head.

Bottles of prescription medication and water sat on the bedside table. After a full-body scan, I realized I was achy but not in pain. Sitting up slowly, I continued to be grateful my injuries were fairly minor.

The note on the bedside table caught my eye, and I smiled.

> *Jack,*
> *You had medicine around 4:00. I'm down helping Sam. Text me when you're awake. Do NOT shower or try to come to work.*
> *Love you,*
> *Henry*

Warmth washed over me.

The wreck, knowing Douglas and maybe Joseph were nearby, and my injuries were a dark cloud, but I knew I was welcome and loved in Haven Grove.

For the first time in my life, when faced with an overwhelming problem, I had no doubt my newly acquired family would help me through whatever came my way.

I just hoped that we could get some answers and bring everything to an end soon. Luckily, my uncle and cousin were impatient and not very smart. So, they'd hopefully mess up quickly.

I made my way to the bathroom, winced at how bad my face looked, and shuffled to the kitchen. Once I had water set to boil for tea, I texted Henry to let him know I was awake.

I immediately heard his big feet on the stairs.

When he blasted through the door, I smiled.

"Jack?" Henry called. "I swear to God if you're in the shower—"

He stopped in the kitchen.

I blinked innocently at him as I put a tea bag into my mug. "What?"

Henry eyed me suspiciously, his arms crossed over his chest. "Did you take a shower?"

"Nope. Just got up."

He moved into the kitchen and looked closely at my hair.

I giggled. "Babe, I woke up, could barely remember how I even got to bed, went to pee, and came in here to make tea. I'm not going to shower without help, at least not today. I'm not going to try to walk down the stairs without help, at least not today." Wrapping my arms around his thick body, I snuggled into his chest as his big, strong arms automatically pulled me close.

"I don't know what this *at least not today* shit is about," he mumbled into my head.

"The doctor said I had to take it easy *today*, and I could play it by ear based on how I feel tomorrow."

Henry growled. "Next week—" He yelped when I bit his pec.

"Next week, nothin'," I said, smiling up at him sweetly. "I will take today to rest. Maybe tomorrow. But then I'm getting back in my kitchen."

"Jack, babe…"

"No, Henry. You said I had to follow the doctor's orders, and I am. If tomorrow feels like too much, I'll rest. But I can't just sit up here for days. I'll go bananas. Between wondering where Joseph and Douglas are and worrying about Cake and Cocktails, I'll be more of a mess if I have to just sit here and stew."

Henry grumbled as he worked over my words.

"Fine. Today. And tomorrow, you have to be honest with me. If you don't feel well, you'll take another day."

"Yes, Papa Bear."

Henry smacked my ass.

"Ow! Be careful, I'm injured!"

He laughed and shook his head. "Let's get you set up on the couch. I'll come back up after lunch to check on you."

By the time Henry headed back down to the bar, I was covered in no less than five blankets, had the remote in hand, and wouldn't be able to consume all the drinks and snacks he'd left for me in a month.

But the sweet kiss and *I love you* he gave me before he left was worth roasting under the covers.

After a movie, I dozed off. When I woke, I checked the time on my phone. Henry would be finishing up with the lunch rush soon, so I dug myself out from the blankets and headed to the bathroom.

Even though I'd promised not to shower, I couldn't *not* wash off a bit. So, I gave myself a bit of a sponge bath with some soap and a washcloth. Once I'd brushed my teeth, I at least felt human.

When I made my way back to the living room, voices caught my attention. I moved to look out the window just in time to see Henry draw back and slam his fist into a man's face.

Without thinking, I yanked open the door. "Henry!"

The man and Henry both looked up at me.

Henry's face raged with fury, but it softened the moment his eyes landed on me. The man he'd punched held his face, but there was no doubt in my mind who it was.

"Jackie," he crooned. "Come give your uncle Joseph a hug."

"You have about five seconds to get your ass off my property before I call the cops," Henry growled.

Joseph ignored him. "Jackie—"

"Don't call me that," I yelled just as Henry charged Joseph and pushed him against the stair railing with a deep warning of, "Don't fucking speak to him."

Joseph held his hands up in surrender. "Okay, okay. I just need my stuff and I'll be gone. Not like we *want* to spend any more time in this hell hole."

"What stuff?" I asked, but Henry shoved Joseph.

"We got nothin' to give you, so you can leave now. I'm callin' the cops either way, just up to you whether they show up while you're here or after." Henry shoved Joseph again. I wasn't a proponent of violence, but I wasn't going to lie, watching Joseph get the grumpy end of Henry's anger soothed something deep inside my soul.

Casey Joe came around the corner just as Joseph nearly face-planted on the concrete. Casey glanced up at me, looked between Henry and Joseph, and then crossed his arms. He'd been putting on some muscle as of late, and he looked just as menacing as his son.

Joseph caught himself from falling and wiped at the blood pouring from his nose as he eyed up Casey Joe. "That's not the way this shit works, man." He turned himself so he could see all three of us. "Jackie-boy took things that belong to me, and I want them back. If I don't get them, *I'll* be the one going to the police. Let's see how well that sissy can run his stupid cake place when he's arrested for theft."

Henry started to say something, but I cut him off. "Theft is when you knowingly take something that isn't yours. I have no idea what you're talking about. I grabbed a suitcase, shoved my life into it, and left. I didn't *take* anything from you."

Sam threw open the door with a phone to his ear. "You want them to send a patrol car?"

Henry nodded, speaking without taking his eyes off Joseph. "Yeah, give them my name. Have them send the two we talked to at the hospital. James and Smathe."

Joseph let loose a string of curses and rushed for the stairs. He hadn't made it three steps before he was on his ass with Henry and Casey Joe both standing over him.

He got himself up on his knees and pointed up at me. "I'm not done with you, Jackie-boy. You won't get away with stealing from me. I was nothing but good to you. Gave you a roof over your head, food in your belly, a car, a college education. Your fuckin' pansy ass had it *good*, but then you had to go and turn into fucking weak-ass thief." He stood up, blood gushing from his nose and elbow. "Mark my words, you'll pay. There are good people in this town who area already suspicious of you, and they'll help me see to that. Nobody likes a thief."

At the blast of a police siren, Joseph's face screwed up. He glanced around and took off, scrambling like a panicked piece of shit.

James and Smathe took statements from everyone.

"I do have to ask, are you sure you don't know what it is he thinks you took from him?" James asked.

I shook my head. "No idea. The car was just one he used from the lot, so I don't think it's that. The phone was in his name, but I can't see him being pissed about that. I mean, I guess he bought me some of the clothes, but I doubt he's throwing this kind of fit over some jeans."

"Well, you let us know if you think of anything," James said.

"And keep your wits about you," Smathe added. "Don't go anywhere on your own." He pointed at me. "You especially, but I mean all of you. He's likely to escalate. He's already proven he's not above vehicular manslaughter, so I doubt he's going to give up and go home."

"He'll probably mess up," James said. "Just be careful so you're not caught in the crossfire when he does."

Henry walked with the officers to their car, and Casey Joe came up the stairs.

"Come on, let's get you inside. I'm sure Henry needs to finish at the bar, and you need to rest." Casey's warm hand on my shoulder steered me toward the couch.

He helped me get settled and then moved to the kitchen to make me some tea. By the time Henry came upstairs, Casey Joe and I were sipping on piping hot mugs of tea while we watched some comedy from Casey's childhood. I was still laughing at his look of indignance when I referred to it as something from the good ol' days.

Henry kissed the top of my head, went to the bathroom where I heard him washing his face and hands, and then reappeared. "You won't be out of my sight until those two psychos are behind bars."

I shrugged. "I'm fine with that. I guess I just wish I

knew what he wants back from me. Hell, if I knew what I'd taken, I'd give it back if it meant he'd leave."

"Fuck that," Casey said. "He's not gettin' shit from you. Whatever it is, it's either worth *a lot* or it's something that could get him in big trouble."

Henry situated himself on the couch and pulled me onto his lap.

"I've been racking my brain for what he thinks I took." I ran through items in my head. "Maybe there was something in the car?"

"But he could track that, right?" Casey Joe asked. "He's probably already found it."

"Maybe someone took something out of the car before Joseph got to it?" Henry suggested.

"I mean, I locked it before leaving it behind the barn, but I'm sure someone might have broken into it. If there was something in the car, it was hidden. There was nothing in the trunk or glove compartment." I rubbed my knuckle over my stitches. The gash was swollen and sore, but I knew it could have been so much worse. "He can't be upset about the suitcase," I said with a huff. "I took the nastiest, oldest looking one just so he wouldn't notice it was gone."

As the words hung in the air, we all froze.

"Was it your suitcase?" Casey Joe asked, his words quiet like we were in a secret meeting.

I shook my head even as I moved to stand. "No. The one I came with as a little kid had been tossed years ago. This one was in the hall closet and had definitely seen better days. I just figured it was gross and old, so it would be the one they were least likely to miss."

Henry gently eased me back down onto the couch. "I'll get it."

There was no reason to protest, so I wrapped the blanket around my shoulders and waited for him to pull the ratty suitcase from the coat closet at the front of the apartment.

He returned and placed it on the coffee table in front of me.

"You don't really think they were ignorant enough to hide stuff in an old suitcase, do you?" I asked.

Henry cocked a brow, and Casey Joe chuckled.

I couldn't help the grin. My uncle and cousin were *mean*, but I'd never heard anyone accuse them of being smart.

The main section of the suitcase was empty which wasn't at all surprising since I'd packed my clothes in it. I would have seen it if they'd hidden something there. I let Henry unzip the pockets and run his hand through them.

Nothing.

"Wait, is it one of those that has a zipper…" Casey Joe mused as he moved closer and examined the case. "Yeah, right there."

A zipper on the inside of the suitcase sat looking as innocent as could be.

Henry opened it and slowly moved his hand inside as if something was going to bite him. His brows shot up, and he pulled a large manilla envelope from the pocket.

"Holy shit."

Chapter 23
Henry

"HOLY SHIT," JACK MURMURED, AND A GIGGLE escaped him. "I've had whatever he's looking for the whole time."

"Open it or give it to the police?" I asked.

Dad and Jack gave me matching *duh* looks, so I shrugged. "Just checking."

Maybe I should have been more careful—put on gloves or something?—but I bent the prongs and worked the envelope open. Dad moved the suitcase, and I dumped the contents of the envelope onto the coffee table.

Dad whistled.

Jack whispered, "Oh my god" over and over.

I grabbed an ink pen and used it to poke around the pile.

At least ten thumb drives, each labeled with years. Pretty innocuous on their own, but the fact they were hidden in a suitcase, and Joseph was frothing at the mouth to get them back, made me think they were likely filled with pretty damning shit.

The sheaf of paper looked to be spreadsheets of some sorts of accounts. I wasn't exactly sure what we were looking at, but the numbers were huge.

When my pen shifted a piece of paper to the side and uncovered the photographs, all the air was sucked out of the room. Picture after picture of Joseph, Douglas, and hundreds of unknown individuals of varying ages and genders. A lot of nudity. Compromising positions. A lot of...other stuff. Whether any of it was illegal or not was going to be for the police to figure out.

But the mixture of so many thumb drives, spreadsheets with what appeared to be money entries, and the photographs had me thinking that Joseph was desperate to get the suitcase back because he and his son might be in some deep shit if any of it got out.

And who knew? Maybe the spreadsheets were connected to accounts belonging to Joseph and Douglas, and they had a lot to lose if those accounts were discovered.

Dad was already on the phone to the police.

"Must be some pretty damning stuff," Jack muttered.

"Yeah, it's definitely not just old tax receipts based on how badly Joseph wants it back," I said. "I want the police to look into the life insurance he took out on you. That should be well-known when he and Douglas are on trial."

Jack's eyes went wide. "You think they'll go to trial? And like, *jail*?"

"Damn, I hope so. All evidence points to them trying to kill you for insurance money. *And* who knows what is on these thumb drives. Hell, the pictures might be bad enough. I think they're in deep shit."

By the time the officers came to the apartment, took *more* statements from us, sifted through the envelope contents, and bagged it all up, Jack's eyes were drooping.

I gave my dad a look, and he nodded in unspoken agreement.

"Hey, babe. Dad's gonna stay with you while I run downstairs. I'll bring some dinner home. Why don't you sleep for a while?"

It was a true testament to how tired Jack was when he didn't even resist. He just tipped his pretty lips up for a kiss and cuddled into the couch with a sigh.

Dad walked me to the door. "I'm gonna let Hudson and Lance know what's going on. We need to all stick close together until this shit is taken care of."

"Agreed." I slapped him on the back. "Thanks for being here and for all your help."

"That's what family's for." Dad glanced at a sweetly snoring Jack. "Sometimes it feels like all my shit fucked you boys up." He scowled at my huff of laughter. "I'm not saying y'all are messed up." He lowered his voice. "Just kinda think maybe I'm getting a chance to do the right thing by him."

"You did your best with us." I always felt bad when I thought about how much Dad missed out on—how much shit he went through—because of the way things went down with him and my mom. "But he's lucky to have you. You're the dad he never got to have."

"Lord knows we don't need him callin' *you* Daddy."

Dad chuckled as I rolled my eyes. "Go on, take care of business. Bring us something good for dinner."

"Keep up with your shit, and I'm bringing you a plate of unsalted broccoli."

Dad groaned. "Man, come on. I'm tryin' to eat better. Lance keeps bringing that pizza with cauliflower shit for crust. And *light* beer. Might as well drink water. At least bring me some grilled chicken with the peach barbeque sauce and a baked potato. Please?"

"You eat the broccoli first."

"Yes, Daddy."

I didn't slam the door on my father, but only because I didn't want to wake Jack.

Everyone had been laying low for a few days. Jack hadn't even argued about one of us being by his side at all times. Which told me he was worried about Joseph and Douglas —as he should be—*and* he was just happy to be back in his kitchen baking cakes.

When Dad came to the Roadhouse at the end of an early shift and told us to pack our bags for a sleepover, I didn't even question it because of the smile on Jack's face. Since my truck was still out of commission, Dad drove us to his place.

As we piled out of the truck, someone cleared their throat, and I whipped around.

Larry Holmes stood there with his grandson, Randy, and the Sanders boy, Pete.

I instinctively moved in front of Jack and crossed my arms over my chest. "Brother Larry, what brings you by?"

Dad joined me, blocking Jack from the preacher. "Can't say I remember inviting you to my home, Holmes."

Larry's cheeks pinked. "Yes, well, it's the responsibility of a good shepherd to check in on his flock from time to time. Especially those who stray."

Dad and I took matching steps forward. Dad was built more like Hudson, not as broad as me, and he had some weight and muscle to put back on after his heart attack had knocked him down, but we made an imposing pair.

Larry stepped back, not even seeming to remember he had two young teens with him. "We've come to make amends. The boys have something they want to say."

Randy pursed his lips and scowled.

Pete cleared his throat. "When my momma found out we'd been messing through your trash, she just about tanned my hide. Sorry. We were just being dumb looking for credit card numbers." He dipped his head in embarrassment. "Didn't know they don't put the whole number on the receipt."

Randy huffed when Larry nudged him. "We thought it was funny to make a mess. Sorry. We weren't thinking properly."

I let my gaze drill into both boys for what I hoped seemed like an eternity. "I appreciate the apology. Don't let me find out you're messing with people's property again."

Both boys nodded, mumbled another apology, and scurried away toward Larry's car.

I kept my arms crossed and cocked my head, just waiting on what Larry might have to say.

"Now, I'm a man of God," he started.

When Dad and I both huffed and rolled our eyes, he held up a placating hand.

"What I was going to say is that I'm not a supporter of businesses that encourage sinning," he went on. At my scowl, he hurried to continue. "But that doesn't mean I'm a proponent for illegalities. I won't succumb to the devil's doing by being a part of that." He straightened his tie. "I just thought you should know."

And with that, he turned and walked away.

"Thought we should know what?" Dad asked.

"He's not a supporter of our business, but he's also not going to succumb to the devil," Jack mused. He snapped his finger. "He means Joseph and Douglas. They've been trying to get information out of him."

I grunted. "He probably told them all they needed to know before he realized they were trying to kill you."

"Good riddance to the good shepherd," Dad muttered. "Let's go. We're meeting Lance and Hudson at the Dairy Palace first. We're sleeping at Hudson's place. He said something about boat races and blanket forts."

Jack's face lit up like a Christmas tree. "I love you guys so much."

I slung an arm around him. "And we love you too."

Dad started walking away from us.

"Where you going?" I asked.

"We're walkin'. I'm supposed to be getting exercise, and if I'm eating ice cream, I need to cancel it out with a walk." Dad hefted his gym bag.

"It's like a mile," I complained.

"Yeah? Well, you're no spring chicken. Walkin' ain't gonna hurt you. Let's go."

So, I hefted our bags onto one shoulder, pulled Jack close, and followed Dad toward the ice cream palace.

Not gonna lie, the walk felt good, and I wasn't even mad Dad made us get our exercise in before we stuffed our faces with ice cream.

Lance and I took orders before leaving Dad, Jack, and Hudson to hold a table in the little outside area. Jack's excited voice talking about boat races in the creek and blanket forts warmed my heart as I followed Lance into the DP.

A little while later, while Dad chatted with someone from town, and Hudson helped Lance clear off our table, Jack took a final bite of his ice cream.

"Thank you for remembering I like plain vanilla," he said, licking the sweet, creamy concoction from his spoon.

I tipped his chin and brushed a kiss over his sticky lips. "I don't care if you want it plain, or you ask for five hundred toppings. You are the smartest, most talented man I've ever met. You deserve a thousand scoops however you want them." Kissing him again, savoring the warm connection between our cold lips, I thanked my lucky stars that Jack found his way into my life. "And I will spend the rest of my life making sure you believe that."

He grinned into the kiss, our teeth bumping. "I love you," he whispered.

"Love you too."

"This is the life." Dad sighed with his legs stretched out in front of the fire at the edge of the creek in the orchard.

Hudson had insisted we set up by the water when Jack had asked if we ever did that as kids. After ice cream, we'd spent the rest of the daylight racing sticks, leaves, and little aluminum foil boats down the creek.

Watching Jack get to relive a part of his childhood that brought him so much joy and reminded him of his mom while he piled good memories on top of the foundation he'd built with us may have been the best experience of my life.

I didn't *let* Jack win.

Okay, I didn't let him win *many* of the races.

Lance leaned more toward my side of things and didn't get too competitive.

Hudson seemed to just be having fun playing in the creek like a kid with his new friend.

Dad, on the other hand, was in full father figure mode: helping Jack shape his boat differently for a better journey through the water, suggesting a little weight to make the tiny craft faster, and stopping just short of giving Hudson and Jack a lecture about the importance of knowing how to just have fun even when you don't win.

I caught Lance looking at his life-long best friend with amusement and pride gleaming in his eyes. When he noticed me watching him, Lance shrugged. "It's just good to see him finally coming out of that hell." He nodded toward Dad. "That's the Casey Joe I remember. Life might have fucked him over, but it didn't knock him out. He's makin' a comeback."

Something warm bloomed in my chest. I hated that a

heart attack and Jack's shitty past had to happen, but if those two things ended up being the catalyst for Dad's phoenix from the ashes story, then so be it.

Hudson had provided everyone with a sleeping bag, and he'd forced each of us to carry two folding chairs. As Dad and Lance built the fire, Hudson, Jack, and I set to work making our blanket fort with sheets from the cabin and clips Hudson had procured from the Juicy Peach.

The rest of the evening had been hot dogs and marshmallows over the fire, warm peach and rum drinks, and laughing at silly stories. The gleam in Jack's eyes wasn't just the firelight, and I was so damn appreciative of my family for helping me give this to him. They loved him and wanted the best for him as much as I did, and that meant the world to me.

When Jack started yawning, I made him take off his boots and climb into our sleeping bag. I'd zipped our bags together for warmth.

Obviously.

Once we'd settled into our cozy cocoon, Hudson and Lance got the same idea. The four of us lay on the ground under the sheets of the little fort while Dad continued to lounge in a chair staring into the fire.

One moment, we were dozing in the peaceful orchard, surrounded only by the crackling of the fire, the hum of insects, and the scent of earth and peaches.

The next second, the wail of a siren pierced the air.

Dad's head jerked up and he jumped to his feet with a curse.

The four of us scrambled out of our sleeping bags—not an easy feat at my size.

As we struggled to yank our boots on, Dad headed off toward the hill.

"Dad! What's wrong?" Hudson yelled.

"CJ!" Lance called out.

"My damn house is on fire!" Dad hollered over his shoulder.

Sure enough, through the trees and up the hill, flames jumped from the back of Dad's house.

"Oh my god," Jack said.

We all took off after Dad. By the time we made it up the hill to his house, the volunteer fire department had arrived and were setting up their equipment. Just as the first arc of water sprayed from the hose, something caught my eye in the shadows to the right.

Dad was bent over holding his stomach, and we had visitors.

"Look out!" I cried, yanking Jack behind me to shield him from the men running toward us.

Dad launched into action, and Lance and Hudson jerked their heads first to me and then to the approaching figures. In moves that couldn't have been smoother had they choreographed them, Lance lunged forward and knocked the first man to the ground, while Dad hauled back and swung hard, landing a blow to the second man's face with a crack of cartilage and bone.

When both men were on the ground, Jack stepped around me. Tears glistened on his cheeks in the orange flames of the fire, but he took a deep breath with his chin held high. He moved closer to the groaning, writhing men. I wanted to hold him back, but I knew he needed to do this for closure.

With Lance pinning Douglas in some sort of wrestling hold, and Joseph incapacitated, Jack knelt near them. "The night I left, it was because I heard you two plotting to kill me for insurance money. I ignorantly thought if I was out of your hair, you'd forget about me. I guess I should have known since you two are nothing but mean and greedy." He dashed at the tears on his cheeks. "Oh, I think I found what you were looking for."

Douglas's eyes finally landed on Jack, and Joseph grunted through his broken nose, "Just give it to us, and we'll leave. No questions."

Jack laughed. "Oh, there will be questions. Plenty of them. I'm pretty sure the police have a whole list of questions they're going to be asking you."

Douglas tried to lunge toward Jack, but Lance tightened his hold.

Joseph moved as if to sit up, and Dad put a boot to his chest.

"Was the fire supposed to smoke me out? Or kill me?" Jack asked, his voice strong but curious. "Was that it? If you killed me in a random fire, you could get the insurance money *and* claim my belongings?"

Jack was cut off when blue lights added to the red ones flashing in the dark night. He stood and moved back into my arms just as our two favorite officers rounded the house a few moments later.

The rest of the scene was a complete blur that somehow passed in the blink of an eye while playing out in slow motion right in front of us.

James and Smathe arrested Joseph and Douglas. The two argued and mouthed off the entire time the officers handcuffed them, read them their rights, and walked them to the car. It was evident they knew they were in hot water and were grasping at straws.

Lance slapped Jack on the back. "I'll call our attorney in the morning. We want to make sure those two are prosecuted to the full extent of the law not only for all the shit in that suitcase but also for attempting to kill you." He glanced at the smoldering remains of the back of Dad's house. "Twice it looks like. Plus, arson."

Jack just nodded, his eyes a bit glassy. "Will all that be enough to keep them in jail? Or do you think they'll post bail?"

I shrugged. "I guess it depends on what the judge thinks, but I'd say there's plenty piled up against them, and they're definitely a flight risk, so let's hope he doesn't offer bail." I held Jack close. "If they can post bail, they'll hightail it out of here, I'm sure."

"So, it's over but not over." Jack's words held an edge of relief, frustration, and sadness.

I kissed the top of his head. "We'll take it one day at a time."

From where we stood, we watched Dad talk to a couple of the firefighters before turning and heading toward the orchard.

"Where are you going?" Hudson called.

Dad spun around and pointed toward the house. "I had a fuckin' heart attack, that piece of shit sucker punched me, and they burned down my house!" He gestured wildly before yelling, "Fuck!" Then he turned and started walking. "Fuck it all, ain't dealin' with this shit tonight. I'm sleeping in the orchard in a fuckin' blanket fort!"

Chapter 24
Jack

I smiled for the picture with the group of ladies who'd come in to celebrate a new grandbaby and a retirement. I thanked them for coming to Cake and Cocktails and told them to be sure they tagged us in the post.

Business had moved from an exciting burst in the beginning to a solid boom recently. I was swamped but so very happy. Like a proud dad, Casey Joe beamed every time someone said they came in to see what the shop was like just because of the *Cake and Cock...* email subject line.

For about two days after everything with Joseph and Douglas went down, I worried about having an online presence since my uncle and cousin had admitted to finding me just by looking for "stupid, pansy-ass cake hashtags."

But when they'd turned on each other and admitted to trying to kill me for insurance money, the judge had opted to hold them without bond for the time being because of the huge amount of evidence against them—the attempted vehicular manslaughter, arson, and a shit ton of items pointing to suspicious, if not illegal, activity in the hidden envelope. According to our attorney, even if the judge opted to free up some space in the crowded county jail, Joseph and Douglas would go back home on strict house arrest and monitoring until their hearings.

So, I'd let Casey Joe and the guys convince me to embrace the social media aspect of our business, and we'd all been having a blast with fun posts, videos, photos, contests, giveaways, and jokes. Customers came from Haven Grove, the surrounding area, and even several states away just to visit and check us out.

"There he is," Casey Joe said with a grin. "The social media darling. I swear, most of these people just come here to get their pictures taken with you."

"Whatever," I huffed, my cheeks heating.

Casey Joe put an arm around my neck and squeezed. "I'm proud of you, kid."

He'd taken to letting me know how proud he was of me a lot more often, and just like every time before, my throat grew tight, and tears pricked my eyes. But I adored having a dad figure in my life.

I gave him a play punch right to the gut. "Thanks, old man."

Casey Joe grunted and put me in a headlock. "Careful, I'm fragile."

Laughing, I poked at his stomach. "Whatever, don't act like you haven't been working out. You're getting all buff and shit."

"And shit is about right," Casey Joe straightened his

shirt and went back to working on some sort of graphic on his phone while I cleared the table. Another large party would be coming in soon, and I wanted to be prepared for the last customers of the day outside of any who popped in from the Roadhouse or just stopped by to see what the cake of the day was.

Casey Joe cleared his throat. "You know I've always been okay with my boys being queer, right?" When I turned raised brows his way, he waved me off. "It's okay to use the word because I don't mean it in a bad way, and both the boys use it."

I gave a nod.

"I want you to know I'm okay with you being queer—or gay, or whatever you choose to call yourself—too." He stared at his tablet for a long time as I quietly put dishes in a tub. "I think it's good that everyone gets the chance to decide who they are—and it's okay to get to know yourself better the older you get."

"Someone had therapy today," Henry said as he came in from checking on the work happening on the future outdoor dining area. He patted his dad on the shoulder before making his way to me for a kiss. "How'd it go?"

Casey Joe wrinkled his nose. "I don't know. Sometimes it feels like I figure a lot of shit out, and other times it's like I take fifteen steps backward." He ran a hand over his face. "All I know is that I *have* to find somewhere else to sleep. Even when they try to be quiet, it's doing a number on my head hearing your brother and my best friend fuckin' through the wall."

Henry barked out a laugh, and I bit back a grin.

I knew Hudson and Lance would never ask Casey Joe

to leave—he'd been staying with them since the fire because the apartment above the Sweet & Creamy was occupied, and the little cabin in the orchard had a recent leak which led to some mold and mildew. Not a huge problem for an occasional shelter, but not suitable for living there. However, I knew having his dad sharing their house was really getting to Hudson.

"Any news on the house?" Henry asked, giving me a secret wink because he was well aware how badly his brother wanted Casey Joe to find a new place.

"No," Casey Joe grumbled. "It's red tape a mile long. At first it was because of those two bozos and the police, then it was the insurance people draggin' their feet. Supposedly, they should be getting me finalized so the work can start soon, but I'll believe it when I see it."

"Damn, I thought you'd maybe be moved back in by the time the Fall Fest rolled around." Henry hefted the tub of dishes for me.

"You and me both," Casey Joe said with irritation.

He touched his fingers to his lips, and I knew he was joncsing for a smoke. Most of the time, he kept the cravings at bay with a sucker, but he'd been complaining about his teeth being super sensitive from all the sugar.

"You want a drink or anything?" I asked, hoping to take his mind off the cigarette.

Casey stood and packed away his tablet. "Nah, I'm good. Gonna head to the gym. Lifting weights and a run usually make it go away—at least until the next one hits."

He waved goodbye and let the door swing shut behind him.

"Mmmm, it's just you and me," Henry said, dancing me toward the kitchen.

"And a party of eight arriving in about fifteen minutes." I couldn't hide the giggle as he spun me around.

"Plenty of time," he teased, leaning in to nuzzle my neck.

"Nope, I have to get everything ready." It wasn't like Henry and I were missing out on alone time. The sex was amazing, but the cuddles and simply being together was just as satisfying. When I stumbled off that bus and made my way to Haven Grove, I never would have imagined in my wildest dreams that I'd find my very own happily ever after in the little town.

But dancing and laughing in Henry's arms, with secret recipe ideas already in place if I ever needed to whip up a certain special occasion cake, and finding the true meaning of family proved to me that I'd journeyed my way to exactly where I belonged.

Henry tipped my chin and pressed a soft, slow kiss to my lips. "Tonight. You and me, peaches and cream cake, and—"

"Lemon drops?" I bit my lip to keep from giggling.

Henry sighed. "Why must you hurt my heart?"

"Go on. You, me, peaches and cream cake, lemon drops..."

"No, no. We have to have the right cake and cocktail— what do you suggest?" Henry leaned back, his arms still tight around me, our hips pressed together as he watched me.

I pursed my lips and thought about it. "How about I

make a dark chocolate cake with chocolate ganache and candied ginger peaches?"

"Oh my god, do you know how much I love you?" Henry shifted to press his forehead to mine.

"Because of my cake?" I hoped my eye lashes batted innocently enough.

"Your cake, your heart, *all* of you."

"Good because I love your cake and cock—" I cut off as Henry's eyes danced with amusement. "Cocktails, obviously."

"Obviously." Henry nuzzled our noses together.

~THE END~

Stay tuned for Casey Joe's story in Snacks & Jockstraps! If you haven't already read Peaches & Cream (Hudson and Lance's story) you can find it HERE.
In the meantime, read on for more from A.D. Ellis.
While you're here, join the A.D. Ellis newsletter and get a free book!

Also by A.D. ELLIS

On Cravenwood Block- the complete four-book series in a box set. Or start with Jett & Leighton in book 1 HERE.

Adore (Remington Place 1) is a steamy, age-gap, bi-awakening, dad's best friend M/M romance with a sassy smartass and a sexy silver fox. It's the first book in the Remington Place series and can be read as a stand-alone.

Crave (Remington Place 2) is a steamy, friends-to-lovers, fake relationship M/M romance with a virgin nursing student and a gruff, grumbly construction worker.

Desire (Remington Place 3) is a steamy, age-gap, hurt/comfort M/M romance featuring a heart-of-gold mechanic and a twink who's a lot stronger than he realizes. *Please note: This story has mention of sex trafficking and sexual abuse.*

Yearn (Remington Place 4)- a steamy, enemies-to-lovers, forced proximity M/M romance between two EMS workers who have hated each other for a decade.

Silver in the City (3 books- meet the Silver crew you read about in Forged in the City) Available on AUDIO!

Forged in the City (3 books- a spin-off series from Silver in the City) Available on AUDIO

Find other books here - https://books2read.com/ap/RWrrNx/ AD-Ellis

About the Author

A.D. Ellis is an Indiana girl, born and raised. She spends much of her time in central Indiana as an instructional coach/teacher in the inner city of Indianapolis, being a mom to two amazing teenagers, and wondering how she and her husband of over two decades haven't driven each other insane yet. A lot of her time is also devoted to phone call avoidance and her hatred of cooking.

She loves chocolate, wine, pizza, and naps along with reading and writing romance. These loves don't leave much time for housework, much to the chagrin of her husband. Who would pick cleaning the house over a nap or a good book? She uses any extra time to increase her fluency in sarcasm.

A.D. uses she/they pronouns.

Sign up at http://www.subscribepage.com/ADEllisNewsMMRomance for a FREE book!

Website http://adellisauthor.com/

My direct buy site https://payhip.com/ADEllisAuthor

My merchandise site https://a-d-ellis-shop.fourthwall.com/

Find me EVERYWHERE at https://www.adellisauthor.com/mylinks/

Connect with A.D. Ellis

Follow my website http://www.adellisauthor.com or find me on Facebook

http://www.facebook.com/adellisauthor

If you want to get updates about releases, interviews, sales, giveaways, and more please sign up for my newsletter http://www.subscribepage.com/ADEllisNewsMMRomance

Find me on Spotify if you'd like to listen to the playlist for this book (mainly just the songs I listened to while writing). Just search for A.D. Ellis.

To make it easy, find me EVERYWHERE here- https://www.adellisauthor.com/mylinks/

Acknowledgments

It's always so hard to write this part because I'm worried I'll forget someone without meaning to.

Thanks to DJ J. for the "Rice Christmas Treats" comment, Charlotte B. for the "gecko/get-go" comment, and Laura H. for the "drier sheep" comment.

Readers- you are the reason I write. As long as you continue reading my stories, I'll continue writing them. Thank you for your support.

Bloggers & Influencers- your support, reviews, and promotion are very much appreciated. Thank you!

My author buddies- I don't know that I could keep doing this without our brainstorm sessions, laughter, road trips, meals, wine, and friendship as my support.

Thank you to my alpha readers, betas, editors, proofreaders, and ARC readers! Your eyes and input are beyond important to me.

Brett and Gage- as usual, I doubt you even grasp how much your support, input, and friendship mean to me. This author journey has brought many wonderful things into my life, and you both are two of the BEST! I'm blessed to call you friends.

My family and friends- thank you for your love and support, always.

Cover Photo by Eric McKinney at 6:12 Photography

Cover Model: Michael H.